D0041847

"Readers will enjoy the hometown feel of this mystery."

—TheMysteryReader.com

"The characters are very interesting and very complex … it is a fun read with lots of twists that will keep you up reading."

—OnceUponARomance.net

In
Sickness
and in
Death

A BROKEN VOWS MYSTERY

In Sickness and in Death

LISA BORK

MIDNIGHT INK
WOODBURY, MINNESOTA

FIRST EDITION
First Printing, 2011

Book design and format by Donna Burch
Cover design by Kevin R. Brown
Cover images: Cooler illustration © Michele Amatrula,
    Diamond ring © iStockphoto.com/George Peters
Editing by Connie Hill

Midnight Ink, an imprint of Llewellyn Worldwide Ltd.

Library of Congress Cataloging-in-Publication Data

Bork, Lisa, 1964–
    In sickness and in death : a broken vows mystery / by Lisa Bork. — 1st ed.
        p.   cm.
    ISBN 978-0-7387-2336-5
    I. Title.
    PS3602.O755I6   2011
    813'.6—dc22   2011015009

Midnight Ink
Llewellyn Worldwide Ltd.
2143 Wooddale Drive
Woodbury, MN 55125-2989
www.midnightinkbooks.com

Printed in the United States of America

For Adam and Chelsea

ONE

I HEARD THE BABY crying, soft whimpers punctuated by fearful wails. My feet slipped off the bed and hit the floor, carrying me across familiar ground even while my eyes remained closed, exhaustion hanging on my body like a shroud. I pushed open the door and crossed to the side of her crib. My arms reached out for her. They met empty air. I searched the mattress, my hands skittering from the center to each vacant corner. The sheets were cold. A cloud of dust tickled my nose. I sneezed. My eyes flew open.

The room stood bare, as it had for almost four months, waiting for the child who would never return. She lived with her birthmother now, only a bittersweet memory for us.

I heard Ray in the doorway behind me. "Are you all right?"

"I heard Noelle crying. She was afraid."

Ray's warm hands cupped my shoulders. He leaned close. "She's happy and healthy. You've got to let her go."

I stiffened. "I did."

Ray released me. "Not really. You've had the dream twice this month already."

I tried to ease the tension with a joke. "I'm making progress. That's half as many times as last month."

The rocking chair creaked as my husband lowered his six-foot-three, 220-pound frame into it. I turned toward him in time to see his hand rub his temple. "Darlin', Noelle didn't die. We took a chance on the adoption, and we lost out. We were lucky to have her as long as we did. But we have to move on."

I slid down to the floor, too tired to support my weight. "I moved on."

Ray buried his forehead in his hands, his dark hair falling forward and hiding his face. "Not true. When was the last time you went into the shop? Cory doesn't even call here anymore to ask your opinion or your permission. He's running the whole show alone."

I shifted, trying to find a more comfortable position on the hardwood floor. "Maybe I should offer to sell out to him. Hawking used sports cars doesn't help the world. I should find something to do that helps people."

"First you have to help yourself."

"What's that supposed to mean?"

Ray raised his head from his hands, his expression etched with concern and something I couldn't quite name. "You don't shower. You don't get dressed. You don't clean or grocery shop. We don't have sex. You don't even know your sister is making a fool of herself all over town. All you do is watch television or stare out the window. It's not normal and it's not healthy, Jolene."

When Ray used my given name, for the most part he was pissed or feeling the urge. I bet on pissed this time.

I fingered my over-sized sleep shirt. It smelled of body odor, and the yellow stain on the area covering my belly button showed up even in the moonlit room. My scalp itched. My toenails were like daggers. I didn't care. My baby was gone.

"Here's the deal, Jolene. Tomorrow morning you are going to get out of bed, shower, get dressed, eat breakfast, and go to work, where you will remain at least half the day. Then you're going to go to the grocery store. I made the list up already. And when I get home, you're going to have dinner on the table. If you don't, I'm calling Dr. Albert and asking him about treatment programs."

"Ray!" Okay, so I'd been a little down lately. He was overreacting, wasn't he? But the creases edging the corners of his brown eyes had deepened over the last few months, giving him the perpetual worried look of a bulldog. Was that my fault?

"I'm serious, Jolene. This shit has got to stop." The rocking chair banged into the wall as he left the room.

Seconds later, our bedroom door slammed.

I stretched out, the floor cool against my flushed cheek.

Resentment simmered inside me. I didn't like being told what to do. Normally I would go out of my way to do the exact opposite, but Ray meant business this time. Worse, he was right.

He wouldn't be enrolling me in any mental health programs. No way. I'd spent too much time in the mental health community while my sister Erica received treatment for her bipolar disorder, suicidal tendencies, and a myriad of other things, including shooting a man four months ago. Not to mention I'd spent three days in the psychiatric wing at the age of twelve after finding my mother's dead body in the family garage. I feared a return engagement. They might never let me out again.

Ray's comment about Erica bothered me. She hadn't been around much lately, but I hadn't given it much thought. Then again, I hadn't given anything much thought for the last few months. I assumed she was working and dating one of the many men who crossed her path at the restaurant bar where she waitresses. She'd held the job for over six months now, a lifetime achievement for her. It seemed like when she got her act together, my world had fallen apart.

What was I missing, hiding out here at home? Had she lost her job and failed to inform me? Was she having public sex, the final frontier for her? Would the word *robbery* soon be mentioned in the same breath as her name, as it had been more than once in the past? Or some worse crime?

I stretched out farther on my stomach, trying to work the kinks out of my spine. It had compressed with all the months of sitting around doing nothing but staring out the window. I might not even be five-four anymore.

Something brushed my cheek. I swatted it away. As my fingers tangled in it, I realized it was a dust bunny. I'd let more than myself go over the last few months. Our bungalow needed a thorough cleaning. So did Ray's pipes.

I reached for the baby quilt draped on the side of the crib. I could handle Ray's ultimatum. It was time to resurface. I wouldn't even bother to point out to him that tomorrow was Monday and my sports car boutique would be closed. But first I needed a few more hours of sleep.

Ray banged the cabinet doors in the kitchen. When I rose onto my knees, my whole body ached. The floor hadn't made for warm, restful sleep.

I snuck past Ray and hit the bathroom. Ten minutes later I'd nicked my legs five times while shaving and washed my hair twice. I was pleasantly surprised to find the brown locks had only a few new strands of gray to betray my thirty-eight years. I could use a haircut though. It took me twice as long to blow dry the wavy hair that fell to my shoulder blades. Then I tackled my overabundance of eyebrow and toenail.

Getting dressed proved more difficult. I hadn't eaten much in the last four months, and my size eight clothes hung on me. I found a long black skirt with an elastic waist, slit the waistband, hacked off several inches of elastic, and safety-pinned the edges together. When I teamed the skirt with a white sweater and my favorite black dress boots, I didn't look too bad. A touch of blush made me look less wan. Mascara made my eyes pop.

I approached the kitchen with trepidation, hoping Ray wouldn't pick up yelling at me where he'd left off last night.

Instead, one of Ray's famous Belgian waffles awaited me, drenched in syrup and whipped cream. He used to make them every Sunday, but I couldn't remember the last time he had. For an all masculine male, he could be very Betty Crocker.

He looked up from the paper, his gaze raking me from head to toe. "You look gorgeous."

I felt immediately forgiven as I slid onto the stool next to him at the breakfast bar. "Like Valerie Bertinelli?" Ray had a thing for her all through high school, with her pictures adorning his locker. My resemblance to her had attracted him.

He twirled my long hair in his fingers. "Exactly. Gorgeous." He tipped my chin and kissed my lips. "Too bad I'm late for work."

He stood and smoothed an imaginary wrinkle from his perfectly pressed county sheriff's department uniform. Deputy Ray Parker. God, I loved a man in uniform, especially this handsome dark-haired stud. I blushed, happy to think this for the first time in months. Then I noticed a few more gray hairs at Ray's temples and worried I had caused them. Or had all his cases been preying on his mind while I'd sat, unwilling to listen?

He smiled at me, clearly pleased to see me up and about and ready to go. "I'm sorry, Darlin'. No strawberries for the waffles. It's not the right season for them, anyway. Here's the shopping list." Ray leaned in for another kiss, lingering as he stroked his thumb over my lower lip. My nether regions tingled in response—not that I felt like doing anything about it. It was just good to know I was still capable of excitement. "Make sure to invite Cory and Erica for dinner Thursday."

My eyes bulged. "Thursday?"

"Yeah, it's Thanksgiving." Ray disappeared out the kitchen door with a wave.

I looked at the list. Turkey. Stuffing bread. Canned cranberry sauce.

My armpits felt damp. I licked my lips. Not only did I have to face the world this morning, but I had to entertain in three days. Although Ray always did the turkey and the stuffing. Maybe I could manage mashed potatoes and a frozen pie. Cory and Erica would bring something. It might work out.

I ate two bites of waffle. Then two more. Then I finished the whole thing. My stomach felt bloated, but I wouldn't need to expand the elastic in my skirt anytime soon. I loaded the dishwasher and wiped down the granite countertops before stuffing the list in my purse and heading out the door.

Driving my Lexus for the first time in weeks reminded me how much I loved the feeling of independence and control behind the wheel. Traffic was light on Main Street, since most of the shops in Wachobe didn't open until ten. Only Asdale Auto Imports opened at nine a.m. Tuesday through Saturday as it had for the last four years under my ownership and the prior forty or so years when my dad ran his garage at this address.

I pulled into the parking lot behind the building and found Cory's BMW parked there. Strange for a Monday.

A cold front had settled in overnight. I held the collar of my white wool coat tight to my neck as I walked along the edge of my cedar-shingled building. The shingles and the white trim could have used a touchup this past summer. I hoped the town fathers hadn't noticed as well. They considered my building an abomination amongst their prized Victorian brick and clapboard storefronts, and my pre-owned but pristine sports cars too modern for their desired tourist town image. In fact, almost a year ago, they tried to force me to relocate to a back street, away from Main Street and the lakefront that attracted thousands of summer residents and cottage rentals. I refused. The Asdale automotive tradition would carry on at this address. If I could get my act together, it might even do so under my leadership once again.

The bell jingled, announcing my arrival. Cory appeared in the showroom, wearing his mechanic's overalls, booties, and plastic surgical gloves smeared with grease.

"Jo. What a great surprise." He stripped off the gloves and threw them in the wastebasket. His arms bruised my ribs as he lifted me off the floor. "I'm so glad to see you."

One whiff of his cologne and I felt the same way. Friends like Cory were hard to come by. "I missed you, too."

He set me down inches from the 2006 F430 Ferrari Spider that had become the bane of my existence. It rested in the middle of my showroom floor, Rosso Corsa paint gleaming under the pin lights, no longer desirable to anyone after I found a murdered man in its front seat almost a year ago now. All my inventory dollars were tied up in the car. Unable to add to my stock on the lot, my only option was to offer customers my ability to locate and broker deals for a sports car of their choice. With the popularity of the Internet and cars readily available for sale online, not many customers took me up on my offer. Without Cory's steady maintenance income, I would be out of business.

I searched his face. "It's Monday. Why are you working?"

He avoided my gaze. "I'm a little behind."

That wasn't like Cory. He always finished his work on time or earlier. I opened my mouth to ask why then thought for a moment. Obviously, it was my fault. He'd been doing his work and mine for months. "I'm so sorry, Cory. I should have been here."

Cory waved his hand as if to say "don't worry about it." He led me into my office and pushed me into my chair. "Good news."

"You sold the Ferrari."

He tipped his head to the side. "Ah, no. But we have two new customers, and one of them needs your expertise."

My throat swelled shut. What expertise? Everything I touched turned into tragedy. "Tell me about the other customer first."

He dropped into the chair beside the desk, looking like I'd punctured his tires. "Okay. Brennan Rowe bought a turbo-charged Mazda Protégé. He hopes to race it this spring, and he wants me to be the crew chief and mechanic for his team." He leapt to his feet. "It's in the garage now. Want to see it?"

Race car support would be a new niche for our business, but not one I wanted to pursue. Too much time at the track. Too many last-minute hassles. Too much tweaking of sensitive engines, brakes, and transmissions. Too hard to hold down expenses. Still, Brennan Rowe reeked of money, especially after the successful construction and lease of his much-contended office building, and he was a lucrative customer with a significant car collection. If Cory had agreed to provide race support, I'd go along with it for now. "Maybe later. Tell me about my new customer first."

Cory stuck his hands in his pockets and swayed on the balls of his feet. Small but wiry at five-one, he always had a lot of energy. Maybe that was why his auburn hair curled poodle-tight. "She's different."

A woman. That was different. Most of my customers were men looking for the power, luxury, status, and speed a fine automobile provided. "How so?"

Cory's girly eyelashes blinked four times in rapid succession. "She read an article on the Internet about the cars that turn men's heads; cars that make men think a woman's hot. You know, a Mercedes 300SL roadster, a Porsche 911, cars like that. She decided to buy one of the cars on the list. She wants to get this guy's attention, and he likes sports cars."

"So which one of the ten did she pick?"

Cory scrunched his eyes as if fearing my response. "The Caterham Seven."

I wished I was home in bed with the covers over my head. "You're kidding me. Aren't they only available in England?"

"They have dealerships in the U.S. now."

"They're kit cars, aren't they?"

"You can buy them and build them. I offered to do that for her, but getting a kit car registered and insured is a hassle. We decided that purchasing a used DeDion model would be the best way to go. It's got the newer Ford Zetec engine, improved suspension, and meets most emission standards."

"Does she know it's an open car, best driven wearing a helmet? Does she think getting soaked in rainstorms and picking bugs out of her teeth will attract this guy?"

Cory sank into the chair again. "Jo, she's not an attractive woman. She's big-boned with hair dyed the color of the Ferrari. Crooked teeth. It's not pretty. But she knows this guy loves the Caterham Seven. He saw it in some Japanese animated cartoons and got all hot for it."

"If she's that big, will she even fit in the car? It's designed for racing." Wouldn't the town muckety mucks be delighted to have Wachobe turn into the new road racing street course? I didn't think they'd send me roses in appreciation.

"Yeah, but it's built for living. She'll fit. I can make her fit, if you can find the car."

I stifled a sigh. "All right. I'll start in the Sunbelt, where people can drive a car like that year-round." Unlike here in New York's Finger Lakes region, where maybe a handful of days over a couple of summer months would be suitable.

"Great." Cory fumbled through a stack of note pads on my desk. "Here's her brother's number. She's staying with him until Christmas. I told her we'd call once we located a car for her."

He sprang out of the chair, ready for action. "I've got a Fiat to service this morning and a Land Rover coming in this afternoon."

I held up my hand to slow his departure. "Cory, one more thing. Did you want to come over for Thanksgiving dinner?"

His eyes misted. "I do, but can I bring a date?"

A date. Cory's life had been busy in more ways than one since I dropped out of sight. "Sure. Who?"

"I'll let you know after I ask him."

How mysterious. Cory had learned the man he loved was a big fat liar in the worst way just a few days before we lost Noelle. He'd handled his depression better than me, pouring his energy into his maintenance work and letting out all his emotion in amateur theater performances at the Broadway-quality theater one town over from Wachobe. Too bad I hadn't taken a page from his book.

I powered up my computer, smelling smoke as the dust burned off. The website for Hemming Motors News came up a second after I typed in the address. They didn't have any Caterhams listed.

A little more searching uncovered two for sale from sports car dealerships in Florida and Arizona. No one answered the phone numbers listed on their websites. I left my name and numbers, office and cell. What more could I do today?

Cory had the bills paid to date, and he'd invoiced all his maintenance customers in a timely manner. An order for parts and supplies went out last week. He didn't really need me here. I'd become superfluous in my own business.

I tried to think of a way to become more important. I stuck my head in the three-bay garage. "I'm going grocery shopping. I'll bring you back lunch around noon."

Flat on his back and smiling, Cory shot out from under the Fiat on his mechanic's creeper. "Can we have pizza?"

———

The grocery store proved to be a nightmare. I couldn't decide between a fresh turkey, a Butterball, or the store brand. Jellied cranberry sauce or sauce with berries? One loaf of stuffing bread? Or two, if Cory brought a guest? Maybe Erica would like to bring a guest as well?

I dialed her cell phone number and waited. She answered on the eighth ring. She sounded half-awake.

"What are you doing?"

"Sleeping. I worked until two a.m. What do you want?"

"I want to make sure you're planning on having Thanksgiving dinner with us."

"I'm surprised you care enough to ask."

I deserved that. I hadn't called her in weeks. "I care. Did you want to bring a date?"

"Are you kidding me? I'm twenty pounds overweight. I look like a cow. No one wants to poke a cow, Jolene."

"That's a nice picture, Erica."

"Better than the picture of all my flab being sucked out. Have you ever seen them do that on TV?"

I had. It grossed me out for days, and the mere memory of it made me want to vomit. "Why are you so gory today? What's wrong?"

"Everything. Not that you care."

"I care, Erica, I care. Why don't you come for dinner tonight and tell me all about it?"

"Fine. But don't serve chicken. I hate chicken." She hung up.

I couldn't decide what to serve for dinner. Ray's list only covered Thanksgiving dinner and a few other staples. I pushed the cart from one end of the store to another, frustrated with my own indecisiveness and shocked at the anxiety this simple responsibility induced. When I saw another woman reach for lasagna noodles, I seized on the idea, purchasing the supplies for it, salad fixings, and a loaf of Italian bread. Only after I was halfway home did I realize I hadn't purchased dessert. Ray liked dessert every night.

I ordered pizza for Cory and me while I unloaded the groceries at home. I didn't feel like driving back to the shop, but I knew he expected me to eat lunch with him today. And I could run into the bakery down the street for a dessert. I would have much rather taken a nap.

But I soldiered on, picking up the pizza and returning to the shop in time to catch a phone call from Ray.

"How's your day going?"

"Okay. I shopped. We're having lasagna for dinner."

"Excellent. Can you set one more place?"

"I'll have to set two extra. I invited Erica."

His silence unnerved me.

"Is Erica a problem, Ray?"

"No, but I have someone I want you to meet."

"I don't need a psychiatrist, Ray. I'm doing everything you asked me to do." Not with any enjoyment or enthusiasm, but I was doing it.

"He's not a doctor, Darlin'."

"Who is he?"

"His name is Danny Phillips. He's twelve."

"Twelve? Where did you meet him?"

"His father was arrested this morning for grand theft auto."

"Not good."

"It gets worse. He's Danny's only parent, and he's not going to make bail. When he's proven guilty, he may be incarcerated for a while."

I noticed Ray said "when" not "if." The Sheriff's Department must have an airtight case. "So why do you want me to meet him?"

"We're his new foster parents."

TWO

ERICA ARRIVED AT OUR home before Ray. I was in the kitchen talking to myself, or, rather, talking to Ray, saying all the things I wouldn't have the courage or stamina to say to his face. Nor would I voice them in front of this twelve-year-old boy, who needed a loving home. Too bad I didn't feel capable of loving him. I wasn't even sure I would like him.

"What are we having?"

"Lasagna."

Erica plopped onto a stool at the breakfast bar. "Great, I wore a white blouse. I'll probably get sauce all over it and look like someone stabbed me."

I stopped slicing the bread, holding the knife in midair. "You're very graphic today and not in a good way."

"Nobody wants me anymore. I'm fat and used up."

"You don't look so bad to me." Her hair could use styling. She could button up her blouse a couple more buttons. Okay, maybe she had a slight roll at the waistline, but nothing crisis-mode. On a good day, she could still give Kate Hudson a run for her money with her sparkling blue eyes and natural blonde ringlets.

"My thighs rub together." She yanked on the blouse. "This is size eight. I'm an elephant." Her eyes raked over my body. "You stole my figure and gave me yours in return."

I resumed slicing so I wouldn't be tempted to turn the knife on her.

"Can I have a beer?" Erica slid off the stool and helped herself to a Corona.

"You shouldn't drink with your medication."

She took a long swing. "I'm not taking it anymore. Mom said I'm cured."

I nicked my finger with the knife. Thankfully, no blood oozed out to ruin the bread.

Erica claimed our dead mother gave her advice all the time. I didn't know exactly how these exchanges occurred since Erica never even visited Mom's grave, but I did know from experience that their supposed conversations tended to precede disaster. "When did you take your last pill?"

Her shoulders hunched. "I don't remember."

"What does Dr. Albert say about it?"

"I haven't seen him lately." She headed toward the living room. "I'm going to watch the news."

Erica had stopped taking her medicine before, claiming to be cured. Her bipolar disorder would never be cured, just tempered to a dull roar. Tomorrow morning I would drag her to Dr. Albert's office and force her to start taking her medication again. She'd come so far in the last year. I didn't want to see her backslide.

I rolled my shoulders and my neck. I'd need to go to bed early tonight to have enough energy to win that battle.

When I set the breadbasket on the table, Erica was watching a talk show. Two women were attacking each other on a stage, pulling hair and screaming while a man held a microphone up to their faces.

Erica pointed her beer at the television. "Women are animals. No wonder men think we're just a receptacle. And when the receptacle shows too much sign of use, they move on."

My lips parted, but no words came to mind. Tomorrow. I'd tackle her tomorrow.

I heard Ray come through the kitchen door and turned to greet him. A mop-headed boy stood next to him, barely waist-high compared to Ray but chin-high compared to me. The sleeves on his red ski jacket were an inch above his wrist bones and his baggy jeans had a hole in each knee. He had on some pretty expensive high-tops, though.

"Darlin', this is Danny." Ray looked at him, reached over and swept the dark hair off the kid's face. I got a glimpse of angry brown eyes before the hair flopped back into place. "Danny, this is Jolene."

"Hi, Danny. Nice to meet you."

The kid muttered an unintelligible reply.

Erica bumped into my back. "Who's the kid, Ray?"

"This is Danny. He's going to be staying with us for a while."

"No shit."

My elbow slammed into her belly roll.

"I mean, that's great."

While Ray hung up their coats in the living room closet, Erica trailed me to the stove. "What's up with the kid? Does Ray want to adopt him? He looks like the Shaggy Dog."

"He's our new foster child. It's only temporary, until his father gets out of jail."

"His dad's in jail?"

I had no doubt that both Danny and Ray had heard her shriek. "We'll talk about it later, when we're alone, okay?"

"Okay, but you better count the silver."

When we sat down to dinner, Ray's glower confirmed that he'd heard everything, and Erica was in trouble. Or maybe I was.

I tried to make amends. "I hope you like lasagna, Danny."

"It's okay."

It must have been more than okay, because he shoveled it into his mouth in seconds flat. Ray smiled at me and served the kid a second helping.

Danny didn't touch the salad I put on his plate. I decided not to press the issue.

Ray made most of the dinner conversation, explaining that he'd delivered Danny's school transcripts and made an appointment with the principal of Wachobe Middle School to register Danny the next morning. Danny would start school the Monday following Thanksgiving.

After dinner, while Erica and Danny watched SpongeBob on the television in the living room, I whispered to Ray in the kitchen.

"Where are his clothes?"

"His father didn't provide an address at the time of arrest. I don't know where their stuff is."

I couldn't believe my ears. "Then how did you get the kid?"

"His father told me he needed to be picked up from school."

"Didn't the school have an address for them?"

"Yes, but it was his father's ex-girlfriend's place. All she said was that they moved out six months ago."

"What about Social Services?"

"Danny's been on their radar before, but they're happy to have us shoulder the burden for now."

"Even though shots have been fired in our home?" This fact had contributed to the judge's decision to return Noelle to her birthmother four months ago. Or maybe it had been the man's blood spattered all over our walls, looking kinda Jackson Pollack, but not in a good way.

Ray frowned. "That wasn't our fault. Let's just say Danny is not the type of kid to be in high demand."

I didn't have the energy to explore this revelation. "Where's he going to sleep?"

"On the couch for tonight."

"Then where?" I started to load the dishwasher.

"We do have a spare bedroom."

A plate slipped out of my hand and shattered on the floor. "Are you talking about Noelle's nursery?" Tears filled my eyes. It was my last link to her. Sometimes I even thought I could smell the No More Tears from her hair.

Ray got the broom and swept up the shards. "I know it's hard, Darlin', but it's time to move on. You said yesterday you wanted to help people. Here's a kid who needs our help."

Words failed me. Ray always liked to take control of a situation and make decisions for me. It was a side to his personality I could live without, but I didn't have the strength or inclination to fight it today.

He took my silence as acquiescence. "I'm on the day shift tomorrow. I'd appreciate it if you took Danny over to school to meet with the principal. Then maybe you could do a little clothes and supply shopping with him? He's looking forward to it. Can you do that for me?"

Before I could tell him I already had my day planned around straightening out Erica, she let out another shriek. Ray and I charged into the living room to find her waving her purse in the air.

"I went in the can and came out to find Danny Boy helping himself to my cash."

"I was looking for a Kleenex." Danny rubbed his nose. "I got boogers."

"Liar! The kid's a thief."

Ray held up a placating hand. "Settle down, Erica. I'm sure it's just a misunderstanding."

"Misunderstanding, my ass. I'm out of here." She grabbed her coat from the closet. Her slam reverberated in the front door glass.

Ray perched on the edge of the couch next to the boy, whose head had sunk into his shoulders. "We have some rules in this house, Danny. If you're going to live here, you have to follow our rules. No stealing, no lying, no swearing, no drugs, no smoking of any kind, no playing with matches, no going anywhere without telling us, and no talking back. We expect you to do your homework and help out when you're asked." He reached his massive hand up and brushed the hair out of the kid's face. "Will you promise to follow those rules, Danny?"

20

"Yes." But his sullen tone and his failure to look Ray in the eye bothered me.

Erica could wait another day. This kid needed me more. But I couldn't let this opportunity pass. "I have one more rule."

Danny and Ray looked at me.

"No hair in your eyes. Tomorrow we'll get you a haircut, too."

———

The principal at Wachobe Middle School, Mrs. Travis, projected warmth in her smile, her handshake, and her guiding hand on Danny's shoulder. I squared away the paperwork with her while a teacher gave Danny some placement assessments. Then the principal took us on a tour. I'd seen the building before. Ray and I both went to school here, and the brick exterior and tan interior hadn't changed much. The library had new blue carpeting, and the gym had a springy newfangled floor made out of recycled rubber. I recognized the smell of Pizza Day wafting from the cafeteria.

With hair masking his face, I couldn't tell what Danny thought of the school. He sat outside in the hallway for a few minutes after our tour while the principal reviewed his assessments with me.

"He tested at grade level, although the teacher thought he showed more potential. I'm going to place him in Mr. Matthews' class. He's a young teacher, and boys seem to relate well with him." Mrs. Travis fingered Danny's transcripts. "Danny's file indicates he can be a handful. I think Mr. Matthews will be up to the task."

I knew why Ray brought the documents over here himself yesterday. He didn't want me to read the kid's transcript. Did he think a twelve-year-old could scare me?

On second thought, Erica at ten had been pretty frightening.

Mrs. Travis didn't seem to notice my involuntary shudder. She kept right on talking as though I was the natural choice to fulfill Danny's needs. "This is the list of supplies we require for fifth graders. It would be helpful if Danny could bring them on his first day."

Maybe she and Ray saw something in me that I didn't. In any case, I was in no shape to argue with either of them, or Danny, for that matter. I rose and picked up my purse. "We're going shopping now. He'll be ready to go on Monday."

The principal shook my hand again and wished us well. I stepped into the hall outside her office, but didn't see Danny. I headed to the left down the hallway in search of him, the click from my dress boot heels echoing off the walls.

I glanced into the classrooms filled with hard-at-work children. At the next hall, I gave up and turned back only to find Danny standing three yards behind me. "There you are. Are you ready to go?"

He nodded and took off at a fast clip. I had to hustle to keep up with him.

The hour drive to the nearest shopping mecca passed without a word from Danny. I commented on how nice the principal seemed and tried to talk up his new teacher. Danny turned his face to the window. I chalked up his silence to natural apprehension about new people and places.

I found a barbershop that catered to sports enthusiasts with televisions tuned to the games while stylists did their magic. Danny didn't express any opinions as to how he would like his hair cut, so I asked the woman to give him a popular cut. His hair ended up covering his ears but not his face. Now I could see he was quite a handsome little fellow with high cheekbones and eyes like a mournful puppy dog. His right cheek had a nick in it the size of a pinhead just underneath his eye.

He picked Wendy's for lunch, but refused to make any sort of conversation, despite my half-hearted efforts. I picked Wal-Mart for shopping. He picked dark-wash jeans and T-shirts with motorcycles on them. Boxers, not briefs, and white crew socks. Pajamas with sports themes. The dark blue parka I picked seemed satisfactory to him. He refused a hat, mittens, or boots, even though I pointed out the snowfall predicted for Thanksgiving Day.

I read the school supply list while he selected the items off the shelf, showing a preference for all things blue and red, especially a red backpack. When we moved to the linen aisle, he selected a twin bed quilt with a sports theme. I got him all the accessories to match. We did all this with minimal conversation. Sometimes I received only a jerk of his head in reply to my questions. I attributed this to his being twelve years old and a boy, who had to shop for his new underwear and sheets with a strange woman.

We bought a bedroom set at a store that promised "zoom delivery" the very next day and no payment for a year, the only kind of furniture I knew for sure we could afford. He liked the walnut. So did I. He picked out sky blue paint at Sherwin-Williams. I was okay with that, too. But Ray would have to roll it over the pink I'd lovingly painted on Noelle's walls. My heart would break if I had to do it myself.

All in all, I considered it a good day. I planted Danny in front of the television when we got home, put the leftover lasagna in the oven, and debated calling Cory. I decided in favor of the nap I'd been craving instead. Cory and I had agreed yesterday that I would return to work full-time next week. This would be a slow week, given the holiday.

The phone rang as my head touched the pillow.

"Mrs. Parker, this is Mrs. Travis. We met this morning at school."

I sat up. "Yes, of course."

"We have a little problem. One of the children brought his Nintendo DS to school this morning in his backpack. That's against school rules, because we do have a theft problem from time to time. Anyway, he reported it missing at lunchtime. We talked to the teachers, and they suspect a boy they saw in the hallway this morning. He matches Danny's description."

Shocked and embarrassed, I couldn't think of a reply.

"I was wondering if you could talk to Danny. The school is closed for the holiday beginning tomorrow, so if he does have the Nintendo, maybe you could bring it in on Monday morning. And of course I'll want to meet with both of you."

I was being summoned to the principal's office for the first time at age thirty-eight. My face burned with shame as I set down the receiver. Although I'd become Erica's surrogate mother at age twelve, her real troubles hadn't begun until after her school years. I'd never had to deal with an irate principal. I felt like an instant failure as Danny's foster parent. What had Ray gotten us into?

Danny was still on the couch where I'd left him. He didn't look up when I sat down or acknowledge my presence in any way. After opening my mouth a few times then closing it just as fast, I decided to set the table and let Ray deal with it when he got home.

I served dinner as soon as he walked in the door. Danny ate two servings of lasagna again, but tried to leave the table without eating the green beans I'd prepared.

I put my hand on his arm. "Another rule. You have to eat vegetables. The vitamins in them are good for you."

He looked to Ray for help.

"Jolene's right. Eat them and you can have two pieces of pie."

Danny ate them and the pie. "Can I watch TV now?"

I shook my head. "I got a call from the principal this afternoon, Ray. After Danny and I left, they discovered a boy's Nintendo was missing. The teachers saw a boy matching Danny's description near the backpack where it was last seen."

Ray got his "good-cop, bad-cop, whatever-you-need-me-to-be cop" expression going, his poker face showing a hint of intimidation this time. "Danny?"

"I found it on the floor. Finders keepers."

"Go get it."

He slinked away from the table and returned minutes later, holding the shiny black box in his hand.

"I'm very disappointed, Danny. I told you in this house we don't steal."

Danny slid his hands into his pockets. "It was on the floor."

"Then you should have taken it to the lost and found. You'll have to take it to the principal on Monday and apologize to the kid you took it from."

I decided not to tell Ray we'd been summoned to the principal's office. Most weeks, he didn't work on Mondays. I could tell him then and let him have the pleasure of facing Mrs. Travis.

Ray pushed his chair back from the table. "I think you should help me clear the table and do the dishes tonight, Danny. Maybe we can assign you some regular chores and pay you an allowance. You could earn enough money to buy your own Nintendo."

I could see Danny mulling this concept over. Ray handed him his dish, and he carried it to the sink. I decided to make myself useful by cutting the tags off Danny's new clothes and washing them with his new sheets.

I could hear Ray's voice murmuring to Danny and the occasional soft reply. Ray would be good for Danny. He was a rock when he needed to be, and a real softie the rest of the time. But what would I do all the hours Ray was at work? I didn't think I could keep up with both Danny and Erica, and tomorrow I had to get my sister in hand.

Over the noise of the washing machine, I heard the phone ring. Ray hung up as I entered the kitchen. I looked at him in question.

"I have to go out."

"You got called in?"

"No." Ray's face was a thundercloud. "Gumby called me. Your sister is drunk and disorderly. She's singing at the top of her lungs at The Cat's Meow and—" he shot a glance at Danny who averted his interested gaze "—flashing people. He said if I hurry, the owner won't make him take her in."

Steven Fellows, better known as Gumby, worked as a county deputy sheriff, too. His wife, the lovely and talented Briana Engle, stripped at The Cat's Meow. The strip joint was located well outside the township of Wachobe but still a pimple on our image.

I pressed my hand against my temple, fearing what tomorrow would bring. "Erica stopped taking her medicine. If you bring her back here for the night, I'll call Dr. Albert and schedule an emergency visit for tomorrow. Do you have to work tomorrow?"

Ray grabbed his car keys and headed for the door. "I do."

I looked at Danny, who'd been swinging his gaze between us. "Then Danny is going to have to go with us to the appointment."

His eyes widened.

I hated to expose him to Erica at her worst, not to mention the rest of Dr. Albert's patients. But then, on the other hand, it might be good for Danny to get a look at the state mental facility. After all, it was a lot like a prison.

And if he didn't stop following in his father's footsteps pretty quick, that just might be his next home.

THREE

By the time Ray dragged Erica into the house, all the song had left her. In fact, she ran to the bathroom and all the drink left her, too. I scraped her off the bathroom floor and tucked her into our bed. Ray would have to take the couch tonight, and the kid would have to make do with a sleeping bag on the floor.

Ray lit a fire and toasted marshmallows with Danny, for whom it seemed a new experience. He torched several before he got the hang of it. Then Ray told him a few ghost stories. The kid didn't scare easily. I left them around ten o'clock to lie down beside my sister, who snored louder than Ray. I wrapped my pillow around my head and tried to get enough sleep to face the next day.

At seven a.m. Ray left for work with a crick in his neck, shoulders hunched from sleeping on the too-short couch, a grim look on his face. He didn't even kiss me good-bye. Danny and Erica arrived at breakfast around ten, both with sour expressions and moans.

"Coffee. Water. Aspirin." Erica rested her head on the table. "Did you get another kid last night?"

I set a cup of coffee in front of her. I'd made it especially for her, knowing that she would want it. I never drank coffee, although I did enjoy the aroma of it. It reminded me of Ray, who could never go more than a couple hours without a cup.

I set juice and pancakes in front of Danny. "What are you talking about, Erica?"

She pointed to Danny. "There's two of him."

Danny rolled his eyes. "You're a drunk."

Erica whipped her head off the table, then put her hands to her temples, blinking rapidly. "I am not."

"You puked last night. You're gross."

"You're a thief."

He shot her the finger.

I banged on the table. Erica moaned.

"Erica, you're thirty-three years old. Stop arguing with the twelve-year-old. Danny, more rules. No swear fingers and no name-calling." I set the aspirin and water in front of Erica. "Drink up. We have a noon appointment with Dr. Albert."

"I don't want to see him."

"Well, he wants to see you. He's skipping lunch just for you. So get it together, because we're going."

The forty-five-minute ride to Dr. Albert's office passed in silence. I couldn't even play the radio, because Erica said it made her head ache.

Danny muttered "boo hoo" in the back seat after she complained. I shot him "the look" via the rearview mirror. He got the message and shut up.

Dr. Albert rented office space in a building conveniently located next to the state psychiatric center, where Erica had spent many months after her multiple suicide attempts. As we pulled into the parking lot, the shadow of "the tower," the nickname for the fourth floor where she'd resided, fell over the car. She slumped in her seat. "I'm not going in."

I opened my mouth to argue, but Danny got his word out first. "Chicken."

Erica whirled to face him. "I am not chicken. I hate chicken."

"Chicken."

As their battle raged on, I got out of the car, walked around to Erica's door, and whipped it open. I grabbed her arm and yanked her out of the car.

"Ow."

I kept hold of her arm and marched her toward Dr. Albert's office. "You're arguing with the twelve-year-old again."

"I don't like him. Can't you give him back to foster care?"

The thought had crossed my mind more than once, but at the moment, I didn't like my sister all that much either. I kept walking.

Dr. Albert was hot, and the minute Erica saw him, she remembered that. She straightened up and smoothed her clothes, smiling at high voltage. He gave her the same wattage in return and ushered her into his office. "Give us an hour, please, Jolene."

I turned and realized Danny hadn't followed us inside. I jogged out to the parking lot. He was in the car. I let out a sigh of relief and climbed into the driver's seat.

"Thanks for riding along with us, Danny. When we get home, your furniture should be coming. And Ray has tomorrow off because it's Thanksgiving. Maybe you guys can start painting the room in the morning."

"Which room am I getting?"

I swallowed. "The second bedroom."

"The one with the baby crib in it?"

Tears warmed my eyes. "Yeah. You guys will have to move all that furniture into the garage."

"Did your baby die?"

I dug a tissue out of my purse and blew my nose. "No. We had a baby from foster care for seven months. We wanted to adopt her, but her mother changed her mind and wanted her back."

"And now you're sad. That's what Ray said."

"He did?"

"He said you were sad, but having me around would make you happy. He said not to worry if you cried, because you'd snap out of it."

That sounded just like Ray. For years I'd soldiered on in the face of my mother's suicide, my father's death, and my sister's bizarre behavior, Ray helpful by my side. But when we lost No-elle and I slumped into depression, Ray accepted two months of my misery before he sat me down. He said he'd never worried about me before when he left for work, because he knew I'd go on whether he came home or not. But now he did worry, and it was affecting his decision-making. I'd told him, "Don't worry, I'll snap out of it." And I would—in time. But it needed to be *my* time.

"He's right. Not to worry." I managed a smile as I stuffed the soiled tissue back in my purse. "I'm okay now."

Danny gave me a relieved twitch of his lips in return. "I don't know what's so great about babies anyway. All they do is cry and mess their diapers. They smell bad."

"They smell really nice after a bath, trust me." I pinched the bridge of my nose to stop the tears from returning.

"I guess." He faced the window. Our bonding was over.

I turned on the radio and listened until it was time to retrieve Erica, trying not to think about Noelle or about Ray's scheme to make me feel better by sticking me with this juvenile delinquent in training. But when the song "You Are So Beautiful" played, I pictured Noelle's sweet face and almost lost it.

I locked Danny in the car while I walked into the office building, explaining it was for his protection. His expression said, "Yeah, right, lady."

A light snow had started. I stuck my tongue out to catch one of the first snowflakes of the season before entering the office building. Maybe in my next life I would be a carefree, drifting snowflake.

Erica handed me her prescription as we stepped into the hall outside Dr. Albert's office. "He said to get this filled on our way home. And we need to pick up my car from The Cat's Meow. I have to work tonight."

I put my hand on her arm to bring her to a halt. "Did you talk to Dr. Albert about your poor self-image, your drinking, and that stuff about being a receptacle?"

"Yes, Jolene." Erica resumed walking, kicking the new fallen snow into the air. "He says my medication helps promote weight loss."

"Really?" I read the prescription. It was for the same stuff she'd been taking for the last year, maybe a higher dosage. The fact sheet from the pharmacy said it could promote bloating. Good thing Erica never read the fact sheets.

"He also said studies have shown that women's hymens can regenerate after months of celibacy. I'm going to be a born-again virgin."

I stopped walking. She took a few more steps, missed me, and turned around.

We couldn't have this conversation in front of Danny, and I didn't want to lose the opportunity. "What are you talking about?"

"I offered to go home with one of the guys at the bar last month. We did it before, a couple years back. He passed. He said my receptacle has been used one time too many and was stretched out like a chicken that had laid too many eggs. Then nobody wanted to go home with me anymore, not even this guy who always sits around until after two a.m. talking to me. And he's not even that good-looking."

This must be what Ray meant when he said Erica was making a fool of herself all over town. She'd been begging men to take her home. Ugh!

I resumed walking. Erica followed.

"A guy over at The Cat's Meow liked me. He wanted to take me home, but Gumby wouldn't let him." She twirled her hair. "Gumby's just jealous. He wanted to make it with me a couple months ago, but I turned him down."

I stumbled and righted myself. Gumby got married five months ago. Was he cheating on his wife already? I shouldn't be so surprised with his track record. But Erica was Ray's sister-in-law. Gumby should show more deference to his comrade-in-arms.

"Dr. Albert said I could be a virgin again if I abstain for a few months. Then my receptacle will be brand new." Erica twirled in circles across the parking lot. "He's so smart. He might even want me then."

I didn't attempt to explain all her faulty logic, nor did I question the quality of Dr. Albert's therapy. Abstaining sounded like a wonderful idea to me. At least it would keep her out of The Cat's Meow.

We climbed into the front seat of the car. I turned over the ignition and glanced over my shoulder as I clicked the gear into reverse.

The back seat was empty.

I slammed the car into park and leapt out of the car. "Danny? Danny?"

My gaze swept the parking lot and the grounds beyond. I couldn't spot any movement other than a plastic bag blowing with the wind.

I raced into the office building and crashed through the door to Dr. Albert's waiting room. No sign of Danny.

I ran back outside. Erica met me at the door. "Did you find him?"

"No."

I darted across the parking lot, threw open my car door, and wrenched my cell phone from my purse. My hands shook as I dialed Ray.

He answered on the second ring.

"He's gone."

"Danny?"

"Yes, yes! I left him in the car outside Dr. Albert's office. I locked him in and told him not to open the doors for anyone. I came out with Erica and he was gone."

My mouth felt dry. A lump formed in my throat. I'd lost another child.

"Do you think someone took him, Ray?"

"I doubt it. I'll issue an Amber Alert anyway. What was he wearing?"

I told him.

"Okay. Stay right there. I'm on my way."

I hit the end button and met Erica by the trunk of the car. "Ray's coming. He doesn't think anyone took him. Danny must have taken off by himself."

Erica kicked a stone across the parking lot. She glanced at me out of the corner of her eye. "You didn't tell Danny I wanted you to give him back, did you?"

———

Ten minutes later Ray arrived. He sent me into the building to knock on all the office doors while he conducted a car-by-car search of the parking lot. The psychiatric center sat a quarter-mile off the nearest artery, so he reasoned that Danny didn't walk away. We would have spotted him.

No one in the office building had seen Danny, nor had the guard inside the psych center. I returned to the parking lot where Ray was talking on his radio.

"Erica said a car was parked next to you when you pulled in. Do you remember what kind of car it was, Darlin'?"

I looked at the spot where Erica stood, outlining a car with frantic waves of her arms. A faint car shape remained in the snow-covered parking lot. "It was a white car, Jo. I remember."

I closed my eyes and visualized pulling into the parking spot. "A white Toyota Camry, a 1996 maybe."

Ray announced that information over his radio.

A male voice responded, "I got a white Camry in sight. Southbound on Pinion Heights. O-o-o-h. Correction, make that stationary at the Charleston intersection. He just rear-ended a Volvo."

"I'm on my way." Ray leapt into his car and took off, siren blaring.

Erica looked at me. "Aren't you going to follow him?"

We chased Ray's sheriff's car, exceeding the speed limit without fear of being stopped since every available officer was on Danny's trail. I did slow down after sliding a few feet through a red light on the fresh snow.

Ray had pulled over about five miles from the psych center, joining a line of parked cars. Danny sat on the side of the road with his head between his knees. A paramedic knelt in the grass next to him, talking to him.

Another sheriff's deputy and a state police officer stood in the road with what looked to be the driver of the other vehicle, a Volvo station wagon. His arms waved as he spoke to the officers.

Erica and I avoided them and approached Danny.

Ray got to him first.

"Danny!"

He looked up and quivered. I couldn't blame him. Ray's nostrils were flaring, his neck flushed.

"Where did you get this car, Danny?"

"It's my dad's."

"Bullshit."

So much for the no swearing rule.

Danny jumped to his feet. "It is."

"Danny, it was parked in the psych center lot, next to Jolene's car. Why would your dad leave his car there?"

"I dunno, but he did. These are his keys." Danny pulled them from his pocket and dangled them in front of Ray.

Ray snatched them from his hand. I could see the initial *P* on the key chain. So could Ray. The flush on his neck started to fade. He marched over to the Camry.

We all chased after him.

He tried the ignition. It turned over.

Ray shut it down and opened the glove box. It was empty.

He checked the back seat, under the front seats and the floor mats, and in the seat pockets. All empty.

Ray walked around to the trunk and opened the lid.

A Styrofoam ice chest sat in the middle of the space. Ray glanced at Danny, who shrugged.

Ray lifted the lid off the chest. A cloud of dry ice rose. It cleared.

We all leaned in.

Erica screamed. She darted onto the sidewalk and gulped fresh air.

I tried to swallow the bile that had washed up my throat and onto my tongue.

Danny took a step back, biting his lip, his body trembling. "My bad. It's not my dad's car. I found the keys in the ignition. Honest."

Ray's eyes reduced to slits.

"Go stand on the sidewalk next to Erica, Danny. Don't say another word."

The other two officers had joined Ray and me behind the car. One of them leaned into the trunk and whipped his head out in the blink of an eye. "What the f—"

What was not in question. It was more *who*.

A woman's forearm sat in the middle of the ice chest, red fingernails embedded with tiny sparkling rhinestones, the index finger sporting a gigantic ruby ring to match, and the wrist, gold bangles, one studded with rubies. It would have been an attractive limb, but for the naked sinew, dried blood, and raw flesh right about where the elbow should have been. That was the image that kept the bile high in my throat.

That, and the thought that somewhere a woman was missing an arm, and I imagined, most likely her life.

FOUR

RAY KEPT DANNY WITH him and sent Erica and me packing. When I saw fear in Danny's eyes, I protested. A bolt of lightning flashed from Ray's eyes into mine. Raising my hands in defeat, I relinquished all custody of the child, giving Danny a light squeeze on the shoulder in support.

As I drove Erica back to The Cat's Meow to collect her car, I hoped that Ray would bring Danny home tonight. Juvenile detention wouldn't do anything to solve his problems, and I didn't like to picture him alone there with all the big bad boys.

Erica and I pulled into the parking lot at The Cat's Meow around three o'clock, after stopping at the drugstore to fill Erica's prescription and have her swallow the first dose.

The strip club had opened at noon. About a dozen cars were in the lot. Erica's black Porsche 944 sat alone, looking forlorn, at the far edge of the lot next to a corn field that still needed to be plowed under. I felt a little forlorn myself, since the Porsche used to be mine. I'd given it to her when I had to buy a four-door Lexus to accommodate Noelle's car seat. Seeing the Porsche now made me mourn her as well as my father. He'd bought the Porsche from an insurance company after it bounced off two trees and a Winnebago. He completed the restoration work himself. The car had been my high school graduation present. Every time Erica ground the gears, I cringed. I'm sure my dad did, too.

Erica slid behind the wheel and backed out. As I followed her out of the parking lot, a woman with fiery red hair stormed out of the strip club and wedged her considerable bulk into a yellow Mustang convertible. Her lips were moving the whole time as though she had someone to talk to, but she was the only one in sight.

A message from Cory awaited me on the answering machine when I arrived home.

"Hey Jo, I'll be bringing a guest tomorrow. What time should we come? Call me. Bye."

I dialed the number at the shop. Cory answered on the third ring.

"How's your day going, Cory?"

"Good. The dealers for the Caterhams returned your calls. They're both headed out of town for the holiday, so you can try them again on Monday."

"Okay. Listen, come by around two tomorrow. We'll eat at four."

"Great. What can I bring?"

"How about an hors d'oeuvre of some kind?"

"Okay. Brennan said he would make candied yams."

"Brennan? Brennan Rowe?"

Cory sounded sheepish when he replied "Yes."

I sank onto the couch. This was an interesting turn of events. We both knew Brennan as a customer, but Cory never let on that he might have a greater interest in the man. "Are you guys dating?"

"Sort of. We went to dinner a week ago, and he came to see me in the show the other night. We went out for coffee afterwards."

"So Thanksgiving will be your third date?"

"Is that a problem?"

"I guess not." But it could be. Danny, the delinquent, might be in attendance. At least Cory and Brennan didn't carry purses for him to pilfer from, but who knows what he might do next? And Erica wasn't exactly Miss Sunshine lately. Neither was I, for that matter. And who knew what kind of mood Ray might be in at the start of an investigation. God forbid, he might even have to work tomorrow and stick me with the turkey and all of them. I started to ask Cory if he really wanted to expose Brennan to all of us, but he had to hang up to take another call.

I would hope for the best.

———

Ray arrived home around six o'clock with Danny in tow. He immediately led Danny into the nursery and sat him in the rocking chair with instructions not to move. He closed the door, and I followed him into the kitchen.

"Why is Danny in there?"

Ray pulled a Corona from the refrigerator, popped the cap, and took a long slug. "Think of it as a timeout. He's not going to sit around and watch television, that's for sure."

"Did you find the owner of the Camry?" Not to mention whoever cut off that poor woman's arm?

"It was stolen from a used car lot outside Geneseo. They reported it missing on Monday. They didn't care if it was ever recovered. Their insurance will pay for the repairs to the front end."

"So how did it get to the psych center parking lot?"

Ray opened the refrigerator and started digging in the drawer. "I'm guessing the thief left it there."

"Could Danny's father have stolen it before his arrest?"

"Anything's possible. He's not admitting to it."

"What about the arm?"

Ray pulled a package of cheese from the drawer and ate two slices. "What's for dinner?"

It always amazed me that severed arms and dead bodies did not keep Ray from food. I tried not to look as guilty as I felt about having failed to prepare him a meal. "I didn't know when to expect you or if Danny would be with you."

He tossed the cheese on the counter. "How about grilled cheese sandwiches and soup?"

I busied myself with opening cans of clam chowder and microwaving them while Ray slathered butter on the bread and sandwiched the cheese slices. I wasn't going to let him ignore the elephant on the table, however. "What about the arm, Ray?"

"They're looking for fingerprint matches. We haven't had any calls about a missing local woman, so we put the word out we have an arm and no body."

"Were there any fingerprints in the Camry?"

"Dozens. They're being matched as well. I'm not holding my breath." He opened the oven and slid the tray of sandwiches under the broiler.

"Did Danny tell you anything else? Why did he take off in the first place?"

Ray leaned against the oven door with his arms folded. "He wanted to see his dad."

My heart panged in sympathy. "Why didn't he ask me to take him?"

"I don't know. He's impulsive."

Was that understatement supposed to be an excuse or a medical diagnosis? I wasn't sure I wanted to know the answer. "Can he see his father?"

"I told Danny I'd take him to see his dad tomorrow, if he behaves himself."

Maybe that would relieve some of Danny's distress. "Was the key in the Camry's ignition?"

"That's what Danny says."

"But you don't believe him?"

Ray peeked in the oven to check on the sandwiches. He flipped them. "All I know for sure is the key was in the ignition when the car was stolen from the used car lot. But it didn't have a key chain on it, just one of those white tags with the vehicle identification number written on it."

"Why would they leave the key in it at the lot? Are they idiots?"

"It needed new brakes. Someone was supposed to pick it up after hours and drive it to the garage."

So Danny wasn't completely at fault for rear-ending the Volvo. "Do you think Danny's dad might have stolen the car, put his key chain on it, and left it at the psych center?"

"Maybe. He won't even admit to stealing the Cadillac Escalade he was caught driving."

I wondered if he'd tried the finders keepers excuse, too. "Did he tell you anything more about where their things are? Where they lived?"

Ray shook his head as he pulled the tray from the oven. "We sent his mug shot and a description of Danny to area homeless shelters, but none of them claim to have housed them. I'm beginning to wonder if they lived from stolen car to stolen car. Danny's father does not have any vehicle registered to him in the state of New York."

What a horrible existence. Again, my heart bled a little for Danny and even for his father.

I scooped the soup into bowls and set them at the breakfast bar. Ray sliced the sandwiches and went to call Danny for dinner while I poured milk.

Danny chose the chair near the wall. He seemed pleased when I sat next to him. Perhaps he feared Ray would fire more questions at him during dinner. But instead Ray formulated a plan of attack for painting Danny's new room that included Danny carrying all the baby furniture to the garage as soon as Ray disassembled it.

I cleaned up dinner while they started working. Then I contributed to the effort by moving the rocking chair into our living room. We would need the extra seats for our guests tomorrow anyway. I also cleaned the bathrooms and vacuumed the whole house, including Noelle's now empty room.

I told myself the dust from vacuuming had caused the tears to form in my eyes.

———

Thanksgiving morning we awoke to find two feet of snow on the ground. Ray sent Danny outside to shovel the driveway and the sidewalk while he stuffed the turkey, a task he took great pride in each year. He planned to keep Danny working all morning, and he did. By the time the doorbell rang at a few minutes after two, the bungalow smelled of fresh paint mixed with turkey, pumpkin and apple pie.

Cory had on tan khakis and a gold long-sleeve polo shirt, untucked. Brennan Rowe, a young Robert Redford look-alike and the best-looking man I'd ever met, wore dark-washed jeans and a crisp white dress shirt tucked in neatly. They made a handsome couple.

I introduced Danny to them. Ray prompted him to shake hands. He did, although without much enthusiasm. Once again, I attributed his behavior to being twelve.

While everyone sat down in the living room, I carried Brennan's dish of yams into the kitchen and retrieved a bottle of wine. Both men accepted a glass. I got Danny root beer and Ray a Corona. Cory uncovered a tray loaded with a variety of mouthwatering tidbits. We dug in, Danny watching glumly.

I started the conversation. "So Brennan, Cory says you're planning to race your Mazda Protégé. Have you decided in what venue?"

"We're looking at the specs for Grand Am Cup racing, although I need more time on the track to qualify for a license in that series."

"Have you raced before?"

"Some dirt track and rally and vintage at Watkins Glen, which is a good way to work myself up."

"My dad used to take me to the track at the Glen all the time." I loved those days, and thinking about them made me miss my dad all the more. Thanksgiving was his favorite holiday.

Erica waltzed in just then, tossing her coat on the rack and leaving her purse by the door.

"I brought cornbread muffins from the restaurant. They're really yummy." She caught sight of Brennan and her eyes widened with pleasure. Then she realized he was with Cory. Her smile faded. She followed me into the kitchen.

"How come all the best-looking guys are gay?"

I lined a bread basket with a napkin and dumped the muffins.

"Excuse me, I think Ray is good-looking."

"Okay, gay or married. All that's left for me is losers."

I considered arguing with her, but given her dating record, it was too much of a challenge. "Your prince will come, don't worry."

"Right, Jolene. When? When is he going to come?"

"I don't know. My crystal ball is broken. But trust me, when you least expect him, he'll arrive." I looked her up and down. "Did you take your medicine today?"

She rolled her eyes. "Yes, Mom. How's our little car thief doing?"

"He's mad. Ray made him work his tail off all morning. I wouldn't be surprised if he falls asleep in his mashed potatoes."

We both grinned at that image.

But when we served dinner, no one fell asleep. The food tasted fabulous, the conversation flowed, and even Danny laughed at Ray's jokes. Thankful for those present at the table, I buried my anguished thought that this would be Noelle's first Thanksgiving, one of many she wouldn't be celebrating with us.

The unidentified woman with the severed arm came to mind. I wondered if her family noted her absence at their holiday celebration, too. Maybe they would file a missing person report, and the police would be able to identify her. If not, I wondered if she would ever be found. Discovering her arm had been quite a shock, but to think of the rest of her lying alone somewhere, abandoned, was unbearable. I couldn't imagine how her family would feel.

After dinner, Ray lit a fire while I made coffee and cut the pies. I had just handed him a slice of pumpkin loaded with real whipped cream when the phone rang. He answered and stepped into the kitchen.

Erica raised an eyebrow. Cory and Brennan didn't seem to think anything of it.

But when Ray appeared wearing his uniform a few minutes later, even their eyebrows shot up in question.

"I'm sorry to break up the celebration. I have to go to work."

I rose to my feet. "What's going on?"

"We may have identified the woman's arm."

Brennan spoke up. "We saw the story on the news last night. Weird. "

Ray nodded. "It gets weirder. Gumby—another sheriff's deputy—told his wife, Briana, about the arm. She works at The Cat's Meow. She thinks it belongs to a girl who worked there sporadically for a month, then stopped coming in on Sunday. The club owner figured she was a transient and didn't think much of it. She wasn't too friendly with the other girls, but Briana said her fingernails were decorated like the ones on the limb we found and the jewelry matches Briana's descriptions. The possible victim lives in a different county, but Gumby and I are going to check out her address with their deputies."

He leaned over to kiss my cheek. "I'll call you later." A blast of cold air wafted into the living room as Ray left.

Brennan shook his head. "How horrific. I suppose they're going to find her dead."

Cory took Brennan's hand in his. "I don't doubt it. Too bad she didn't have anyone who cared enough about her to know she was missing."

Brennan nodded. He gave Cory a look that spoke of his affection.

Erica sighed and helped herself to another piece of apple pie.

Danny got a look on his face like he might throw up. He stood and raced into his bedroom. I followed him.

"What's wrong?"

He pointed toward the living room. "They're fag—"

I slapped my hand over his mouth, shut the door, and dragged him to the far side of the room. "We don't use that word in this house. They're our friends."

I took my hand off his mouth.

"My dad says—"

"Lower your voice, Danny."

His eyes flashed with anger, but he lowered his voice to a whisper. "My dad says to stay away from guys like that. They like little boys."

"Men who like little boys are called pedophiles. That's a mental illness." Or at least I thought it was. Erica might know for sure, given her time at the psych center. "Danny, most men like women, but some men like men, grown-up men. They're born that way. It's not an illness."

"My dad says that's sick."

I lost my patience. "Your dad isn't here. This is my house, and Ray's, and those two men are our friends. You'll be polite to them."

"I don't want to."

"Then stay in your room." I walked out and left the door open behind me, but only because I feared the paint fumes might kill him. My head ached already. I didn't know if it was from the confrontation or the fumes, maybe both. I did know I could live without this kid in my home, needy or not.

We chatted by the fire for a while longer before Cory offered to help me do the dishes. I declined his offer, but he and Brennan gathered the pie plates and took them into the kitchen anyway. Erica and I followed, carrying the coffee tray and the pies.

Brennan approached me. "Thank you for a lovely evening, Jolene. My mother has been dead for years and I'm an only child. I was going to be alone. I really appreciated the invitation."

"We're happy to have you."

The front door slammed. It sent a shock wave through the house. We all jumped in surprise.

A car motor turned over in the driveway. A lump formed in my throat as I raced to the window.

Danny backed Erica's Porsche out of the driveway. His aim was true, but his speed too fast for the slippery conditions. The car spun out of control on the road, colliding first with Brennan's Mercedes then bouncing into the snowbank.

He floored it, trying to horse his way out of the snowbank. The Porsche smoked but refused to budge.

Erica appeared at the window beside me. She screamed.

"That little shit. He smashed my car."

Brennan and Cory took one look and grabbed their coats, racing across the two-foot-deep snow in our front yard.

I dug out a pair of boots and slid into my coat, silently cursing Ray for bringing this nightmare home.

Cory and Brennan were examining the damage to the rear quarter panel on the Mercedes. I darted past them and crossed the road to Danny, who had his head down on the steering wheel. The car was shut off.

I noticed the keys in Cory's hand. He must have wrenched them away from Danny while I got on my coat.

Danny's shoulders heaved up and down. I grabbed his bicep.

He raised his head from the steering wheel, sobbing, "I want my dad. I want to see my dad."

Erica skidded to a stop next to me, arms flailing to catch her balance. "You little shit. Get out of my car."

"Erica!"

She shoved me aside and dragged Danny out from behind the wheel. "I've had it with you. Don't you ever touch my stuff again, you little brat."

He stood in the road sobbing as Erica collected her keys from Cory. The two men pushed her car out of the snowbank. She took off down the road without even a thank you.

Cory looked at me. "I can fix both cars. Don't worry."

I nodded, feeling numb. Was chaining a child to a bed frowned upon in modern society? What the hell was Ray thinking bringing this boy home?

Cory glanced at Brennan then back at me. "Do you need me to stay?"

"No, go on. We'll be fine." Too bad I wasn't as sure about that as I sounded.

After I apologized profusely, Brennan and Cory climbed into the Mercedes, Brennan seeming unperturbed by the damage to his car. I watched him creep down the slick road, thinking perhaps Cory had finally gotten it right.

I turned my attention back to Danny, who used his fists to dry his eyes and the arm of his coat for his nose, leaving a long trail of mucus on his sleeve. "Danny, what were you thinking?"

"Ray said he'd take me to see my dad, but he left. He's not going to take me."

True, Ray would not be back in time to take him as promised. "That's no reason to steal a car, Danny. If you wanted to see your dad, all you had to do was ask me. I could have taken you."

His eyes brightened then dimmed again. "Oh."

If Ray had been home, he would have made Danny sit in his room or wash the dishes or some other punishment. But he wasn't, I was. And I felt sorry for the kid, even though he'd ruined an otherwise lovely day, not to mention two very nice cars. He was twelve and without his father. I knew all about missing a parent and wanting them desperately.

I sighed. "Promise me you will not drive any more cars. You don't have a license."

"Okay."

His hands were in his pockets so I couldn't see if his fingers were crossed. I wouldn't hold my breath. "Do you want to go see your father now?"

He lit up like a Christmas tree. "Can we?"

"Sure." I wanted to get a look at his father anyway.

I wanted to see the man who had created this monster.

FIVE

Thirty minutes outside Wachobe, in a much less touristy and upscale town, the county's public safety building housed the sheriff's office, county court, and a forty-cell jail. The imposing brick and cement facility seemed impervious to the hustle of traffic in and out of the hospital and convenience store flanking it. Every time I entered the place, I got the creeps.

When Danny and I walked into the building, Gumby was on his way out. He was the one man I knew taller than Ray, and the first man to ask me out after Ray and I separated four years ago. I passed then, and I cringed now as he stooped to give me a kiss on the cheek.

"Hey, Jo, Happy Thanksgiving. Ray's not here."

"Happy Thanksgiving to you, too. We're actually here to visit Danny's father." I gestured to him. "Have you met Danny?"

Gumby studied Danny. "Nice haircut, kid."

Danny studied his feet.

"Can he see his dad?"

"Visiting hours are over."

"It's Thanksgiving and he's twelve. Can we make an exception?"

"It's not my rule. It's the sheriff's."

"Is he here?"

"Hell no."

I gave Gumby "the look." He bugged out his eyes right back at me. I tried a new tactic.

"Gumby, I can't believe you won't make an exception for a holiday and a twelve-year-old boy. You didn't have any qualms about making an exception to your marriage vows with my sister." I raised an eyebrow.

His chin jerked up. "Is that what she said?"

"She tells me everything." This time I had my fingers crossed in my pocket for two reasons.

He muttered something under his breath. "Let me ask."

Gumby led us down a number of corridors into the law enforcement division, filled with empty desks. He told us to wait and leaned into an office to speak with someone. I couldn't hear what was said, but Gumby made a number of gestures, not all G-rated. When Gumby stepped out of the office after five minutes, he had a ring of keys in his hand. "You're lucky he's still in pre-arraignment detention. Otherwise, you'd be SOL. Come on."

We went through a doorway into a hall then through a locked doorway into yet another hall. Gumby unlocked the next door a few feet down and stood aside to let us pass. We stepped into a four-cell holding area.

The cell to the right was empty. To the left a man lay on his back, sleeping. His chest rose and fell as he alternately whistled and snorted. I figured him for a drunk.

"Come here, kid." Gumby patted Danny down, then took him by the arm. I followed.

The next cell on the right was also empty, but to the left, a man sat with his back against the wall and his legs outstretched on his bunk. Now I knew where Danny got his good looks.

His father's hair was held back in a ponytail and his face had a few mores lines on it around his eyes and mouth, but otherwise, their facial features were almost the same. But this man had a scar on his neck as though someone had tried to slice it open and finish him off. It made Danny's nick on the cheek look as insignificant as a pimple. On his right arm, Danny's father had a tattoo of a heart with a sword running through it. A scroll beneath the heart was solid black.

When he spotted Danny, he leapt to his feet with a broad smile and moved to the cell door. "Danny."

Gumby rattled the keys in his hand. "Back against the wall, Mr. Phillips. Danny can come inside if you wait against the wall."

Mr. Phillips rushed to the opposite side of the cell. Gumby unlocked the door. Danny stepped inside. He and his father met in the middle of the cell, his father's arms encompassing him in a hug that lifted Danny off the floor. Then his father covered his face with kisses. I heard Danny sob.

Blinking back my tears, I walked back to listen to the drunk whistle and snort. Gumby remained outside the jail cell, leaning against the far wall with his eyes averted.

He gave them five minutes then five more. I didn't think even he had the heart to separate them.

When the door opened behind me and the other officer stuck his head in, Gumby asked Mr. Phillips to step back while Danny left the cell. Gumby had to tell Danny to come out three times before he did so, but only at his father's urging. I was relieved to see Danny had stopped sobbing. He asked to use the restroom before we left.

I waited in the lobby with Gumby. "Ray said Briana identified that woman's arm."

Gumby nodded. "It's her. The apartment manager let us in her place. At first, everything looked fine. Living room had an open magazine on the coffee table like maybe she'd just put it down. Kitchen clean and neat, flowers on the table. But her bed was soaked in blood, spatters all over the walls. No body though. We're going to work with that county and the State Police on the investigation. Our first priority is to find the body. No one at the apartment building saw or heard anything, and no one remembers ever seeing the woman with anyone. It's hard to tell if they're being honest or refusing to get involved. Briana said the girls at the club don't know anything about her either, other than she may have offered to meet a few guys outside of work for a price."

So the dead woman was a prostitute as well as a dancer. "What was her name?"

"Josie Montalvo."

"Why would the killer cut off her arm?"

Gumby ran his hand over his hair. "Guy might be a psycho who likes trophies. Or maybe he did it for the jewelry. The ruby ring and the gold bangles are worth a few thousand. The medical examiner said the ring would have to be cut off her finger."

"Why keep just one arm?"

He shrugged. "It's not so easy to chop off an arm. Maybe he only had time for one. Besides, Briana said Josie only wore the ring and bangles on one arm."

"So you're sure the killer is a man?"

"Guys are the only ones sick enough for dismemberment. It's probably some psycho who took her home, then did her in."

Before I had a chance to get a mental image of that, Danny reappeared.

I smiled at him. "Ready to go?"

He kept walking right past me and disappeared into the parking lot.

I took that as a yes.

———

In the middle of the night, I awoke. The clock read four a.m. Ray slumbered peacefully beside me, but I heard crying. I swung my feet to the floor and stumbled over familiar ground. When I opened the door to the nursery, the sobbing grew louder. I stepped forward and smashed my toe.

"Oh. Ow. Oh. Oh. Shit!"

I hopped around the room, holding my toe in my hand as the pain telegraphed over and over to my brain.

The crying ceased. "Jolene?"

"Yes, Danny?"

"Are you okay?"

"No." I dropped onto the end of the bed, which now extended into the middle of the room. "I stubbed my toe. It hurts like he—. It hurts."

"You swore."

The pain in my toe eased. I lowered my foot to the floor. "Yes, and see how awful it sounds when someone does."

He sat up in the bed. "Why are you here?"

"I heard crying. I thought you needed me." Truthfully, I thought Noelle needed me, but once again, I'd been mistaken. Danny didn't need to know all that, though.

"Oh."

"What's wrong? Are you worried about your dad?"

"Yes ... no ... yes."

"Do you want to talk about it?"

"Yes ... No."

I slid up next to him. "Let's talk anyway. It will make me feel better."

"Okay."

"Are you worried he's not going to get out of jail?"

"Yes."

"Are you worried something bad will happen to him there?"

"Like what?"

Perfect. I'd led myself right into a trap where I could build his fears. "I don't know. I've never been in jail. Has your dad?"

"Yes. He said he'd never go back."

I processed the implications of that statement. Ray seemed confident Mr. Phillips would be convicted. I didn't know the sentence for car theft, but I imagined a couple of years at least, more since the man had priors. I didn't see how Danny's father could avoid doing time if he did get convicted. Prison escapes were pretty passé around here. Maybe he should have thought of that before he stole the Escalade.

I decided to change the topic. "Where did you live before your dad got arrested?"

"We moved around. We stayed with my dad's friends sometimes."

I wondered if they were all car thieves, too. "Where's all your stuff?"

"In my dad's car."

"A Toyota Camry?"

He didn't answer. I took that for a yes.

"Where's your mom?"

"I don't know."

"Have you seen her?"

"I'm not sure."

What an odd thing to be uncertain about. "You're not sure because it was so long ago?"

"No. My dad won't talk about her."

The information must be on his birth certificate, although we'd learned the hard way with Noelle that legal documents were only as accurate as the source. Surely Ray must know his mother's name. I would ask him in the morning.

"Jolene?"

"Yes, Danny?"

"You know that lady's arm … the one in the cooler?"

As if he could be referring to any other arm. "Yes?"

"Do you know that lady's name?"

"Josie Montalvo."

"Did she work at The Cat's Meow?"

"Yes. How did you know?"

Again, he remained silent. But my suspicions grew.

"Danny, do you think that lady was your mother?"

"No … maybe. I don't know."

"Did you meet her?"

"No. I had to stay in the car."

"Do you mean your father went to The Cat's Meow to see her and you waited outside?"

"Yes."

"When?"

"Saturday night."

"What time on Saturday?"

"After nine, I think."

Ray had said that Josie didn't come to work for the last several days. Did that include Saturday night? I was tempted to get him out of bed to ask, but I wanted to keep Danny talking for as long as he was willing.

"Was your dad driving his Camry?"

No answer once again, which was as good as a "yes." But the Camry with the arm in the trunk hadn't been stolen until Monday. Or was that just the day the used car lot discovered it was missing? They probably didn't work on Sunday. I would have to ask Ray.

"Why do you think she might be your mother?"

"Because that's the name my dad used to have on his tattoo."

"Josie?"

"Yes."

I pictured the heart tattoo with the sword running through it and the blacked-out banner underneath. I should have realized the blacked-out banner represented a lady who had fallen out of favor with her knight in shining armor. "Are you sure?"

"Yes."

"Did your dad ever say your mom's name was Josie?"

"No, but he said he loved Josie. And once he told me that he loved my mom."

I didn't want to argue with Danny's logic, but it was possible his father had loved two different women in one lifetime. He'd probably loved many if he and Danny moved around a lot. If Ray didn't know Danny's mother's name, I could ask his school for the name on the birth certificate. I hoped they would tell me.

If it was Josie Montalvo, then Danny's father would be tied to her murder by virtue of their relationship. If it wasn't, his visit to The Cat's Meow might be enough to connect him to the murder. And if convicted of murder, Danny might never live with his father again.

That might be for the best, but I sure didn't want to be the one to separate them. Danny seemed to love his father, and from all appearances, his father loved him. Could a man capable of killing and chopping up a woman also feel love? I preferred to think not.

"Danny, how long did your father have his white Camry?"

"He bought it on Saturday."

"Were you with him?"

"No. He left me at Chuck E. Cheese's while he went to pick it up."

"By yourself?"

"Why not?"

If tested, I could think of a hundred reasons why not. I kept them all to myself. "No reason. So when he picked you up, he was driving his new Camry?"

"Yes."

"Then you went to The Cat's Meow?"

In the dim light, I saw him nod.

"And you waited outside. Then what?"

"My dad took me to his friend's house and dropped me off."

"You slept there?"

"Yes."

"What's the friend's name?"

Danny crinkled his brow. "I don't remember."

Must not be a close friend. Who would leave their child with a virtual stranger? Mr. Phillips' parenting style hit rock bottom in my estimation. "Where did your dad go?"

"I don't know."

"When did he pick you up again?"

"He was there in the morning when I woke up."

So Danny's father may have had the opportunity and means to kill Josie Montalvo. Did he have a motive, too? What a nightmare. Poor Danny. He had no idea the information he'd shared could lock his father away forever.

"Jolene?"

"Yes, Danny?"

"I'm cold."

I stood and gathered the covers from the end of his bed. "Let me tuck you back in. It's too early to get up."

"Okay." He laid his head on the pillow while I pulled the sheet and blanket up to his neck. I bent over and kissed his cheek. "Go back to sleep, Danny."

His voice was small when he replied "okay."

I scurried across the cold wooden living room and kitchen floors to slide back in bed beside Ray. I pushed on his shoulder. No response.

I pushed again, whispering his name. The man could sleep through a bomb raid.

He rolled over and threw his arm over my chest. "Go back to sleep, Darlin.'"

I kept my voice to a whisper so Danny wouldn't hear me. "I can't sleep, Ray. I need you."

He massaged my breast. "Mmmm." He nuzzled my neck and started to move downwards.

I shoved his shoulder again. "Ray, I need to talk to you about Danny."

He lifted his head. "What's he done now?"

"Nothing."

Ray dropped back onto his pillow. "Then why wake me up? I'm tired."

By the time I finished whispering to him, he wasn't tired anymore. In fact, he jumped out of bed, showered, and pulled on his uniform.

"I'm going to have another talk with Danny's father and the bartender at The Cat's Meow."

"It's only five a.m., Ray. I'm sure the bartender's not there. He just went home a few hours ago."

"I've got his home address."

I'm sure the guy would be thrilled to have Ray wake him minutes into his R.E.M. sleep.

Then I started to worry Danny's information sharing would make his father angry with him. "Can you keep Danny out of it? I don't want his father to feel betrayed."

Ray pressed his lips to mine. "Don't worry. One thing I'm sure about with this case is Danny's father loves him. I doubt anything can change that."

"What else are you sure about?"

"That we have a dismembered dead woman floating around somewhere."

SIX

Ray worked the next three days, interviewing everyone connected to The Cat's Meow, the car dealership, and Danny's father, of course, who exercised his right to remain silent. In conjunction with the State Police and the next county, Ray's department combed the area surrounding The Cat's Meow and Josie Montalvo's apartment, looking for her body. They found nothing.

The bartender at The Cat's Meow, however, did confirm that Danny's father had spoken at length to Josie Montalvo Saturday night, the last night she reported to work. His impression was the conversation had been intense, but not violent, although he had no idea what they talked about.

In the meantime, Ray left Danny at home with me and the instruction not to watch television. He hid the stolen Nintendo DS.

I felt like I was the one being punished. I didn't know what to do with a twelve-year-old. After two days of washing windows, cupboards, baseboards, and anything else I could think of as well as sorting out old clothes and accumulated magazines and mail, all the easy jobs were done in our tiny two-bedroom bungalow. I couldn't bear the thought of stripping and waxing the wood floor even though it needed TLC.

We played Monopoly. Danny won twice. We played Scrabble. I won, by a landslide. Danny refused to play again. We played crazy eights. The game lasted two hours. Then I needed to get out of the house.

So I took advantage of the library's Sunday hours and let Danny roam the stacks.

Fifteen minutes later, he asked if he could check out some movies. I knew the movies wouldn't go over with Ray.

"Didn't you find any books that interest you?"

"No."

"What about this?" I pulled a Hardy Boys book off the shelf.

He curled his lip.

I took offense. I'd loved the Hardy Boys and Nancy Drew as a child. I tried not to snarl at him. "What are you interested in?"

"Cars."

Couldn't fault him for that.

I asked the librarian for books about cars. She led us to the non-fiction area. Danny agreed to read books about racing and race car drivers. I breathed a sigh of relief and took him home.

While Danny read, I hid in the closet we called an office and surfed the Internet for more Caterhams as well as individuals interested in purchasing a Ferrari. I felt certain the Ferrari would sell someday, but to someone who hadn't heard of its history. Since our town loved to gossip, only an out-of-towner might not hear. I say "might" because those gossip vine tendrils can grow for miles.

The phone rang around five o'clock.

"The butterflies are so pretty."

"Erica? Where are you?"

"See the blue one?"

Panic clamped onto my heart and gave it a painful squeeze. "Erica, answer me. Where are you?"

"I don't know." Her voice sounded hoarse. "Mom, where are we?"

I gripped the phone tighter. Erica had never addressed our mother within my hearing, not since Mom died, of course. "Erica, are you home?"

"No-o-o-o."

"Are you in a house?"

"It's dark."

"Are you sitting down?"

"Lying."

"On a bed?"

"Cold. Where are my clothes?"

My hand shook. The phone struck my temple. She hadn't gotten her medication fast enough. She was either hallucinating or talking in her sleep. She'd been known at times to walk, talk, and chew gum while asleep. No one could say she wasn't a woman of many talents. "Is there a window?"

"Y-e-e-s."

"Okay, Erica, get up and go to the window. Look outside and tell me what you see."

"Can't."

"Why not?"

"My wrist is stuck."

"On what?"

"Ahhh ..."

Clearly, she was stumped. "Okay, Erica, hold on."

I ran from the office into the living room and grabbed my purse, fumbling for my cell phone with one hand. I hit speed dial for Ray's cell.

Danny watched me from the couch, his brow furrowed.

I turned my back to him.

"Yes, Darlin'?"

"Ray, Erica called me from this number." I checked the caller readout and repeated the incoming phone number to him. "She doesn't know where she is. She's completely out of it."

I could hear him keying into a computer, looking for the address to go with the number.

"Keep her on the phone. I'm on my way."

I clicked my cell phone shut. "Erica, honey, Ray is coming to get you. Just sit tight."

Nothing. "Erica? Erica? ERICA?"

All I got in response was a dial tone.

———

Ray called twenty minutes later. "It's a motel room. She's not here. There's no sign of her. The desk clerk says he didn't see her, but four different guys checked in today. Glen Burton, Maurice Boor, Richard Scott, and Mickey Dean."

"Mickey Dean's is a restaurant."

"I know. The names may all be aliases."

I didn't think so. "Is Boor spelled B-o-o-r?"

"Yes."

"Erica went to high school with a Maury Boor. He used to put notes in her locker all the time. He freaked her out, always calling and asking her on dates."

"I don't know him."

I pulled the phone book out of a drawer and thumbed through it. Maurice Boor wasn't listed, nor anyone else with the same name. Just my luck, his family had moved away. "I think he was a year younger than Erica, so six years younger than us."

"What does he look like?"

"I haven't seen him in years. In high school, he was short and scrawny with dark hair and horn-rimmed glasses. Sort of geeky." I would have to dig out Erica's old yearbooks to find his picture.

"The desk clerk couldn't remember which guy was which, but he said two of them were dark-haired, one balding, one with a gray ponytail. All of them were taller than him, and he's around five-eight."

Maybe Maury had a growth spurt after high school. "Are any of them in their rooms?"

"No. This is an hourly sort of motel, Darlin'. It's about a mile from The Cat's Meow. They draw their regular crowd."

"Can you go see if she's there?"

"No. I'm supposed to be looking for a one-armed woman, Jolene. I cannot chase your sister around town."

"Ray, Erica was talking about butterflies. She spoke to Mom like she was in the room with her. She's not well."

"She hasn't been well for a long time. There's no sign of any foul play here, or any kind of play. I don't know why she called you, but I have to get back to work. I'll check and see if Maurice Boor has any priors."

I couldn't believe he hung up on me. I resisted the temptation to slam the phone on the receiver over and over again only because of Danny's watchful eyes.

While it was true Erica had been sick for years and known to disappear for days at a time with men, her hallucinations usually involved someone being after her, making her afraid to leave home. She lost several jobs because she failed to show up for work, too afraid to drive there for fear someone would be in the back seat of her car waiting to attack her. I'd never really thought of her conversations with our mother as hallucinations, since Erica never said she saw Mom or heard Mom's voice. She just quoted her, which I'd interpreted as Erica trying to garner support for her own ideas by attributing them to Mom. After today, I wasn't so sure.

I tried to convince myself that, like so often in the past, I had no real cause for concern about Erica's safety. But Erica had a thing for butterflies. She coveted their short life span. And images of the severed arm lying in the ice chest kept pushing their way into my mind. We might have a psycho killer running loose in our county, one who preyed on women from The Cat's Meow. Erica had recently become one of those women. While not a dancer, she had been there the other night, offering herself to men in the bar. Had one of them decided to take her up on her offer? Was he keeping her against her will? I couldn't sit idly by and wait to find out, not when she'd called me in distress.

I glanced at Danny, who tried to avert his eyes back to his book before I caught him watching me. "Are you hungry?"

"Yeah."

"How about pizza?"

"Okay."

"Get your coat and shoes. We're going out."

———

I pulled the Lexus into the parking lot of The Lincoln House, the restaurant and bar where Erica worked. Erica's car sat in the far corner of the lot. My heart rejoiced. Could she have shown up for work?

Danny studied the picture of Abraham Lincoln in the lobby of the log cabin restaurant while I scanned the bar. I didn't see Erica, but the place was full.

The hostess seated us near the fieldstone fireplace. When the waitress arrived, I ordered sodas and sent Danny to get his pizza from the salad bar. I hustled into the barroom and caught the bartender's eye.

"Hey, Jolene. Did you and Ray come in for dinner?" Bernie, the bartender and half-owner, went to high school with us. He was a star on our high school football team, but his renowned brawn had since aged into paunch.

"Ray's at work. I brought our new foster child, Danny. He's twelve."

Bernie swiped a towel over the bar. "I got a twelve-year-old. Jacob. Maybe they'll be in the same class."

"That would be nice. Is Erica working tonight?"

He folded the towel in his hands and looked at it. "She's off tonight. She was here last night." He didn't sound too happy about it.

"Her car's in the parking lot."

His gaze remained trained on the towel. "I noticed."

"Do you know if she went home with someone last night?"

He frowned. "Not for sure. She walked out with a new guy."

"An employee?"

"A customer. He's been in a couple times this month."

"Do you know his name?"

"No. He's quiet. Not really her type."

"What do you mean?"

He gave his nose a nervous swipe. "Your sister likes excitement. Lately she's been spoiling for a fight."

"In what way?"

"She's irritable. She's jumpy. She gets mad if things don't go her way. I had to sit her down the other day and tell her that she needs to sweeten up or she's outta here."

"I'm sorry to hear that. I thought she was doing well here."

He brought his gaze to meet mine. "She was, Jolene. She was. I knew her record when I hired her, and I warned her then. She did fine for a while, but the last few months ..." He trailed off and avoided my eyes again.

"What about them?"

"To be honest, since you lost your baby, she's been different."

I shouldn't have felt surprised. Erica did shoot a man the day before we surrendered Noelle. Surely that had affected her, whether she admitted to it or not. "Different in what way?"

"It's like she's desperate for attention." He washed a few glasses in the sink under the bar. "I think she misses you."

"Misses me?"

"Yeah. She talked about you and the baby all the time. Then suddenly she didn't have anything to talk about anymore. I'd ask her how you were doing and she didn't know."

Guilt washed over me. I'd neglected my sister, my surrogate child. Erica needed support, and I hadn't been there to give it to her. "What does this guy she walked out with look like?"

"Dark hair. Maybe six foot. Okay looking, for a guy."

"If he comes in again, can you call me?"

Bernie stopped drying the glass in his hand. "What for?"

"I don't know where Erica is, and she's been off her medicine. I need to find her and make sure she's all right."

"Sure. Sure. If he comes in, I'll call you. And if Erica comes in, I'll let you know, too." He leaned closer. "I gotta tell you, though, if she doesn't come in for her next shift, she's through."

"Fair enough." If that happened, I would pay Erica's bills just like always.

After thanking Bernie, I rejoined Danny at the table. He had four slices of pizza stacked on a plate with a side of heavily buttered bread. No vegetables.

I let it go. "I'm going to grab a piece of pizza and some salad. Then we need to go to Erica's apartment, okay?"

Danny nodded, his cheeks bulging with pizza.

———

Erica lived in the apartment I'd leased when Ray and I separated four years ago. He and I'd been unable to come to terms over his desire to have a baby and my desire to avoid perpetuating my bloodline's mental health issues. When Noelle fell into our arms and Ray and I reconciled after three years, we bought the bungalow, and Erica had moved into this old Victorian on Wells Street. She lived in the first floor apartment, and the landlord lived on the second floor. This time of year, the landlord was most likely holed up in a hunting lodge somewhere with his old war buddies. The entire house was dark when we pulled into the driveway.

I rang the bell then used my key. The apartment smelled musty. Danny followed me in and waited while I turned on the lights.

"Wow. Cool." The dozens of fake butterflies dangling on fishing line from the ceiling captured Danny's attention immediately. "She likes butterflies."

I nodded. My fears grew.

The kitchen was clean and orderly. No one had cooked here in days, maybe months. Her bed was made, her clothes hung. Her suitcases remained tucked under the bed. Erica wasn't here, and I couldn't find a clue as to where she might be.

I tried to find her yearbooks, but failed. I'd have to go by my dim memories of Maury Boor for now.

I shut off the lights and led Danny out to the driveway again. "Danny, I need to go to The Cat's Meow. Would you mind staying in the car while I go inside?"

He shrugged.

"Will you promise to stay in the locked car and wait for me? I don't want to come out and find you missing again like at Dr. Albert's office."

He gazed at the floor. "I promise." He lifted his head. "Do you think Erica is at The Cat's Meow?"

I slid into the car and started the engine as he scrambled into the back seat. "I don't know. She was there the other night. She was at a motel near there this afternoon. I just have to ask if they've seen her." With any luck Briana Engle, Gumby's wife, would be there to answer my questions. I didn't feel like sidling up to anyone else in the place.

I backed out and headed out of town.

"What's wrong with Erica?"

"What do you mean?"

"She's weird."

"She is *not* weird." I glanced at Danny in the rearview mirror but couldn't make out his features in the dark. "Why do think she's weird?"

"I don't know. She's just different."

I had to give him that. Erica was different. When depressed, she was unapproachable. But with the right medication and phase of the moon, she was exuberant, charming, outgoing, and talkative. These days, she seemed dark and restless, a precursor in the past to hospitalization. Her heavy drinking was new. She'd stayed away from alcohol in the past because of her medications. I mentally kicked myself for not paying more attention to her. I'd fooled myself into believing her days in the psychiatric center were over.

But Danny didn't know Erica was different from the usual. He meant she was different from everybody else, and not in a good way.

I couldn't decide if he was very intuitive or just becoming a bigot like his father.

Either way, my number one priority was to find my sister.

SEVEN

Sunday night at The Cat's Meow didn't draw a full house, judging from the parking lot. Only a dozen cars sat in it, surrounded by the dead cornstalks that looked on like sentinels. In one vehicle, a couple was steaming up the windows. I parked as far from them as possible and crossed my fingers Danny wouldn't notice them.

I turned around to look him in the eye. "Now remember, you promised to stay in the car. Do not get out. Do not unlock the doors. Do not speak to anyone. Okay?"

"Okay." Again, I heard the "yeah, right, lady" in his voice. I knew my fears for his safety far exceeded his confidence in his ability to care for himself.

I ran across the muddy parking lot and opened the front door. A bouncer sat alone in the foyer.

"You got ID?"

I pulled out my driver's license, flattered he thought I might be underage.

He looked at my picture. I had long hair when it was taken several years ago. "You were hot." He handed it back to me.

In an instant, I felt old and ugly, two things only amplified by the interior of the strip club.

At first, the loud music and disco lights stunned me. It took several seconds for my eyes to adjust. Then I spotted the dancer gyrating on the stage with a G string, feather boa, and pasties, sporting boobs the size of cannonballs. I felt shortchanged, overdressed, and embarrassed for her and me.

The half-dozen men seated around the stage paid no attention to me, perhaps because I had all my clothes on, but more likely because their eyes were riveted on the stage. I crossed the room to the bar and asked for Briana Engle, Gumby's wife. The bartender sent the half-naked waitress standing at the bar to get Briana from her dressing room.

"What else can I getcha?" He smiled at me with two broken front teeth.

"Nothing, thank you."

He hitched his pants up and walked to the other end of the bar to watch the football game.

"Hey, Jolene. I haven't seen you since the wedding. How are you?" Briana enveloped me in a hug that brought me in contact with her own two cannonballs. They didn't flatten an inch under her red silk robe as her chest met mine.

"Worried. My sister, Erica, is missing. I know she was in here Tuesday night. Did you see her?"

Briana pursed her lips, which were as red as her robe. "I saw her singing at the top of her lungs and hitting on all the boys. She stole my thunder. I didn't make any tips that night. Gumby finally called Ray."

So he called because his wife was losing money, not because my sister needed help? Surely Gumby was a better officer than that. "I'm sorry about your tips. Has my sister been back since?"

Briana called the bartender over and asked him. He shook his head. Briana shrugged. "Guess not."

"She wanted a man to take her home that night. Do you know his name or what he looked like?"

"No name, but he's a big, redheaded guy. Really big. Meaty. Erica kept asking him if he was big all over."

Lovely. And unfortunately, not the same man as the one from The Lincoln House. Now I had two potential suitors for her affections, and no name for either one.

"If Erica or the redheaded man comes in again, can you call me?"

"Sure, Jolene. No problem."

"Thanks, Briana." I started to turn away then felt Briana's hand on my coat sleeve.

"Can you do me a favor, too?"

"Of course."

"When you find your sister, tell her to stay away from my husband."

———

After Danny went to bed, I climbed into the bathtub and tried to soak off the lingering sleaze dust I'd picked up inside the strip club. I hadn't been able to think of anywhere else to look for Erica when we left there, and I knew Danny should be in bed by nine before his first day at Wachobe Middle School.

I must have dozed off in the tub because the next thing I knew Ray was sitting on the side of the tub, giving me a soapsuds beard.

He bent to kiss me on the nose as I wiped away his handiwork.

"How was the rest of your day? Did you find Josie Montalvo's body?"

"Not even a lead. She rented her apartment a little over a month ago. Her landlord didn't require any information from her, just a $500 deposit, which he's now going to have to use to hire a professional service to clean the blood off her bedroom carpet. They released the scene today."

"I went to The Cat's Meow to look for Erica tonight."

"I heard. Briana called Gumby."

"I have no secrets, do I?"

Ray gazed down at my body. "Not without the soapsuds."

My cheeks burned. I tried to attribute it to the hot water, but the temperature of my bath had turned cold long ago. "Could you hand me a towel?"

He rose and pulled a bath sheet off the rack, holding it out so I could step into it.

I would have preferred to have him hand it to me and leave the room. Even though we'd been together for over fifteen years, I felt a little shy to step out naked in front of him. I knew where it might lead, and I couldn't remember the last time we'd had sex. Most likely it had been in the days following Noelle's departure, when I'd been inconsolable no matter what Ray tried.

I could tell from the look on Ray's face what he'd like to try tonight. My hands started to shake even as I told myself how ridiculous it was to feel nervous with Ray.

Erica's nonsense about becoming a born-again virgin crossed my mind. Absurd. Totally absurd.

I stood and stepped over the side of the bathtub with as much grace as I could muster. I slipped on the wet tile. My leg went out from under me. I flailed my arms in an effort to catch my balance.

Ray's arms and the towel enfolded me, holding me upright. He picked me up and set me on the rug in front of the mirror then tucked the edge of the towel in securely, brushing the top of my breast with his dry hand. He met my gaze in the mirror.

"Tired?"

His voice was husky.

A tingle rippled down my back. "A little."

I grabbed another towel and wrapped it around my head, careful not to bump him in the shrinking room. "I took Danny to The Lincoln House for dinner and asked Bernie if any guys had shown an interest in Erica."

Ray's hands pushed mine aside as he took over gently toweling my hair. "And?"

"Bernie said she left the other night with a quiet, dark-haired guy. He didn't know his name."

"A quiet one, huh?"

Ray always says to watch out for the quiet ones. I pulled the towel from his hands and nodded. "What if the guy is a serial killer? What if he's the guy you're looking for?"

He took off his badge and laid it on the countertop. "Then he picked too small a town. We'll find him fast."

"Briana said Erica tried to take home a redheaded guy at the club. Do you know any guys with red hair?"

He wrestled off his belt and laid it next to his badge. "I don't even know any redheaded women."

I started brushing my hair. "I might. Cory said our new customer is a redhead. He said she had a brother. In fact, I saw a redhaired woman come out of The Cat's Meow the day Danny stole that car. I took Erica there to pick up the Porsche."

"What's her name?"

"I don't remember. Cory wrote it down for me. I'll have to go to the office tomorrow." I put my hairbrush back in the drawer. "Which reminds me, are you off tomorrow?"

"I'm not off again until we find Josie Montalvo and her killer."

"Oh."

Ray stopped unbuttoning his shirt. "What's wrong?"

"It's just the principal wanted to see us about the Nintendo. I was hoping you could handle it."

"Sorry, Darlin'. You'll have to handle it." He reached for the towel encasing my body, wrapped his fingers in it, and pulled me toward him. "You can handle anything."

I slammed my hand onto his chest, bringing me to a halt inches from him. I could feel the heat of his body, and my own body's reaction to it. It had been a long time.

But I wasn't feeling the love at that moment. "Ray, you just stuck me with Danny. Whatever made you think bringing him home was a good idea?"

His gaze roamed over my shoulders and the tops of my breasts. "You said you wanted to help people."

"I did, but I wanted to do it in my own way, not yours."

He released my towel and took a step back. "Do you want me to call Social Services and request another placement for Danny?"

My heart leapt with relief. Then I felt the all too familiar waves of guilt and responsibility. "Not now. He's got a room here and clothes and books and … and … we're committed to him. That's not my point. My point *is* you should have consulted me first."

"You're right. I'm sorry. I saw his need, remembered what you said, and went with my gut."

I didn't see any point in arguing with him about it any further. "I understand."

He bent and ran his lips down my neck and along my shoulder, sending chills down my spine. "So am I forgiven?"

I rested my hands against his chest, feeling his heartbeat.

Mine accelerated. "Yes."

He leaned in to kiss me. His lips grazed mine. The pressure increased, drawing me in. I almost let go.

Then I heard crying. I shoved at his chest.

It was like trying to move a mountain, but he stopped. Irritation flashed in his eyes. "What?"

"I hear crying."

Sadness replaced the irritation. "Jolene, Noelle is happy and healthy with her mother. You have to stop this."

I slapped his chest in frustration. "No, Ray, I hear Danny crying."

He tilted his head and listened with me. Through the open bathroom door came the distinct sound of sobbing.

Ray glanced at my towel. "I'll talk to him."

I pulled on my pajamas and slippers and chased after Ray.

When I entered Danny's room, his lamp was on. I could see his red face and the tear stains on his pajamas as he sat sniffling. Ray had one hand on his shoulder, patting it soothingly.

Danny's anguished face turned toward me, and he burst into a fresh onslaught of tears. "My dad's going to jail. It's all my fault. He told me to stay in the car, but I didn't. I didn't."

Ray moved over so I could join them on the bed. "Danny says he got out of the car at The Cat's Meow and tried to sneak inside to see who his dad was talking to. He tried the back door and the side door, but they were locked. He even went into the foyer, but the bouncer kicked him out."

Danny hiccupped. "Then I went back to the car. It was open. The driver's door and the back door. I figured my dad came out and couldn't find me. So I got in the car and waited for him. But when he came out, he didn't act like he knew I'd gotten out of the car. He just hopped in and took off."

I moved closer to Danny and hugged him. "I don't understand. What did you do that was so terrible?"

Danny looked at Ray, who replied. "He left the car, Darlin'. Danny thinks someone came and planted the woman's arm in the car while he was circling the building."

"Oh." I thought about that for a minute. "But the person would need a key to get in the trunk or a remote. Your dad's key chain didn't have a remote on it."

Danny's eyes widened. "He had a remote. I know he had one."

Ray and I exchanged glances. I'm sure he was thinking the same as me. What happened to the remote? The key chain Danny claimed to have found in the car at Dr. Albert's office had just a key and a metal letter P. Was the car the one his father had been driving or not?

Ray patted Danny's shoulder. "You know what, bud, we're not going to be able to solve this tonight. You have school tomorrow.

You need to go to sleep. Don't worry. I'll talk to your dad tomorrow and we'll figure this all out."

Danny seemed satisfied. He allowed us to tuck him in bed. Ray and I kissed his cheeks and turned off his lamp.

When we got to our bedroom and climbed into bed, Ray and I conversed in whispers.

"What do you think happened to the remote, Ray?"

"I have no idea."

"Do you think it fell off the key chain?"

"It's possible."

"Do you think someone stole it and planted the arm in the car?"

"Also possible. Anything's possible, maybe just not probable."

"What did Danny's father say about the Camry?"

"Nothing. His lawyer's trying to work some kind of a deal for his release, and, in the meantime, Danny's father isn't answering any questions."

"But it was his car."

"It was the dealership's car. He may have stolen it. From what Danny says, he did. But none of what Danny tells us is going to be admissible in court, and Danny will never testify against him."

"So what do we do now, Ray?"

He pulled me close and spooned. "We sleep."

I wiggled out of his arms and sat up. "I can't sleep. I can't stop thinking about this."

"We can't do anything tonight, Jolene. Go to sleep."

"I can't."

"Then do me a favor. Sit there quietly so I can sleep."

EIGHT

I AROSE ON MONDAY still filled with dire thoughts regarding Erica's whereabouts, Danny's father, Danny's future, and, of course, my future. To top it all off, I had to face Principal Travis.

My day only got worse when I realized I couldn't wear the stretch pants I'd had on for the last four days. My two-size drop meant I had to put on the same skirt I'd worn when I met her last week. Hopefully she wouldn't notice.

At 8:55 a.m. the principal's secretary escorted Danny and me to Mrs. Travis' office for the second time within a week. This time I was exhausted, annoyed, and embarrassed. I had the Nintendo DS in my hand.

Danny managed to enter the office hiding behind my back. I could tell from the way Mrs. Travis craned her neck to catch sight of him. I stepped to the side so she could give him the full effect of her wrath.

Instead, she greeted us both warmly and offered us the chairs in front of her desk. I offered her the Nintendo, and she accepted it. She sat on the edge of her desk, holding it in her hand and towering over Danny, her warm smile still firmly in place.

"So, Danny, how did you come by this Nintendo?"

"I found it." His eyes didn't meet hers.

"Where?"

"On the floor, in the hall."

"I see." She turned it over in her hands. "Danny, you're new to our school. We'd like to see you get off on the right foot. In this school, when we find something that doesn't belong to us, we bring it to the office, and my secretary places it in the lost and found. I know a Nintendo is an exciting toy, but in the future, I hope you will remember to bring anything you find on the school grounds here. Is that fair?"

Danny nodded.

Mrs. Travis stood. "All right, Danny. You can head off to class. Mr. Mathews is looking forward to meeting you."

With a final unreadable glance at me, Danny left. I stood to follow him, relieved that Mrs. Travis had let us both off so easily.

Mrs. Travis held up her hand. "Do you have just a few minutes more for me, Mrs. Parker?"

"Sure." I sat again with reluctance.

Mrs. Travis rounded her desk and took her seat. She opened a file and flipped through the pages inside. "After I spoke with you last week, I read Danny's file more carefully. I even placed a call to his old school. Danny is an unusual boy. His school attendance record is perfect. He's never missed a day, not even for an illness. He's been late only once or twice. Danny hands in all his homework. It's not always correct, but it's always done. His grades tend to be above average. His father attends every teacher conference.

His father signs every report card. In those aspects, Danny is a model student."

She closed the file and leaned back in her chair. "On the other hand, Danny never rides the bus. His father transported him to and from school. His old school does not believe Danny had any friendships outside of school. Some weeks, they suspected the only showers Danny had were the ones he asked to take after his physical education class. On occasion, Danny fell asleep during lectures. His classmates often couldn't find their lunch money. Sometimes they couldn't find other things as well. No one could prove it was Danny, but he was the prime suspect. It led to several fights."

She fiddled with a paperclip lying on her desk. "I know you and your husband have only had Danny in your home for a few days. Your husband indicated Danny's father might be in jail for some time to come. I think it's important we all work together to make sure Danny benefits from this move to our school and your home."

I nodded and waited for her to say more. She didn't. She just smiled at me.

I wasn't sure what she was trying to tell me. Wasn't it a given that we were all working together in Danny's best interests? Was she letting me know that she knew Danny was a thief? Was she trying to tell me Danny should ride the school bus? That I should help him make friends outside of school? Or was this her carefully worded way of letting me know this school wasn't going to tolerate any nonsense from Danny?

Mrs. Travis continued to smile at me, clearly allowing me to draw my own conclusions. Instead, I decided to take the opportunity to find out what more she knew about Danny.

"We share your concerns about Danny, Mrs. Travis. In fact, Danny was very upset last night. He said his father won't talk to him about his mother. Is there any information in the file about her?"

She tapped the file. "According to this, she passed away when he was two. At least, that's what his father suggested to Danny's kindergarten teacher during a teacher conference."

So maybe Danny's mother really wasn't dead? "What was her name?"

Mrs. Travis flipped through the file and stopped at Danny's birth certificate. "Jennifer James. She had Danny at age nineteen. She and Mr. Phillips lived at the same address in Newark. I don't know if they were married."

She flipped the file closed and seemed to hesitate before plunging on, "I don't know if this information will be helpful to you or not, but Danny's teachers weren't certain Mr. Phillips knows how to read. They would show him samples of Danny's completed assignments during the conferences, and he didn't seem to comprehend the work."

"Oh." I didn't know if it was important or helpful either, but instantly I felt sorry for the man. The inability to read would be a huge deficit in life. "Is there anything else in his file that you think might be helpful?"

"I'm afraid not. Most of it is Danny's report cards and standardized test results, all of which tend to be above average, as I said. I think Danny's old school worried more about what they didn't know about Danny than what they were able to document."

I thanked Mrs. Travis for her time and walked into the hallway. I had the overwhelming urge to peek into Danny's classroom, just to make sure he was okay. I started to turn back to ask the secretary for permission then decided just to find my way.

The teachers' names hung on the wall above their classroom numbers in the hallway. I walked down one hall without finding Mr. Mathews' name. In the next, his door was second on the right. It was closed.

I sidled closer until I could see inside through the three-inch-wide window beginning a foot above the door handle.

Danny's desk was in the third row, between two other boys. Danny was reading a book, as was the rest of the class. He looked… absorbed. I guessed that was the best we could hope for on his first day.

Inside the room, a man moved past the door. I jerked away from the door and speed walked around the corner, hoping no one had spotted me. I didn't know if a twelve-year-old would appreciate his "mother" looking in on him or not. I was quite sure he wouldn't appreciate having his teacher whip open the classroom door and catch me in the act.

In the school parking lot, I used my cell phone to call Ray.

"Hey, Darlin'. How'd it go with the principal?"

"Okay. She said Danny's old teachers suspected him of stealing from his classmates."

"I heard when I picked up his file."

"What else did you hear that you neglected to tell me, Ray?"

"I heard he was a good student, and his father was attentive."

"Did you hear that the school wasn't sure his father could read?"

"No."

"Maybe he's a thief because his prospects are limited."

"That's no excuse."

"What's the penalty for stealing a Cadillac Escalade?"

"He's been charged with grand larceny in the fourth degree. That's a Class E felony. For first offenders, the maximum sentence is four years in a state prison."

I watched as a woman pulled into the space next to mine and hustled into the school carrying a tray of cupcakes. Would that be me one day? "Is his father a first offender?"

"He's been in prison for armed robbery, when he was seventeen. He served nine years."

"So he's prone to violence."

"His partner in crime pulled the gun. Even the bank clerk testified that Danny's father seemed surprised."

I felt some relief. "Is prison where his neck got sliced?"

"Yes."

"Stealing cars seems like a step down from armed robbery."

"Auto theft is a multimillion dollar business, Jolene. It's the most expensive property crime in the U.S. More than a million cars are stolen every year, dismantled in chop shops and the stolen parts sold. Nationwide, only a little over ten percent of those thefts are cleared by arrest."

Like he was telling me something I didn't already know. "But why is Danny's father stealing cars here in Wachobe? Most of New York's auto thefts occur in the New York City area."

"We think he planned to put the Escalade in a semi bound for the city."

But instead, he got caught sitting behind the driver's wheel, and now he faced more time in prison. Would Danny want to visit him there, too? If his father let him, Ray would have to take him to visit. The county jail already gave me the creeps. I couldn't take a state prison. But surely Danny had to have other relatives.

"Principal Travis also told me Danny's mother died when he was two, or at least, that's what his father implied to his kindergarten teacher."

"I can try asking his father again. He's smart enough to take his right to remain silent seriously."

Just our luck that criminals are getting smarter. "Doesn't he have any other relatives?"

"Not that I've heard."

"Mrs. Travis said the birth certificate listed the same Newark address for both of Danny's parents. Do you think they might have family still living there?"

"Newark?"

I detected more than a hint of interest in Ray's voice. "Yes, Newark. What about it?"

"The Escalade was reported stolen by a woman who gave a home address in Newark."

"What was her name?"

"Hold on a minute."

I heard Ray's fingers clicking on the keyboard. "Her name's James. Jessica James."

Now we were getting lucky. Any chance she was related to Danny's mother, Jennifer James?

NINE

WHEN I MENTIONED IT to Ray, he hung up on me so fast that I didn't get to ask him to call me when he found out the answer. No matter, I would get it out of him later.

I drove straight from Danny's school to Erica's apartment, hoping to see the Porsche back in the driveway. It wasn't. I did see tire tracks on the driveway and footprints in the dusting of snow leading to her door.

I leapt out of the car and rushed onto the front porch. No one responded to my hammering on the door. I fished out my key and unlocked it.

Inside, the living room appeared the same, just dusty and un-occupied, as was the kitchen. Her bedroom and bath were another matter.

The mirror over her dresser now lay in pieces. Her dresser drawers hung open and empty. The bathroom vanity mirror had also been smashed. I surmised that the stiletto heel lying in the sink had been used to do the deed.

All of Erica's toiletries were missing. Only their lavender scent lingered in the air. Her suitcases were gone too. The remaining clothes lay strewn about the bedroom floor, still on the hangers, as if they'd been considered for packing and dismissed. Her discarded shoes were heaped in a pile in front of her closet.

I sank onto the corner of her bed and surveyed the damage.

If I called Ray, he would ask if I saw signs of foul play. In all honesty, I did not. When it came to Erica, breakage was commonplace. Once, she'd even put an umbrella through her television set. With the exception of the mirrors, the room just looked like she'd packed to go somewhere in haste. I crossed my fingers it wasn't Las Vegas to marry one of the unknown men in the Elvis chapel.

I dropped to the floor, crawling about on my hands and knees, trying to discern if she'd taken summer clothes or winter, beach or ski chalet, fashionable or serviceable. I came to no conclusions.

I did, however, spot her new prescription bottle under the bed. A count of the pills told me she'd stopped taking them two days after we'd had the prescription filled.

"Oh, Erica, how can I help you if you won't help yourself?"

———

I trudged across the driveway and knocked on the door of my old neighbor and nemesis Mr. Murphy. During the years I'd occupied the apartment next door, he'd made an almost weekly trip to my door to complain about the placement of my trash cans on garbage day. With his attention to detail, I hoped he might have noticed Erica's departure and perhaps her departure companion.

He wasn't home.

I got back in my car and drove by The Lincoln House. Erica's Porsche sat right where she'd left it days ago. It was too early for the restaurant to be open for lunch. I doubted any of the lunch shift employees would be of much help anyway. Erica worked the five to close shift. Maybe I would come back later and question some of her co-workers about Erica's mystery man. I could only suspect that she'd either run away or moved in with him. Surely psycho serial killers didn't have their victims pack suitcases.

Asdale Auto Imports was closed, according to the sign in the window. I was pleased to find the parking lot behind the building empty. Cory had stayed home or gone out on the town today as he should. But I needed to find the name of the redhead who wanted to purchase the Caterham. I wanted to find out if she was the same woman I saw at The Cat's Meow the other day. And I wanted to know if her brother had red hair, too.

But first I had to call the two dealers and discuss their available cars so I would have a reason to contact this woman.

That took me an hour. At the close of the hour, I wasn't excited about either car. The condition and maintenance records for both sounded satisfactory, but the prices were not. I didn't feel like flying Cory to either dealership's location to examine the cars. I really couldn't imagine how owning one of them was going to turn this woman's love life around.

Cory had written her name in his tight script on a pink Post-it Note. Leslie Flynn. He'd noted her brother's phone number underneath her name and the message to find her a Caterham DeDion.

I dialed the number. A man answered.

I identified myself and asked to speak to Leslie.

"This is she."

Now I heard the slightest hint of femininity in her otherwise gravelly voice. Dear God, did the woman have no attractions at all? "I understand from my mechanic Cory that you're interested in purchasing a Caterham DeDion. I've located two for sale."

"Excellent. How much are they?"

"Around forty thousand."

"Who do I make the check out to?"

I pulled the phone from my ear and looked at it. She must be nuts. No bargaining? No negotiating? I put the receiver against my ear again. "Leslie, I wanted to talk with you more about these cars. I'm not sure they're the best value for your dollar."

"I'll be right over."

"Leslie?"

She'd hung up on me.

I sat at my desk and waited for her arrival, finding myself in the awkward position of not wanting to make the sale. These Caterhams didn't merit their asking price, and the dealers didn't seem inclined to bargain. Hiring me to broker the deal seemed silly, especially considering the fact that Leslie could locate these guys by herself if she just got online. And, even though it wasn't my concern, I didn't think owning a Caterham would be the answer to her prayers. If this man she desired was so shallow that he could be won over with the purchase of a British sports car, he couldn't be worth having in the first place.

Had I become the love police? Maybe I should just let Leslie and, for that matter, Erica, decide what was right for them.

Nah. My new mission was to help people, whether they realized they needed help or not.

When the yellow Mustang convertible pulled into the shop's parking lot a half hour later, I knew Leslie was the woman I'd seen at The Cat's Meow.

She entered the showroom through the front door, stamping snow off her tan work boots. I walked out to greet her, thinking Cory had described her quite well.

Leslie Flynn had thinning sunburst red hair. I would have said it was a dye job, but the abundance of freckles visible even on her tanned skin suggested it was natural, or, at least, a simulation of natural. Her teeth were not only crooked but stained, and the brown Carhartt overalls and matching jacket she wore emphasized her unfortunate weight. As Cory had said, it wasn't pretty. And she smelled kinda funny, too.

She looked me up and down. "You're a cute little thing, aren't ya?"

I felt my cheeks flush. "Thank you. Please, come in and sit down in my office."

Her work boots clunked across the floor behind me. She dropped with a whompf, expelling all the air from the seat cushion.

I wasn't sure quite how to begin, never having tried to talk a customer *out* of buying a car. "That's a nice Mustang you're driving now."

She straightened and beamed with pleasure. "It handles well."

"It's a popular car. More popular than a Caterham."

Her head bobbed up and down. "I know, I know. But have you ever seen Gatekeepers or eX-Driver?"

"No, I'm not familiar with those."

"They're Japanese animated cartoons, and they feature the Caterham. The man I'm interested in loves the Caterham and those cartoons."

"You've talked to him about the cars and the cartoons, then?"

"Many times."

"So you two already have a relationship?"

Her lips parted and her eyes narrowed as she appeared to consider my words. "I sell him eggs. Fresh brown eggs."

"I see." I didn't really.

Leslie must have sensed my confusion. "My brother and I run a dairy farm. We have chickens, too. We also sell flowers and planters."

Now I recognized her perfume. Eau de Manure.

Farms covered the hills and valleys of the Finger Lakes countryside, most run by Mennonites with family names like Weaver and Hoover who spoke with German-like accents. In fact, the Finger Lakes region had received the dubious distinction of hog-farming capital of New York, dubious because the swine aromas didn't mix well with the fine wine aromas that the dozens of surrounding vineyards preferred to promote. The Mennonite farmers were tourist attractions, however, given their farm stores that sold homemade cheeses and fresh eggs as well as quilts, jams, wooden toys, and handcrafted furniture. Their simple clothes, refusal to use electricity or phones, and use of horse and buggy transportation or bicycles, which gave them their lean muscled physiques, also intrigued visitors to our area.

With her bright yellow Mustang and her less than toned body, I didn't figure Leslie Flynn for one of our more touristy farmers.

She went on, "The farm has been in our family for a hundred years. My brother and I still work it. We have hired help, too."

I wondered why Cory had made it sound like she was only visiting the farm. She seemed fully immersed in it on a daily basis. "Is farming a lucrative business?"

Leslie's eyes rolled back in her head. "It's a living. We can supply most of our own food needs. I can wear coveralls every day, so we have money for other things like cars, don't you worry."

"I wasn't worried about that. I'm just curious. I haven't spent time on a farm."

"You haven't missed much. I'm planning to spend less time there in the future. I want to see the rest of the country. I just have to find a bookkeeper for my brother. He's a nightmare when it comes to organization and paying bills."

I could understand her desire for a different setting. After living in Wachobe all my life, I'd started to wonder what else was out there. Maybe her plans to leave had given Cory the idea she was only visiting her brother. I wondered what her brother thought about her plan to seduce a man with a Caterham. It was the kind of idea Erica would come up with. I thought it best not to ask, but I couldn't let the opportunity pass to ask Leslie about her brother. "Is your brother a redhead, too?"

"He sure is. We're twins, born two minutes apart. I'm the older, wiser twin."

"The women are always the wiser ones."

Leslie bellowed. "I'm learning that more and more every day. My brother's a bit of a hothead. It's all I can do some days to keep our help from quitting when he gets the notion to light into them."

"My sister met a red-haired man the other night … at The Cat's Meow." I rushed on, embarrassed to admit my sister was hanging out at a strip club. "She took quite a liking to him. Do you think it might have been your brother?" Perhaps their lack of organization and ability to pay bills had brought them together.

Leslie scratched her cheek. "He spends a lot of time there, I know that. I had to go over there the other day and cover a check he bounced. If you tell me her name, I'll ask him about your sister when I get home and let you know. Now, how about you tell me about these cars you found?"

I supplied Erica's name, then spent the next half hour comparing and contrasting the two vehicles, emphasizing their selling points as well as their drawbacks. Overall, I hinted to Leslie that no matter how fun a sports car the Caterham might be, it would not buy her a boyfriend.

She leaned back in her chair when I finished and hooked her thumbs around the straps of her coveralls. "You don't seem keen on me buying this car, Mrs. Parker. What's wrong with a Caterham?"

"Nothing, and please, call me Jolene. If you have the money and you think you'll enjoy driving the car, then you should buy it. It's just—"

"You don't think it's going to get me a man."

"No, I don't."

Leslie examined her dirty and cracked fingernails. "I read an article that said men find women who drive these cars attractive. I know he likes these cars already. I just thought he might notice me as a woman if I drove one, too."

"If I had to guess, Leslie, I'll bet the article you read was written by a man trying to lure more women into buying sports cars. Most of them are bought by men."

Leslie's knee bounced up and down as she appeared to consider my words. "You're a married woman. Tell me, how did you attract your husband?"

I smiled. "He thought I was pretty." Just like Valerie Bertinelli, but I kept that to myself. I didn't want Leslie Flynn to try to remodel herself to look like a Caterham. She'd have a hard time becoming sleek and racy.

Leslie glanced down at herself with a rueful grin. "I ain't pretty."

Although I'd just had that thought myself, I felt obligated to disagree. "Nonsense. A new hairdo, a little makeup, clothes that emphasize your womanly assets—he's sure to notice a change in your look." I sounded much more confident than I felt. He would notice, but who knew if he would find her attractive? I tried to push that thought out of my mind. Something about Leslie Flynn made my heart go out to her. I felt the need to help her in any way I could.

She fiddled with the buttons on her flannel shirt. "I don't know how to pick out clothes. I get my haircut at the walk-in place for eight bucks." She darted a glance at me from the corner of her eye. "Can you help me pick out some clothes?"

I laughed. I'd be no help there.

Leslie stiffened. Her brow furrowed.

I held up my hand to appease her. "I'm sorry. I'm laughing because I don't pick my clothes out, either. I buy them at Talbots across the street. The manager picks them out for me."

Leslie's eyes brightened. "She's a nice gal? She might help me?"

I laughed again. "Nice might be too strong a word, but, yes, she will help you."

TEN

I PUT ON MY coat and walked Leslie across the street to Talbots. The sun had come out in full force today, melting away all traces of last week's snowfall. In fact, the temperature felt downright warm, and my wool coat felt too heavy for the day.

As we approached the store, I could see Celeste Martin through the window. She was waiting on a customer. From her gestures and facial expressions, I had no doubt she was telling the woman exactly what to buy. Celeste had a gift for fashion. She also had a gift for gossip and attracting men. I was hoping I could get at least two of her gifts to work in my new friend Leslie's favor. From experience, the gossip would always work against me.

By the time we entered the store, Celeste was ringing up her customer's purchases. Leslie and I hovered in the vicinity of the cash register while I waited to catch Celeste's eye.

She handed a tiny red and black envelope to her customer. "Here's your receipt. And here's your bag." She caught sight of me. Her eyes narrowed, but her smile remained firmly in place.

"Thank you, Mrs. Dean. Please be sure to stop back next week. Our fall clearance prices will be in effect."

She walked around the counter. "Jolene, I haven't seen you in months." Her gaze traveled down my body to my dress boots. "You've lost weight. You're a size four now. Your sister must be jealous."

"Have you seen Erica lately?"

Celeste nodded. "At the restaurant. She's put on a few pounds."

"Have you seen her this week?"

Celeste raised an eyebrow. "No. Is she missing?"

I swallowed my pride. Celeste knew all about my family's mental health issues. In fact, last year I'd learned she even dated my father for a while shortly before his death, a revelation that came as quite a shock to my world. Even more shocking was the fact that no one in town told me about it while it was happening. They usually loved to spread "news" as soon as they heard it. "Yes."

She glanced at Leslie, looking her up and down. "I'll keep my eyes open."

"Thank you." I gestured to Leslie. "This is Leslie Flynn. She wants to have a new look. I told her you would be able to help her."

Leslie pointed to Celeste's head. "You have beautiful hair. I'd like to have hair like yours."

Celeste raised a hand to her blonde, perfectly coiffed hair that always brushed her chin but never, ever would dare to get in her eyes. It might not even have the nerve to grow, since it always looked the same. I'd never seen a dark root on her, but we had gone through school together. Celeste was a natural brunette. However, knowing her, she was a blonde all over now. "It's not your color. I don't think this cut would suit you, either, but I can give you the name of my stylist. He's been known to work miracles."

Leslie's head bobbed up and down, an excited grin on her face. Clearly, she'd missed the insinuation that a miracle was required.

"Celeste, can you help Leslie pick out a few things? I'm going to try on some pants."

Celeste moved toward the stairs leading to the Plus size department. "I'm sure we can find ... something for you, Leslie."

Leslie clapped her hands together, smiled at me, and lumbered after her. The two disappeared into the loft.

I moved to Petites and selected a few pairs of pants. I slipped into the dressing room to try them on. The floor overhead creaked. A few minutes later something thumped onto the floor. I finished my try-on quickly and started in the direction of the stairs.

Celeste came down, holding a mannequin's arm in one hand and the leg in the other. "That woman's a menace."

I cringed at her hiss. "She needs you, Celeste."

"She needs to lose weight. She needs veneers. She needs a new dye job and extensions." Celeste dropped the mannequin's parts on the counter behind the register. "And she needs a bath. I might have to fumigate."

She looked at the three pairs of pants in my hands. "How did those work out for you?"

"I'll take them."

"You'll need sweaters to mix and match. I've got the winter styles in the basement."

I didn't really need or want the sweaters, but Celeste liked to manage a top-selling store. And Leslie needed her goodwill. I could always return the items on Celeste's day off.

An additional six sweaters and a hip-length quilted jacket later, I left the store laden with packages and Celeste's promise that Leslie would be a new woman when she came into my shop tomorrow to continue our discussion about the Caterham.

I sat in the Lexus and dialed Ray for a second time today. He didn't answer his cell phone. The department operator said he was out of the building. With any luck, he was hot on the trail of Danny's mother and potential aunt. If anyone could sniff them out, it would be the hound dog named Ray.

I started the car and headed back to Mr. Murphy's house in the hopes he'd returned home and could answer my questions about Erica.

His car was in the driveway when I pulled in next door. I dashed across his soggy lawn, my heels sticking in the grass, and raced up his front steps.

He pulled open the door before I had the chance to ring the bell. "You're here about your sister, aren't cha?"

Thin and sprightly as ever, Mr. Murphy now had tufts of hair growing not only above his ears but out of them. Coupled with his enormous earlobes, it made it difficult to focus my gaze on his wizened face. I did my best.

"She's packed her bags. I can't find her. Did you see her leave?"

"Sure did."

"Was she with someone?"

Mr. Murphy's hair tufts wafted up and down as he nodded. "Tall boy, with dark hair."

"Do you know his name?"

"Never seen the boy before. Never seen any of those wild boys visit her more than once."

"What kind of a car was he driving?"

"White one. One of those foreign four-doors. They're everywhere."

"Can you be more specific? A Honda Civic? A Hyundai Sonata? A Toyota Camry?"

Mr. Murphy waved his hands. "I don't know names. Not the boy's name. Not the car's. No names."

I tried to keep the smile on my face. "Can you tell me what time she left?"

"Morning. After the first two hours of the Today show. You know, when Regis comes on."

As I struggled to think of something else that might be helpful, Mr. Murphy started to close his door. My time was up.

I held my hand against the door, halting its progress. "Can you think of anything else, Mr. Murphy? Anything at all? Erica hasn't been taking her medication. I'm worried about her."

He rolled his lips and looked toward the porch roof. "Boy had on a Syracuse Orangemen sweatshirt. That's all I know."

That was enough. I let go of the door.

He slammed it shut.

The "boy" was Maury Boor.

———

I checked my watch. I didn't have time to look for Maury and Erica now. The day had slipped away from me. It was now quarter to three. School dismissed at five minutes after three. Danny would be waiting for me in the turnaround.

As I drove toward the school, I recalled Maury's fascination with the Syracuse University basketball team. For a short guy, he'd been obsessed with the mighty tall ones. Maybe because he'd never had a chance of making the team himself. Maury must have asked Erica at least twenty times over the course of high school to attend a game with him. His parents had been season ticket holders. Maybe they still were. Maybe Ray could get the campus police to provide an address to go with those tickets.

I drove into Danny's school's turnaround and pulled up to the curb behind a woman in a minivan. She had a bumper sticker that read "Soccer Mom." Would that be me someday, too? I'd never drive a minivan, but I could do soccer. Maybe. Depending on the weather.

Ray didn't answer his cell. I didn't bother calling the department. He'd be home for dinner soon enough.

Danny came out of school with his backpack over his shoulder, dragging his new coat through the wet grass and puddles. I cringed.

He climbed into the back seat.

I turned to look at him. "How was your first day?"

"Okay."

"Was Mr. Mathews nice?"

"He's okay."

"How were the other kids? Did they talk to you?"

"Yeah. They're okay."

"Okay" was the word of the day. I started the car and eased my way out of the parking lot, trying to avoid the other more hurried moms and the kids jaywalking across the street.

When we got home, Danny plunked in front of the television. I headed into the office and fired up my computer, searching for Maurice Boor in the on-line white pages. The only listing I found was for an elderly man in another state. I dialed the number, hoping to find Maury's dad.

He wasn't a relative.

Faced with another dead end, I turned off the computer and headed into the kitchen to pull out all the remaining Thanksgiving leftovers. If I really was a super soccer mom, I'd be able to mix them all into a delicious casserole. I gave that thought all of a minute then shoved them as is into the oven to reheat.

Ray came through the door just after five, as he did most days. "Where's Danny?"

"In the living room, watching TV."

He motioned toward our bedroom. "Come talk to me."

I followed him, noticing his pant cuffs were filthy. "How'd you get so dirty?"

"Crawling around the parking lot of The Cat's Meow." He took off his pants and threw them in the clothes basket. "I wanted to see if I could find a remote in the parking lot. The bartender said no one had turned one in."

"Did you find one?"

"No, but the bartender and the bouncer remember Danny's father going out of the bar and coming back in again to look for something. The bouncer figured at first it might be Danny, but his father was looking on the bar and the floor."

"Maybe for his remote?"

"That was my thought. But that's not what I wanted to tell you." Ray pulled on a pair of jeans. "I called Newark and checked out Jessica James."

"And?"

"They sent officers to her house. She wasn't there. They talked to the neighbors, who said they hadn't seen her for at least a month. The description they gave matches Josie Montalvo's description, right down to the rhinestone fingernails. DMV provided a picture of Jessica James. It matches the picture on Josie Montalvo's license. We found it in the apartment where we think she was killed. The two women appear to be one and the same person. But DMV never issued a license to a Josie Montalvo, and the Social Security office says the number on her card doesn't exist."

"So Josie Montalvo was a fake?"

Ray nodded. "The neighbors knew her sister, Jennifer, too. And Danny and Danny's father." He started to flip through his shirts, considering and dismissing them in turn.

"What else did they know?"

He pulled a thick rugby shirt off a hanger. "They all lived with the aunt in that house for two years after Danny was born. Then his mother died. The neighbors weren't sure, but they thought it was from complications related to pneumonia. They did say the family was devastated. Danny and his father lived there with the aunt for another year or so—then one day he and Danny were gone. Jessica continued to live there until about two months ago when she bought the Escalade. The neighbors said she put her bags in her old gray Cavalier a month later and disappeared. She left the Cadillac in the garage. They thought she'd taken an extended vacation or something."

I watched Ray pull his shirt over his head. Danny had thought that his aunt, Josie Montalvo, might be his mother. At age three, maybe he had believed she was. His memories from that time of life would be cloudy at best.

106

"So what does it all mean?"

Ray reached out and pulled me into a hug. His shirt smelled dusty. Yet another area of housework I'd neglected.

"Danny's father knew Josie Montalvo. He was found driving the Escalade that she, as Jessica James, reported stolen. He was at The Cat's Meow, which suggests he knew where she worked. He may have known where she lived as well. He's now the number one suspect in her death."

I wiggled out of his arms and gazed up at his face. "So you think he killed her?"

Ray rolled his neck and shoulder. "No."

I couldn't believe my ears. "You don't?"

"No. The first thing we did was light up both the Escalade and the Camry. There's no trace of blood in either vehicle. The guy has no real history of violence. His prison record is exemplary. His parole officer said he followed the rules of his parole. Even the neighbors said he was a good father and a good neighbor. He appeared genuinely shocked to hear Josie Montalvo was dead."

"He's talking now?"

Ray heaved a sigh. "He's still not talking, but I could tell from his body language. His attorney wanted a deal. I think Jessica James' death threw a monkey wrench into it."

"Will you investigate Danny's father for her murder?"

"No. When the sheriff heard the definite connection to Danny, he took me off the case. I'm back on patrol duty for the month."

The sheriff's office in our county was fortunate to have only tenured members. The sheriff had decided that every deputy would have the chance to work investigations, so they took turns. When a deputy was not assigned to an investigation, he was on patrol, usually in hopes of finding another investigation to pursue. The sheriff must know what he was doing. Employee morale in his department was exceptionally high.

"So you're not going to be involved?"

"You can bet I'll be looking for her body under every bridge and haystack."

Ray'd probably find it, too. "What should we tell Danny?"

"Nothing. His father's not in the lockup any more. He's in the jail. I'll take Danny to visit him tomorrow. He can tell Danny what he thinks is right."

I felt a niggling of suspicion. "Are you hoping he'll come home and share the story with us?"

Ray ran his finger down the bridge of my nose. "Only if it helps the two of them, Darlin'. Only if it helps."

ELEVEN

OVER OUR DINNER OF leftovers, I told Ray and Danny about Mr. Murphy witnessing Erica's departure from her apartment in the company of the man I believed to be Maury Boor.

"And he was driving a white car, a four-door import. Mr. Murphy didn't know which make or model. What are the odds it could be another white Toyota Camry?"

Danny choked and sputtered on his milk as his gaze shot to my face.

Ray studied Danny. "What do you think, Danny?"

"I don't know." He focused on his mashed potatoes.

Ray turned to me. "Camrys are one of the most popular cars on the road, especially white ones. They last forever, and they don't show the dirt as much. We must have several dozen in this county alone."

I knew that. But I'd been hoping Ray would tell me something different—I'd been imagining all sorts of scenarios involving my sister, a psycho killer, and a white Camry, not to mention dry ice in a cooler.

Ray continued, "After dinner, I'll make some calls to Syracuse. See if I can find a season ticket holder named Boor. I'll call the DMV and see if I can find a Camry registered to a Boor, too."

Danny finished his plate and rose from the table.

Ray fixed an eye on him. "I didn't hear you ask to be excused."

"May I be excused?"

"What's the magic word?"

Danny wrinkled his brow and thought for a moment. I began to despair in earnest for his upbringing. Finally, he got it. "Please?"

"First take your dishes to the sink."

Danny carried them over, then disappeared into the living room. I expected to hear the television again. Instead, he reappeared with his backpack in hand. "I have homework." He stared pointedly at the table.

I scrambled to my feet. "Let me clear the dishes and you can sit here to do it."

Ray helped me carry the dishes to the sink. He leaned close to my ear. "Good to see him showing some responsibility. I'll go make those calls."

I started to load the dishwasher. "I need to run over to The Lincoln House and ask some of the dinner shift crew about Erica and Maury Boor. Maybe one of them knows more about Maury."

"Go ahead. I'll babysit."

I wanted to tell Ray that it's not babysitting when it's your own child, but, then, Danny wasn't really our child. He was definitely temporary; just how temporary, Social Services and the penal system would have to determine. Four years for car theft was a far cry from a murder sentence. I wasn't naïve enough to hope Jessica James was still alive. I could only hope Danny's father wouldn't be convicted of killing her. Danny wanted to be with his father, and, even with his obvious faults, his father did love Danny.

Just like I loved my sister. But, boy, could she be a pain in the ass. As I guided my Lexus over the roadways in the direction of The Lincoln House, I thought about the dozens of other times Ray or I had set off in search of her. The last time she'd been released from the psych center, Dr. Albert had said she wouldn't ever come back. Of course, he might not have anticipated her "cure" and subsequent decision not to take her meds. Maybe he should have, though. It wasn't all that uncommon for patients to think they no longer needed their medicine. Was he not as good a doctor as I thought? Maybe his statement had even given her the impression she was cured. Would I have to find her a new shrink, too? I hoped not.

The Porsche still shone under the street lights at the back of The Lincoln House's parking lot. I peeked inside to see if she'd left any clues. I saw piles of beer caps and wine corks on the back seat. Erica collected them and stored them in shoeboxes. She labored under the delusion that her collection would be sold for money some day. I also spotted half a matchbox. The label was covered by a cork. I tugged on the door handle. Of course, she'd remembered to lock it. I'd have to look for the spare key in her apartment.

I went inside the restaurant and introduced myself to the hostess, an older woman who seemed to recognize me. When I explained about Erica, she expressed her sympathy.

"She's a sweet girl, but lately she's been a little ... cranky. I tried to help clear a table in the barroom last week, and she bit my head off. Accused me of trying to steal her tip, which was ridiculous. I did see her leave with that dark-haired man. One of the girls said she knew him." She pointed her index finger at me. "Wait here a minute."

She returned, followed by a brunette with a ponytail, wearing the black pants, white shirt and the tie of a server. "Patty knows him."

The brunette's ponytail swished behind her as she nodded. "Maury Boor. Class of '90. He sat next to me in homeroom and at graduation. Real quiet. He's grown a couple feet since then. He's kinda cute now."

"Do you know where he lives?"

"I thought he lived outside Buffalo, but I'm not sure. Try the phone book."

"I did, online. I couldn't find him."

"Did you use his real first name?"

I tipped my head. "I thought it was Maurice."

"No, it's Emerson. That was his dad's name, too, so they called him Maury. Maurice is his middle name."

I thanked her for the information and headed for home. When I walked in, I found Danny in front of the television. Ray was in our office, on the phone.

He motioned me inside as he hung up. "Syracuse issued one season ticket to an Emerson Boor. He gave an address in Geneseo. Could that be Maury's father?"

"It could be Maury. One of the waitresses who graduated with him said he was named after his father, Emerson. But she thought he lived in Buffalo."

"The basketball season started over a month ago. I'm sure the University sent the ticket out months before that. Maybe he moved. I'll call the department and have him run through DMV and check for a record on Emerson Boor. He's somewhere close by." Ray picked up the phone again.

I sank into an armchair to wait.

Ray didn't seem to like the answers he got. A muscle in his cheek twitched as he listened. I leaned closer, trying to hear.

"Good work. Thanks for checking." He hung up and rubbed the five o'clock shadow on his chin, making a rasping noise that sent shivers down my spine.

"DMV's last known address for Boor is Buffalo. They're sending his picture. I can start showing it around tomorrow. But there's bad news, Darlin'. Emerson Maurice Boor, age thirty-five, has an arrest record in Geneseo for stalking a female co-worker."

———

Tuesday morning I awoke after another nearly sleepless night, rolled out of bed too fast, and had to grab the bedpost because the room swayed. In fact, my whole life swayed. My sister was in the hands of a stalker, and my foster child might be about to learn his father was a murderer—and I didn't think I could do much to protect either of them. I hated to be so helpless.

Ray had kissed me goodbye around six, eager to check out Erica's apartment and hunt for Maury Boor. While he hadn't been interested in Erica's disappearance days ago, the fact that he was now on patrol, coupled with Maury's record, made her top priority. I think he figured Maury had psycho killer potential, but he didn't want to alarm me. He never liked to alarm me. Hence, he tended to hide things from me. This time it was too late—I had already made the leap myself.

I drove Danny to school and waited until he'd vanished into the stream of children walking through its front doors. He seemed to have a spring in his step this morning, maybe because Ray had asked me to bring Danny to the public safety building at seven p.m. tonight to visit his father. When I told Danny the plan at breakfast, his eyes had lit up, and he couldn't wait to go out the door and get the day started. Perhaps he thought it would pass more quickly if he got the jump on it. I, on the other hand, dreaded what his visit to his father might bring, fearing Danny wouldn't hold up well to learning about his mother's and his aunt's deaths, not to mention the fact that the police now considered his father to be their number one suspect.

At nine-ten I walked into the showroom. The door was unlocked. The bells jingled to announce my arrival, but Cory did not appear. I headed toward the garage entrance.

"Over here."

I jumped. My purse dropped to the floor. I turned to find Cory sitting behind the wheel of the Ferrari in the middle of the showroom floor.

He waggled his fingers at me. "Sorry."

I picked up my purse and walked over to climb into the passenger's seat.

The moment my butt hit the seat, I remembered that a dead man had been the last one to … ah … rest on it. I blocked that memory out of my mind and closed the door. If I couldn't get past it, how could I expect a customer to?

"Why are you sitting here, Cory?"

114

"Brennan and I watched some old black and white movies last night, the kind where the couples sat in the cars as though they were driving and the scenery moved past them."

I smiled. "Ah, yes."

"I don't have anything to work on this morning, so I'm pretending Monte Carlo is moving past."

I leaned my head against the seat rest. "Is it hot out?"

"Very. Not a cloud in the sky."

I closed my eyes and felt the sun on my face, which wasn't too tough since it was pouring in through the showroom window. The temperature today in Wachobe had risen to fifty degrees already. We were looking at a second Indian summer. Must be all that global warming.

"And they're racing today. We're in the lead."

I opened my eyes and glanced over at him. "You've gotten the racing bug all of a sudden, haven't you?"

He grinned back at me, his teeth glittering ivory from all the whiteners he used on them. According to Cory, a stage actor must have gloriously white teeth. I'd wondered more than once if he'd reached the point where they glowed in the dark. "Brennan's excited to race this Mazda. The turbo's got a lot of power."

"Do you see us getting involved with other race teams, or just Brennan?"

"Just Brennan, unless you think differently."

I closed my eyes again. "I don't. To be honest, I've been wondering if I should get out of the sports car business altogether. You're the moneymaker here. I haven't sold much this past year and I still have this lemon."

Cory touched my forearm. I turned toward him again.

"I think the time is coming for this car, Jo. People have forgotten about the murder. And now that fuel economy standards mandate a corporate average fuel economy of 35 miles per gallon by 2020, America isn't going to be manufacturing the sports car classics like the Corvette. Pretty soon it will be all about imports. Our knowledge and skills will be in demand, you'll see."

Everything I'd read gave me the same idea, but still … "I thought about offering you the business."

His head wagged back and forth. "I don't want the responsibility, Jo. The last few months sucked without you. I was afraid you weren't coming back. I wouldn't have time for Summer Theater without you. I love cars, but I love the theater, too. I want the time to do both. Besides—" he slid his hand into mine "—we're a team. Batman and Robin. The Lone Ranger and Tonto."

I tapped the Ferrari's dashboard with my free hand. "Laurel and Hardy."

His girly eyelashes batted. "I don't do slapstick comedy."

"Fair enough. How about you take the day off? I owe you a few days off."

"What are you going to do?"

"Leslie Flynn's coming to see me at eleven. She's going to unveil her new look." I explained to Cory how I had enlisted Celeste's support to makeover Leslie.

Cory wrapped his fingers around the steering wheel. "I'm not going anywhere. I have *got* to see that."

"Fine, but be advised I'm also talking her out of buying the Caterham."

———

The two-hour wait passed as if it were ten minutes. I used the time to tell Cory about Erica and Danny. I had plenty to tell and he was a good listener.

Ray stopped by at ten-thirty with a copy of Maury Boor's DMV photo. He'd already started to show the photo in all the convenience and grocery stores plus the motels in and surrounding Wachobe, along with a photo of Jessica James.

He leaned against the Ferrari, never asking why Cory and I were sitting inside it, which was good because I didn't want to explain about Monte Carlo. "So far, no one's seen either of them."

"Do you have their pictures on you?" Cory asked. "Maybe I've seen them around."

Unfortunately, Cory was not acquainted with the elusive Maury Boor or Jessica James.

I wasn't surprised no one had seen Jessica. For all we knew, she was six feet under somewhere. Even though I avoided the gossip vine, I think even I would have heard if a one-armed woman was wandering around town.

Ray twirled his keys around his finger. "A number of the checkout counters in the convenience stores had sale displays of silver initial key chains just like the one Danny said his father owned. The letter P appears to be popular. Some of the displays didn't have any left."

Great. So maybe it was Mr. Phillips' key chain, maybe it wasn't. I sank a little farther into my leather seat, disappointed that Ray's investigative efforts hadn't paid off.

Ray's radio squawked and a string of codes followed. He listened and eased himself off the Ferrari.

"I talked to the Buffalo PD. They're going to send a car by Maury's address and see what they can find out. I gotta go. I'll call you later." Ray kissed my cheek and left.

I stuffed the photo in my purse. I wanted to help with the search, but Leslie was on her way. As soon as she left, I'd start asking around town about Maury, too.

At one minute to eleven, the showroom bells jingled again. "Ta da."

Cory and I looked up. He gasped.

If I hadn't *known* it was Leslie Flynn, I wouldn't have recognized her. Her hair now had a more subtle auburn color and appeared longer than the day before. Her eyes appeared darker and with thicker lashes. The red lipstick made her mouth full and lush and set off her new teeth, which were straight and white but also a little wide and long. The V-neck of her blouse drew the eye away from her broad shoulders, and its empire waist de-emphasized Leslie's thick middle. Her fingers were manicured to match her lipstick. I had no doubt her toes matched as well.

Her wide-legged black pants swished over her black pumps as she sashayed across the room. "Celeste taught me how to walk, too."

All I could say was "Wow." Celeste had accomplished this magnificent transformation within twenty-four hours. No way could I return the extra six hundred dollars of clothes she'd forced on me yesterday. It would be downright disrespectful.

Cory remained speechless.

Leslie pointed to her hair. "It's a wig. Celeste's stylist said my hair needs a rest from all the dye and sun."

I had a sneaking suspicion that her hair had been too thin to style, but I kept it to myself. "You look amazing. Ah-mazing."

She hugged herself.

Cory hopped out of the car and hugged her, too. "Jo's right. You look fabulous!" Fabulous for Leslie, that was. She still looked a bit horsy, but at least she was on her way to thoroughbred. Nevertheless, the transformation merited celebration.

I climbed out of the Ferrari. "How about I take everybody to an early lunch?"

TWELVE

We locked up and headed across the street to the Coachman Inn, a historic village landmark. In addition to serving meals, the inn operated paddleboat dinner cruises on the lake and rented tastefully decorated rooms with comfy poster beds and gas fireplaces. It was perfect for a romantic weekend getaway in the Finger Lakes and a delightful spot for a celebratory lunch.

In the lamp-lit, pine-floored entryway, Leslie spotted the restrooms. "I'll meet you at the table. I was so excited this morning, I forgot to whiz."

Cory and I waited for the hostess to seat the two groups ahead of us. Apparently, everyone in town had decided to have an early lunch. While we waited, I spotted Celeste's best friend, Mindy something, come out of the ladies' room. She flew into the dining room so fast that I didn't get a chance to say "hello." I feared Celeste might be lurking nearby as well.

The hostess greeted Cory and me. We followed her to a table near the stone fireplace.

"Jolene Asdale."

I turned to find Celeste and her friend Mindy sitting in a booth. Both wore skirts and blouses I swore had been on the cover of the most recent Talbots' catalog. Mindy got her hair styled at the same place as Celeste. She even had the same style, although she was a brunette. I wondered if Celeste had to give that her stamp of approval. She'd certainly never given her approval on my marriage to Ray, not when she wanted him for herself. That was why she always called me Jolene Asdale instead of Parker.

Cory continued on to the table while I stopped to thank Celeste for transforming Leslie so beautifully.

Celeste examined my pants and blouse. "I think that blouse was supposed to go with black pants, not tan."

I resisted the impulse to bump her table and upset her drink into her lap. "I'll remember that next time. Listen, Leslie looks fabulous. Thanks so much for your help."

"Ugh, it took a team, Jolene. My dentist opened up at six this morning to work on her."

"Thank him for me, too. It was worth it. The change in her appearance as well as her confidence is miraculous."

Celeste tapped her French nails on the table. "She's an odd one, that's for sure. In fact—"

I held up my hand and glanced over my shoulder to make sure Leslie wasn't in hearing distance. "She's joining Cory and me for lunch. We're celebrating her makeover."

She pursed her lips. "Don't let her overeat. There's not much room left in those pants."

I fumbled in my purse for the DMV picture of Maury Boor, pulled it out, and smoothed it on the table. "You two know almost everyone in town. Do either of you know Emerson Maurice Boor, Maury Boor?"

Celeste and Mindy cranked their heads sideways to study his picture. Both shook their heads.

"He's not too bad to look at." Celeste leaned back. "Let me guess. He has something to do with Erica's disappearance."

"She may be with him. I'm not sure."

Celeste exchanged a meaningful glance with Mindy. "We'll keep our eyes open."

From experience, I knew that was as good as my posting a sentry on every street in Wachobe to keep watch for my sister. Celeste had the whole town and beyond on her friends and family network.

The waitress appeared next to me with their drinks.

I stepped aside to allow her access to the table.

As she passed out their glasses, she glanced down at Maury's photo on the table. "Hey, that's a nice picture of Maury."

I glanced up at her in surprise. "You know him?"

"Sure. He's our linen rep. You know, the guy who delivers our tablecloths and napkins and uniforms and aprons and stuff. He comes here once a week, usually on Wednesdays."

I couldn't believe my good luck. "So you're saying he'll be here tomorrow?"

She shrugged. "He should be." She said Maury worked for a company called In-house Textiles.

I tried not to dance with excitement over the new lead and excused myself to call Ray right away with the news. He didn't answer. Impatient, I decided that if he didn't call me back by the time lunch was over, I would call the company and see if I could locate Maury myself.

I joined Cory at our table and filled him in on what I had discovered about Maury.

A minute later Leslie appeared, her lipstick and hair retouched. When she spotted Celeste, she raced across the room, pulled Celeste from her booth, and drew her into an embrace. "You're the best."

She released a visibly shaken Celeste. "Look at me." She twisted from side to side. "I'm a babe."

Celeste gave her a weak smile. "Yes."

"I'm going to ask him for a date when he comes to the farm tomorrow. I'll wear the green and say exactly what you told me to say." Leslie threw her arms around Celeste again and squeezed her so tight Celeste's eyes bugged out.

"Good. Good." Celeste's voice sounded more like a squeak.

"Thanks again for everything, Celeste."

As Leslie trotted over to join us, Mindy pointed at Leslie and leaned forward to speak to Celeste. I thought I heard her say, "That's her."

Celeste's eyebrows shot up in response.

Was it my imagination or did I see gossip tendrils sprouting from both their mouths?

The dining room was beginning to fill up by the time Leslie sat down with us. "What a great girl she is."

Cory winked at me. "Yep, that Celeste is one of a kind."

The two glasses of champagne I drank to celebrate Leslie's new look took the edge off the fact that Celeste and Mindy kept looking over at our table and whispering to each other all through lunch.

I couldn't imagine what the two of them were talking about, and I wasn't sure I really wanted to know. My family had been "newsmakers" in this town for years. People loved to look at us sidewise like we were specimens under the microscope. I'd long ago decided that it was best not to ask too many questions. The answers were almost certain to depress me. This time their interest seemed to focus on Leslie. I couldn't decide whether or not to be relieved.

Leslie drank three glasses of champagne. With her size, they didn't seem to faze her a bit. She told Cory and me all about her visit to the hair stylist and the dentist's office, and how excited she was to unveil her new look to her friends and family—all punctuated by exuberant gestures, much batting of the eyelashes, and multiple fluffs of her wig. Overnight, she'd transformed from a rough cowhand into a radiant flower. And no one was more excited about it than she was.

"Wait until Dr. Albert sees me."

I looked at Leslie over my wineglass. "Dr. Albert? Dr. Simon Albert who has an office next door to the psych center?"

She nodded. "Do you know him?"

I set my glass down. "My sister has been a patient of his for a couple years now."

Leslie forked her last bite of cheesecake. "I've known him about that long. We're almost finished with our sessions."

Cory lifted his eyebrow and looked at me. I knew he was wondering if I would be so bold as to ask Leslie what she was in treatment for.

I would. But as open as Leslie was, I hoped she'd just spit it out before I had to ask.

Her cell phone rang instead. She pulled it out of her black leather backpack and flicked it open. "Hello ... okay, I'm on my way." She pushed back from the table. "I am so sorry, Jolene, Cory. I have to leave. The milking machine is on the fritz and my brother is losing it again. Thank you so much for lunch and for everything. Y'all have been wonderful. It's so nice to make some new friends."

She hugged me and Cory in turn, smothering me with her breasts and cutting off my oxygen.

Halfway across the dining room, she turned and waltzed back to the table. "And I'm going to hold off on the Caterham for now. I'm going to use the ideas Celeste gave me instead."

I wouldn't ask what those were, not ever. It would be too much like shaking hands with the devil herself. But let poor innocent Leslie use whatever tricks she could live with to attract the man of her dreams. "Okay, good luck. Keep us posted."

"Don't you worry, I will." With an excited wave and a couple funky chicken dance steps, she was gone.

Cory glanced at me. "Is it only me, or do you think she has some future in the theater?"

———

Cory headed for home while I sat at my desk in the shop and dialed Information for the number of In-house Textiles, which, come to find out, was based in Buffalo. When I asked their receptionist for Emerson Boor, however, she said he was no longer with the company.

"Since when?"

The receptionist sounded like a young girl. "His last day was yesterday."

"Did he resign?"

"I can't say. You'll have to speak to Human Resources."

"Did he get fired?" I could be so much bolder on the phone than in person. Hell, I hadn't even given this girl my name.

"I really can't say. Would you like to speak to someone in HR?"

I scrambled for a way to get more information, knowing HR would just hang up on me. "No, it's just ... he's been dating my sister. If he hasn't got a job anymore, I don't think they should get married, do you?"

"Maury's getting married? Does your sister ... hold on, I have another call."

I listened to the music while I waited for her to return.

"Hello, listen, I really can't talk. I'm sorry."

"But you don't think my sister should marry Maury?"

"He's not so bad. He brought me roses for Secretary's Day."

"So you think he's an okay guy?"

"He brings lots of girls roses. He's a little creepy. I have to go. Bye."

A little creepy. That wasn't news. That was the way Erica had felt about him in high school. She'd wanted to like him, because he'd always been so nice to her. But he was so persistent in his pursuit of her that he'd freaked her out.

It didn't help me to know he wasn't employed by In-house Textiles anymore, either. Now he wouldn't be showing up at the Coachman Inn tomorrow, where I'd been hoping to meet him.

Maybe the manager of the Coachman Inn could help me. Maybe he knew more about Maury, like where he lived. I headed back across the street.

The hostess summoned the manager, who I knew ever so slightly from the Wachobe Business Association meetings. He and I both appeared at those meetings sporadically.

I explained about Erica's disappearance and the connection to Maury.

"Gee, Jolene, I'm sorry, but I don't really talk to the guy. He brings in our order and takes away the laundry. That's about it. I don't think any of the guys in the kitchen really talked to him. He's in and out of here pretty fast."

Another dead end. I thanked him for his time and stepped outside onto the sidewalk, holding Maury's picture in my hand.

I tried to think of all the places in town that might utilize Inhouse Textiles' services. The yacht club and a couple other upscale restaurants came to mind. Given the warm day and the sunshine, I decided to walk from place to place and ask about Maury.

By two-thirty, I had pink cheeks from the sun's rays and no more answers than when I started. My last stop was The Lincoln House. I didn't hold out much hope there, because Bernie, the owner and bartender, already said he didn't know Maury. If he was delivering linens to the restaurant, surely Bernie would know him.

I took a seat at the bar and waited for Bernie to spot me.

"Hey, Jolene, are you here for lunch?"

"No, but I could use a Pepsi."

"Coming right up." He filled a glass and set it in front of me. "I haven't seen or heard from Erica, if that's what you're here to ask. I hired a new girl to take over Erica's shifts this morning. I haven't seen that guy again, either."

I sucked down half the Pepsi through my straw, then pulled out Maury Boor's picture.

"Is this him?"

Bernie accepted the photo. "That's him. A little younger."

I explained what I had learned about Maury. "I also found out Maury worked for In-house Textiles. Do you use them?"

"We use somebody else less expensive. Sorry." Bernie filled a bowl with pretzels and set it in front of me. "Hey, my son Jacob is in the same class as your boy Danny."

Danny wasn't my boy and he never would be, but I didn't want to miss an opportunity to check up on him. "Did Jacob give you any idea how Danny was fitting in?"

"I heard he has a good arm for football. They played at lunch yesterday."

"That's good."

"You should have him try out for the team in the fall. I'm a coach."

"We're not really sure how long Danny will be with us."

Bernie popped one of the pretzels in his mouth and chewed. "Is it true his father is in jail for car theft?"

I finished my soda and pulled out a five. "Yes. Where'd you hear that?"

Bernie waved off the money. "Jacob told me. He heard it on the bus. One of the other kids' mothers knew."

Word traveled fast in Wachobe. Some of the deputies had wives and mothers who didn't know when to keep their mouths shut. "I hope that doesn't cause problems for Danny at school."

"I'll tell Jacob that Danny needs a friend. Jacob's a good kid."

"Thanks, Bernie." I gathered my purse and stood. "Call me if you hear anything else, about my sister or Danny, okay?"

He swiped my glass from the counter and dunked it in the sink below the bar. "Sure thing, Jolene. Don't worry."

But worrying was one of the things I did best.

———

I called Ray on my cell phone as I walked back to the shop. My feet had started to burn and ache in my dress boots. I think I even limped a little.

"What's up, Darlin'?"

I filled Ray in on Maury Boor's old job and my quest to learn more about him. "It's a dead end. Have you had better luck?"

"He drives a white Honda Prelude, not a Camry."

"That's good news, I guess. Right?"

"It means it isn't likely that he parked a white Toyota Camry with a woman's arm on ice in the trunk outside the psych center, if that's what you mean."

It was. "But everyone keeps saying he's creepy."

"I talked to the arresting officer about the stalking charge. He was leaving roses for a girl on her doorstep nightly. She asked him to stop, but he didn't."

"Not such a big deal, right?" But it was. It was. I knew it was.

Ray must have agreed. "I don't like it. I'll call the HR department at In-house Textiles and see what they're willing to share with me. I'll see you at home later."

He hung up before I had a chance to ask him if they'd gotten any more leads on Jessica James' body.

I checked the clock and realized I had just enough time to get over to the school for dismissal. I hopped in the car and hightailed it over there, successfully inserting my Lexus sedan into the last parking space behind a rainbow assortment of minivans.

While I watched for Danny to appear in the stream of children exiting the school building, I tried to make sense of what we knew so far. A Camry had been stolen from a used car lot outside Geneseo. That same car, based on the VIN, had been parked outside the psych center with Jessica James' arm inside the trunk. Danny claimed the keys had been in the ignition when he took it. He also claimed the keys belonged to his dad, until he saw the woman's arm and changed his mind. Ray said they hadn't been able to get any clear prints from the keys to match Danny's father's prints, so maybe his father had stolen the car, maybe he hadn't. But from what Danny said, his father had been driving a Camry with all their things in the trunk. So, where were all their things? Had someone removed them from the car and replaced them with Jessica's arm in a cooler? What for? And what happened to their things?

The psych center or the doctor's office building figured into this somehow. Had the person who had stolen the car been in an appointment with their doctor or visiting a patient when Danny spotted the car and took it? If so, Danny's father couldn't be that person. He'd been in the county jail at that time. Were we blaming him for a car theft he hadn't committed? Were we looking for another car thief? Maybe one in treatment?

That seemed like a bit of a stretch. Car thieves didn't get treatment like kleptomaniacs. They got jail time. But I'd bet stalkers got treatment. Maybe Maury Boor had been required to seek treatment. Maybe Maury Boor had been at the psych center that day, driving a stolen Camry instead of a Prelude. He'd worked as a deliveryman. Maybe he had a customer close to the used car lot from which the Camry had been taken. He wouldn't want to mess up his own car with a dead woman's body, but he might have a preference for cars like his own. If so, was my sister in the hands of a murderer?

I squeezed my shoulder blades together to stop from trembling. My imagination was getting the best of me. Lots of people were in and out of that doctor's parking lot and the psych center every day. Even Leslie Flynn said she was a patient there.

I kicked myself mentally for not asking her about the nature of her treatment. But she didn't drive a Camry. She didn't live in Geneseo. In fact, I got the impression that prior to now she'd stayed pretty close to the farm most of the time. But she had been at The Cat's Meow—supposedly to pay off her brother's bounced check. Her brother had been there, too, talking with my sister on Tuesday before she disappeared. I'd forgotten to ask Leslie whether her brother had admitted to meeting Erica or not. I wondered what kind of car he drove. Maybe Ray could look it up.

The back door of my car flew open. Danny dropped onto the seat, his head bowed.

"Hi, Danny. How was school?"

He dug in his backpack and pulled out a yellow slip of paper. "Here."

His head lifted. I got a good look. "What happened to you?"

He had a shiner on his right eye, a dark, purple-red one, and a touch of dried blood under his nose. "I got in a fight. You have to meet with the principal in the morning. I think I'm going to be suspended."

THIRTEEN

I READ THE YELLOW slip. It was a request from Principal Travis for Ray or me, preferably both, to bring Danny to her office at eight o'clock in the morning. "Oh, Danny. What were you thinking?"

"I don't know."

I could hear the frustration in his voice. It matched mine. "What was the fight about?"

"Nothin."

I twisted around farther in my seat. "It was not about nothing. Did someone say something to you about your dad?"

Danny's eyes grew frightened. "What about my dad?"

Once again I'd led myself into a trap. "Nothing. I just thought... never mind. What was the fight about? You might as well tell me now, because you're sure going to have to tell Ray later."

Danny's eyes filled with tears. "This kid, he kept making these snorting noises every time he walked by my desk. At lunch, he got right in my face. I asked him, 'What's your problem, dude?' He said, "'Your foster father's a pig, and pigs stink.'"

The fight was about Ray? I couldn't believe it. Ray talked to the kids at this school every year about the D.A.R.E. program. It wasn't quite that time of year yet, but he'd never said that any of them had been anything other than respectful in prior years. And I was shocked that the old "pig" label had come up. I'd never heard anyone refer to any police officer or sheriff disrespectfully in this town, especially in that ridiculous way.

I wanted to ask if the other kid had gotten the worst of it, but I settled for a different question. "What's this kid's name?"

"I don't know." Danny pressed his head against the window. "Can we go home now?"

I sighed, partly delighted that he thought of our house as "home" but also a little distressed because I had to stop at the grocery store first. All I wanted to do was go home, too.

Danny refused to come in the store with me, which didn't matter. Everyone would just stare at his eye, then at the two of us, wondering. A few would even be bold enough to ask what had happened to Danny, if they knew me. In this town, sometimes they had the nerve to ask even when they didn't know you. I wouldn't miss the attention.

The store wasn't busy this time of day. I wheeled the cart around the store as quickly as I could, grabbing anything that looked good to me.

As I grabbed a package of spaghetti off the shelf, a flash of red from the end of the aisle caught my eye. It was Leslie, carrying a shopping basket and looking right at me.

"Hey, Leslie." I waved and started toward her.

Her eyes widened. She darted around the corner.

I chased after her in time to see her climb into a Ford pick-up truck in front of the store. Seconds later, she pulled out of the parking lot and disappeared.

Then I realized she hadn't been wearing her new wig. In fact, it probably wasn't Leslie at all. It must have been her brother. Funny he'd run away. People must get them confused all the time. Maybe he wasn't a people person? I shrugged it off.

My bill came to over two hundred dollars. I handed over my credit card and pushed the cart laden with grocery bags out the door.

I unlocked the trunk of the Lexus and deposited all my bags inside. Then I started toward the cart corral.

As I shoved my empty cart into the mass of other carts, a shot rang out. Something whizzed past my ear and pinged against the back end of the stainless steel corral frame. Seconds later, I heard another shot and another ping, this time against the car parked next to the corral.

I looked at the round hole in the trunk of that car. It could have been in my torso instead.

I hit the deck between the car and the corral and fumbled for my cell phone in my purse.

As my shaking fingers pressed 9-1-1, another bullet zipped past my ear. I scrambled toward the front end of the car, away from the shooter.

The 911 operator answered.

"I'm in the parking lot of the Wachobe P&C. Someone is shooting at me."

"Ma'am, are you in your car?"

"No, I'm on the ground between a car and the cart corral." An awful thought hit me. "But Danny … my boy … is in my car on the other side of the parking lot."

"All right, ma'am. An officer is on his way. Stay low to the ground and seek cover until he gives you the all clear."

"But my boy—"

"Stay where you are, ma'am. The officer is coming. I'll stay on the line with you."

I eased my head up to peek over the hood of the Acura I'd taken cover behind, trying to spot Danny. Another shot whizzed past me and cracked the windshield of the truck behind me as I dropped back to the pavement.

"Ma'am, are you taking cover?"

"Yes, yes! Where's the officer? Can you call my husband Ray Parker? He's a sheriff deputy."

"I'll contact him now. Stay down, ma'am."

I heard a car turn over. It sounded familiar. The driver accelerated and squealed out of a parking space.

Another shot connected with the back end of the Acura. Was the shooter trying to hit the gas tank?

I dug in my heels and crab-walked closer to the truck behind me. If the Acura blew, the truck and I would go with it, not to mention the cart corral.

A car flew past the rear of the Acura, spun around the end of the line of parked cars and slammed to a stop in the lane behind me. "Get in, Jolene, get in!"

I scrambled to my knees and crawled to the Lexus. Danny opened the rear passenger door. I dove into the back seat. He hit the gas. We peeled out of the parking lot. He made a hard right onto the road which threw me to the floor. I heard the police siren coming from behind us as Danny raced down the road.

The siren faded.

"Pull over, Danny. Pull over. We're safe now."

He jerked to a stop by the side of the road. I climbed over the console and into the passenger seat. Then I grabbed him and hugged him tight. "Thank you."

He wiggled his way out of my grasp. "I didn't see the guy, but I heard the shots."

"And you came to save me."

He blushed and refused to meet my eyes. "Yeah."

I looked down at my hands. The cell phone was still clutched in one hand, my purse in the other. "But I have the car keys."

He nodded.

"Danny, did you hotwire this car?"

He didn't respond, but his eyes shifted about as though looking for escape.

"You know how to hotwire cars?"

A tentative nod told me he did.

"What else do you know how to do, Danny?"

He bit his lip and considered for a moment before replying. "I can jimmy a car door and pick a lock."

"Did your dad teach you all that?"

His eyes grew proud. "A man has to have some skills."

I grinned. "Is that what your father says?"

"Yeah."

"Next time you see him, you tell him I'm not sure what he was thinking when he taught you all that, but I'm sure glad he did."

Danny beamed with pride. "Okay, I'll tell him."

"Ma'am? MA'AM?"

I glanced at my cell phone in surprise. The 911 operator was still with us, just as she promised.

I raised the phone to my ear. "Yes?"

"The Wachobe police chief and your husband are now on the scene. They want you to meet them there. It's all clear."

"Did they make an arrest?"

"No, ma'am. The suspect appears to have fled."

"Okay, thank you." I ended the call and flipped my phone shut. "We have to go back."

Danny's hands slid under the wheel column.

I pulled the car keys from my purse. "I think you better let me drive."

———

Danny and I stood in the sun making our statements to the police chief and Ray while a team from the sheriff's office dug the bullets out of the cars, picked up the others, and plotted trajectories. Whoever it was must have been following me. I hadn't notice a tail, but then, I hadn't looked either. He could have been the worst tail in the world, and I never would have known he was there. They concluded the shooter had been in the trees in front of my Lexus. Unable to get a clear shot with my trunk open, he'd taken a shot as soon as I stopped in front of the cart corral.

Lucky for me, his aim was off.

Danny didn't want to talk when we got in the Lexus to drive home, which was fine with me because all my thoughts ended in, "Oh my God, someone tried to kill me."

Even though I had a trunk full of groceries, Ray offered to order pizza. He must have figured I couldn't cook since my hands were still shaking.

While we waited for the pizza, I went into the bedroom to change my clothes. My new tan dress pants were ruined with black grease marks and a tear in the knee. It was a small price to pay for my life. Besides, Celeste would be only too happy to sell me another pair, especially if she got to hear about my drama firsthand.

Ray appeared in the closet doorway. "Are you all right?"

"I think I'm still in shock." I studied his face and couldn't read it. "Why? What else happened?"

"That's what I want to know."

I reached for my dirty stretch pants. "I'm not following you."

"I saw your sister's car at The Lincoln House. You didn't tell me it had a dent in it."

Uh, oh. I hadn't told Ray about the damaged cars because I knew he'd be unhappy with Danny and with me for taking him to visit his father when he should have been disciplined for his actions on Thanksgiving night instead.

I pulled on the stretch pants, trying to think of an explanation that wouldn't make Ray angry. Nothing came to me, so I told him the truth about Danny stealing Erica's car and backing into Brennan Rowe's. "Cory can fix both cars. Like you said, Danny's impulsive."

"Let me make sure I have the story straight." He folded his arms. "Danny stole Erica's car to go see his dad, backed out of the driveway, smashed into Brennan's car, then the snowbank, and you took him to see his dad as a reward."

"Not as a reward. As a stress-reliever. He's twelve. He misses his dad. You can understand that, can't you, Ray?"

Ray's eyelids flickered. He'd lost his dad, a firefighter, when he was a teenager. While his father's death had occurred due to a heroic effort to save a family of four from their burning home, it hadn't lessened the pain for Ray and his family.

He cleared his throat. "At first, when I saw Erica's car, I thought someone might have attacked her, too. You should have told me what happened. We're supposed to be a team when it comes to Danny, Jolene. You can't keep things from me. I have to know what's going on. And we have to discipline him. He can't just steal a car, smash up two, and have no consequences."

"Okay, but today, he really came through for me." Even though I'd told him not to drive any more cars without a license, I would never consent to disciplining him for ignoring my direction now.

Ray's lips twitched. "He did, didn't he?"

I smiled. "He did."

We both started to laugh. Ray stepped inside the closet and closed the door behind him. "He's something else, isn't he?"

"He is. He is." I laughed so hard that tears came to my eyes.

Ray pulled me into his arms. "Gotta love a kid like that." He met my gaze and held it.

Then he whispered, "He saved you."

The laughter left me in an instant. "He did, Ray."

A flame flickered in his eyes. He bent to kiss me.

As his lips brushed mine, I felt a familiar tingle. It built into a slow burn. My tongue entwined with his as I molded my body to his, frustrated not to be closer.

He must have shared my frustrations because seconds later my back was against the wall, my legs wrapped around his waist, as he fought with his zipper.

A knock sounded on the closet door.

Ray whipped his head up and growled, "Yes?"

Danny's voice came from the other side. "The pizza's here. I need twenty bucks."

FOURTEEN

WHEN THE LAST SLICE of pizza disappeared, Ray took the empty box and threw it on the breakfast counter. Then he hitched his chair closer to the table and fixed his gaze on Danny.

Danny didn't seem to notice. He was too busy watching the clock. "Am I still going to be able to visit my dad tonight?"

I held my breath and prayed. Say "yes," Ray, say "yes."

Ray glanced at the clock over the stove. It read quarter to seven. "Visiting hours are from seven to nine weeknights. We can still make it, but, first, we have to talk."

Danny tried to read his face and failed. "I'm sorry about the fight at school."

"We can talk about that later. Right now I want to talk about Thanksgiving night when you smashed Erica's and Brennan's cars."

Danny swallowed. "I'm sorry."

"Sorry isn't enough, Danny. You have to take responsibility for your actions. Jolene and I have talked it over. You need to pay for the damages to those vehicles, at least the insurance deductibles. You're going to have to work at Jolene's sports car boutique after school, helping Cory with the repairs and anything else he or Jolene ask you to do."

My mouth dropped open. We had no such discussion. This was Ray at his best, solving the problem and making decisions for me. "Ahh …"

Ray paid no attention to me. "Are we agreed, Danny?"

"Yes, sir."

My lips compressed into a thin line of anger. If Ray had asked me, I would have told him how Danny felt about Cory and the complications that might arise from forcing them to work together. Now I would have to deal with that, too.

Ray patted Danny on the shoulder. "Good. Do you have any homework tonight?"

"Just one math sheet."

"Get it done by seven-thirty, and we'll head over to the jail."

As soon as Danny left the room, I whacked Ray on the arm and hissed, "We never talked about any of that. You're sticking me with him again."

"Remember that the next time you forget to inform me about Danny's behavior."

Why did I feel like I was being disciplined too? "Fine. Then you can take him to school tomorrow and deal with Mrs. Travis."

"I'm planning on it. I want to get a look at this kid who called me a pig. He bears watching." Ray wiggled his eyebrows.

When I didn't laugh, Ray reached over and took my hand in his. "Let's talk some more about who might have wanted to take a shot at you this afternoon. Have you been pissing off anybody besides me lately?" He smiled to take the edge off his words.

I pulled my hand from his anyway. "I don't know, Ray. I've been asking around town about Maury Boor. No one admitted to knowing anything about him, but maybe they were lying."

Ray let out a heavy breath. "I took his picture into The Cat's Meow and showed it to the staff. He's been in there before, but none of them remembered if he was there on Josie ... Jessica James' last night."

"Were any of them receiving roses from him?"

"No."

"Other women at In-house Textiles did. He had them all pretty freaked out."

"Their HR manager mentioned that when I spoke to her." Ray rubbed his forehead. The lines on it seemed deeper than a few months ago. Had I contributed to the tension that caused them? When had he started looking so tired?

I grabbed his hand as he lowered it to the table and held on tight.

He glanced at me, seeming both surprised and pleased. "Maury resigned two weeks ago. He just finished out the month to get a few more dollars in vacation pay. He'd only worked there since August anyway."

"Did he get another job?"

"She didn't know. He gave his two weeks' notice and left. I got the impression they were glad to see him go, considering his effect on the women in the office."

"I'm surprised they didn't fire him."

"They had reassigned him to a territory that required him to come in early to get the deliveries. That way he didn't see any of the women. The HR manager said that made most of the problem disappear.

"The Buffalo PD stopped by the address listed on his registration. It's a furnished apartment. The landlord hadn't seen Maury in a week or so, but the rent is paid up through today. He promised to call if Maury showed up."

I stifled a sigh. "So we're no closer to finding Maury or Erica."

"I'm afraid not."

"What about Jessica James' body?"

Ray squeezed my hand. "It's hunting season. We're hoping someone will stumble over her."

I got a visual of that in my head. A bit of bile burned the back of my throat.

Danny appeared behind Ray wearing his jacket. "I finished my homework."

Ray slapped his hands on the table and rose to his full and intimidating height. "Then let's go."

———

I sat down and tried to concentrate on reading the newspaper, but the words blurred and jumbled in my mind. Ray's question came back to haunt me. Who had I pissed off this week?

If Maury Boor had made off with my sister for either good or nefarious purposes, he might not like to have me hot on his trail. But which of the many people I'd spoken to about him had leaked my questions back to him? No one had really had a kind word for him. It was hard to imagine any of them secretly passing information about my visit on to him. Still, stranger things have happened.

Or maybe Erica had told him I would never rest until I found her. Maybe Maury thought he'd put me to rest instead.

I rose and closed the living room shutters. No sense making a target of myself.

I dropped back onto the sofa.

My only other new acquaintance this week was Leslie Flynn. From all appearances, she now loved me. She had a new style, more confidence, and no further interest in purchasing a Caterham at this time. All that and I hadn't even charged her a penny. In fact, I bought her lunch. Although I never sold her anything, I'd list her as a satisfied customer. Surely she wasn't mad at me for talking her out of buying a Caterham.

But I had asked her about her brother and if he knew Jessica James a.k.a. Josie Montalvo. She never got back to me on that question. What if she had asked her brother and mentioned my name during the course of the conversation? Would he come after me for some unknown reason? It seemed strange he would run from me in the grocery store then come back to shoot at me. Could he have a connection to Jessica James' death? He was known to frequent The Cat's Meow. I would have to ask Ray if he could get Leslie's brother's DMV picture to show the girls who worked there. Maybe he'd been one of the men Jessica had arranged to meet outside of work.

Otherwise, I was at a loss to figure out who would want to take a shot at me. Whoever it was must have seen Danny sitting in the Lexus, but hadn't had any interest in him. Or were the shots fired because of him? Ray hadn't interrogated Danny about his father, because he couldn't be the bad cop and the boy's foster father, too. But I had asked Danny a lot of questions and gotten some pretty interesting information about his father in return. Ray had questioned his father after that. Did Ray let it slip that Danny had confided in me? Had his father spoken with one of his friends and sent one after me to prevent Danny from confiding in me any further? I would have to ask Ray if Danny's father had received any other visitors at the jail.

Danny's father must know that Jessica James was dead and that he topped the suspect list. Maybe the attack had been designed to frighten me into asking Social Services to place Danny with another family. All the shots had missed, after all. Or maybe someone thought having shots fired at me would cause Social Services to take Danny away from us, preventing him from sharing any more information that might point to his father as a killer. Shots fired in our home had been one factor in the judge's decision to award custody of our sweet foster baby, Noelle, to her birthmother. Anyone who read the local paper would know that.

I got up and started to pace, watching the clock and waiting for Ray to come home. Did Danny know more that might incriminate his father? What would his father tell Danny tonight about his mother and aunt? Were Ray and I dismissing an obvious link? All I had was unanswered questions.

And where the hell was Erica? Did Maury Boor figure into all this somehow? Was my sister in danger from him, or just herself like usual?

I started straightening stacks of magazines and blowing dust off the mantel, anything to take my mind off my worries. It didn't work.

When Ray and Danny walked through the door hours later at nine-thirty, I was in the kitchen making a cup of Chamomile tea to calm my overwrought nerves.

I darted into the living room just in time to see Danny's bedroom door close behind him.

Ray hung up his coat and followed me into the kitchen. He took a stool at the breakfast bar. "Danny wants to be left alone."

"Why?" I offered Ray tea, which he declined. Then I climbed onto the stool next to him. "What happened?"

"Danny saw his father in the visitor's area. I waited outside in the lobby."

"Did Danny tell you what they talked about?"

"No, but I could tell he'd been crying when he came out."

"Did you ask him why?"

"No, Jolene. Danny was trying to hide the fact he'd been crying. Maybe it upset him that he could only see his father on the other side of the glass. Maybe it's dawning on him that his father isn't going to be released, and he's stuck with us. It could be he's just sad. I wasn't going to ride him about it. You ask him tomorrow when I'm not around. He'll tell you."

"But, Ray—" I stopped short and told myself it wouldn't do any good to ride Ray, either. Instead, I filled him in on my tortured thoughts from earlier in the evening.

He heard me out and gave my ideas a few minutes of thought.

I started to get antsy, squirming on my barstool. "So, what do you think?"

"It's not Danny's father."

"How can you be so sure?"

"Danny's father doesn't know Danny confided in you, unless Danny told him. And even if Danny did, the guy hasn't had any visitors other than Danny. He hasn't placed any phone calls. His only contact has been with his public defender, who would never help arrange for a hit on you, Darlin'. It doesn't fit.

"But I will look into Leslie Flynn's brother. Leslie may have gone home today and asked him about Erica and The Cat's Meow. Maybe that tipped him off. He might have denied the whole thing to her, but now he knows you're interested in him. He may also know you're married to me. That fits."

Ray stood and stretched his arms toward the ceiling. "I'll check him out first thing in the morning. And I have the whole department on the lookout for Erica. She and Maury are bound to turn up soon."

His shirt slid out of his waistband and hitched up, exposing his hip bones and muscled abs and the fine dark hairs around his belly button.

I couldn't take my eyes off him.

He noticed. His hand slid under my chin, lifting my face. His normally copper-colored eyes looked black. "I'll keep everyone safe. I promise."

I smelled coffee on his breath. I didn't drink coffee, but I sure loved the smell of it. It always reminded me of Ray.

A shiver racked my body.

He rubbed his nose against mine and planted a wet kiss on its tip. "What is it?"

I was thinking Ray never liked to go long without sex, either. It had been a couple months now. He'd been awfully patient with

148

me. Maybe he'd been a little depressed after Noelle's departure, too. He'd just chosen to work through it differently.

He stepped back, waiting for my answer.

I pulled my legs up onto the stool and slid onto my knees, bringing my face level with his. I held out my arms.

He stepped into them.

I wrapped my legs around his waist and whispered in his ear.

His arms tightened around me with alarming intensity.

"A born-again virgin? Awesome."

FIFTEEN

THE NEXT MORNING I couldn't get the stupid grin off my face. I felt like Scarlett O'Hara the morning after a drunken Rhett ravaged her. Even Ray had a new spring in his step and added warmth to his voice. We were back in the groove as a couple.

Danny kept sneaking looks at us over breakfast, but he didn't say anything. Hopefully Ray and I hadn't made too much noise last night. I wondered what Danny knew about sex. Wasn't sixth grade the year the kids lost their innocence about that issue forever when the school health teacher showed up? Would Ray and I still be his foster parents when the time arrived to talk about sex? When Ray and I went to school, they told us about the birds and the bees. Now we have the birds and the bees, the bees who preferred bees, the birds who preferred birds, the birds that looked like bees but liked birds and vice versa and versa vice-a, then the birds who actually had the surgery and took the medication to become bees or vice versa. Who could explain all that with a "don't-worry-it's-all-part-of-growing-up and growing-up-is-great" face?

I pushed that intimidating thought out of my mind. Nothing was going to ruin my day. It didn't even bother me when Ray suggested I accompany him and Danny to see Principal Travis in her office. I had a new pair of pants to wear.

Ray followed my Lexus to the school parking lot and kept his eyes open as we entered the building. With all the buses circling, the masses of kids milling about, and Danny inches from my elbow, I doubted anyone would take a shot at me on the school grounds anyway.

When the secretary ushered us into Principal Travis' office, we found another boy and his parents waiting with Mrs. Travis. The boy's nose was in a splint, both eyes red, purple, and black. He reminded me of the riddle what's black and white and red all over?

I tried to arrange my face into a sympathetic expression as I sat down.

Principal Travis introduced us to the other boy's parents and the boy. His father rose and shook Ray's hand. His mother gave me a tentative smile. Neither of our sons acknowledged each other.

Danny's left knee bounced up and down, up and down, up and down. I couldn't watch it anymore. I stilled it with my hand and shook my head.

He frowned.

Mrs. Travis folded her hands and leaned forward. "I met with Danny and Scottie yesterday. Scottie admits to taunting Danny and referring to Deputy Parker as a 'pig.'"

She gave Ray an apologetic smile before continuing, "Danny admits to punching Scottie first. According to the teachers who broke up the fight, it was pretty much a free-for-all after that. I did sit down with the boys yesterday. They apologized to each other and shook hands."

She glanced between Danny and Scottie. "How are you boys feeling today?"

Both shrugged in response.

She nodded and began to alternate her gaze between Ray and me and Scottie's parents. "Danny and Scottie will receive a mandatory three-day suspension. If they are involved in any sort of fisticuffs again, with each other or anyone else, they will be expelled.

"Do you understand, boys?" She shifted her gaze to the boys in turn.

Danny and Scottie nodded.

"The boys can return to school on Monday. In the meantime—" she tapped two piles of books and folders in front of her, "—their teacher assembled their classroom work for the rest of the week. He'll correct it all on Monday then test them on it. Do you have any questions?"

Oddly enough, none of us did. I think we didn't dare.

Outside the school, Danny climbed into the Lexus while Ray and I shook hands with the other boy's parents one last time. I hoped I'd never see them again.

We watched them get in their car and drive off. Ray shook his head. "You know who they are, don't you?"

I shook my head. "Who?"

"They own the vineyard on the west side of the lake, the one next door to the big hog farm. They've been very vocal opponents of hog farming."

"So you're not the only pig they're against." I smiled.

"Nice, Darlin', really nice." Ray leaned on his patrol car. "Can you take Danny to the shop with you?"

"I guess I'll have to."

"When he needs a break from his schoolwork, he can start helping Cory."

I didn't look forward to that. Maybe I'd take a leaf from Principal Travis' book and develop my own good behavior policy. "I'll have Cory call Brennan and ask him to bring in his car. Maybe I'll pick Erica's car up from The Lincoln House, too." If I couldn't find her spare key in her apartment, I could always have Danny hotwire it. A man should practice his skills, right? That would be our little secret.

Ray followed my car to the shop and pulled his patrol car into the drive behind me. "I didn't see any tail. I'm going to drive by as often as I can, just in case."

He waved. I blew him a kiss.

Danny observed us with a glum expression.

I didn't think now would be the time to ask him about last night's visit with his father, not while he was still reeling from the meeting with Principal Travis this morning. I decided to give him a few hours to regain his confidence instead.

Danny followed me into the shop, shoulders slumped and feet shuffling. But when we walked into the showroom, Danny's eyes lit up at the sight of the Ferrari. "Is that yours?"

"It's for sale. Until then, it's mine." Or the bank's. I can share.

He ran over to the car and leapt into the driver's seat. "It's so cool. I can't believe nobody bought it."

I couldn't tell a twelve-year-old the story of the dead man in the passenger seat, could I? He'd have nightmares. On the other hand, Ray's ghost stories hadn't bothered Danny the other night.

I filled him in on the ghost now riding shotgun. "So, that's why it may never sell. It makes people too uncomfortable."

"I'd buy it. It's awesome."

"I'm glad you like it." That made one of us, sadly not one with any income. "Come on, Danny. You can sit here and do your work." I led him behind the showroom reception counter and set him up with pencils and pens.

He gazed at the pile of books and folders without much enthusiasm.

I sat on the edge of the desk. "Cory will be here at nine. Ray said you can work with him after a couple hours of schoolwork. When you do, you will be polite and respectful. You will respond when spoken to and do exactly what he says. We can't afford any more mistakes."

Danny's eyes darkened.

I waited for an argument. It never came. "Okay. Get started on your work. I'll be in my office."

A stack of mail waited for me. I sorted through the payments, invoices, and junk, watching Danny out of the corner of my eye. He'd opened his books and his pencil appeared to be moving across the page. Poor kid, nothing had gone right for him lately, but we couldn't risk having him expelled from school. Wachobe only had one school, and I wasn't the home schooling type.

Cory breezed through the door at one minute to nine, stopping in the middle of the showroom when he spied Danny.

"Hey, Danny, what're you doing here?"

"I got suspended."

"For fighting?"

Danny nodded.

"Bummer." Cory peered over the top of the reception desk. "Geez, they make you do homework when you're suspended? That stinks." He entered my office and dropped into the chair across from me, leaning forward to whisper, "Nice shiner."

I rolled my eyes. "The other kid's got a broken nose and two black eyes."

Cory whistled.

I moved on. "Listen, do you think Brennan wants to bring his Mercedes in for repairs? Ray would like Danny to help you complete them, you know, to pay off the deductible."

"Brennan's not worried about the deductible."

"At least he's still speaking to you. I bet he doesn't want to eat Thanksgiving dinner at our house again."

Cory stood and waved his hand at me as if to say forget-about-it. "He had his own wild childhood. The Danny thing didn't faze him as much as you. I'll call him now and see if he has time to drop off the Mercedes."

I picked up the phone as Cory disappeared into the garage. I dialed Leslie Flynn's number. After seven rings, I almost hung up. Then I heard her voice.

"Hi, Leslie. This is Jolene Parker. How are you?"

A few seconds passed then the voice said, "This is her brother. I'll get her for you."

I heard him put down the receiver and walk away. Then I heard footsteps moving toward the phone. "Hey, Jolene, what's up?"

"You and your brother sound just alike."

"We are twins."

"I guess so. Listen, I hate to bother you, but did he ever tell you if he'd talked with my sister?"

"He did! I think she scared him a little. He likes to look at girls, but he's afraid to talk to them. She came right up and hit on him. She ah … came on a little too strong."

Like when she asked him if he was big all over? "Sometimes she scares me, too. Did he know the missing girl, Josie Montalvo?"

"No."

Her answer was a little too fast for my comfort. "How do you know?"

"I read about her disappearance in the newspaper, and I asked him. He saw her on stage, that's all. Like I said, he never talks to girls. He just looks."

I wondered about a guy who just looked, but not as much as I wondered about a sister who knew all about her brother's desires to look. It seemed like an odd thing for a brother and sister to discuss over the breakfast or dinner table. Of course, Erica and I talked about things like that, but we were both girls.

Leslie went on, "I meant to call you. We didn't get to really talk until late last night. We spent most of the day fussing with the milking machines and milking the cows by hand. We didn't eat supper until after eight."

The shots had been fired at me around four in the afternoon. Leslie's brother hadn't known I was interested in him then. He'd been milking cows. He wasn't the shooter. I sighed.

"Something wrong, Jolene?"

"No, not a thing. Hey, what about the guy you were interested in? What did he think of your new look?"

"He didn't come by today."

"I'm sorry."

"Eh, the eggs are available every day. My time will come."

"I'm sure it will."

After we said our goodbyes, Cory appeared in my doorway. "Brennan's going to take me out to lunch later, then we'll stop by his house for the Mercedes and I'll drive it back here. In the meantime, I'm going to keep taking his Mazda apart."

"Why are you taking his new race car apart?"

"He bought it used. I want to go over it thoroughly and make sure it's not only going to run well on the track but that it's safe. I'm going to check every line, wire, and bolt."

"Anything I can do to help?"

He pointed his index finger at me. "I was hoping you'd ask. I could use a donut, a fried cake with chocolate frosting."

Cory and I had a tight relationship with the bakery down the street. A donut for breakfast one day, a cupcake for lunch the next. I could gain back all my weight loss by just thinking about what I'd consumed from them in the past. Still, a donut did sound good. I could walk down to the bakery and back to offset the calories.

"I'll go get some."

Cory gave me two thumbs up. "Thanks."

I walked out to the reception desk. "Danny, I'm going to the bakery for donuts. What's your favorite?"

For the first time today, he smiled. "I like powdered with raspberry jelly."

"Okay. I'll be back in a few minutes. Cory's in the garage if you need anything."

I set off down the sidewalk, walking as briskly as two-inch heel dress boots allowed, enjoying the sun at first. Halfway there, I realized I was in the open air, easy pickings for any sniper who might be watching me. I should have driven.

I walked faster, keeping an eye on all the approaching cars. It would be hard to shoot me from the far lane, wouldn't it? Who would take the chance at this time of day, with all the other cars and people around? Darn it, did we really need donuts anyway?

By the time I reached the bakery, I'd broken out in a sweat, and not from the weather or my exertion. I could feel my heart pushing against my chest.

My eyes must have looked a little wild, because the clerk hurried to get my donuts and rushed me out the door, right back into the full view of anyone who wanted to kill me.

I walked home on the opposite side of the street, so I could watch the oncoming cars again and glance over my shoulder to make sure no one was sneaking up behind me. In the end, I was side-stepping like a crab.

"Ugh." I smacked into someone on the sidewalk, knocking the wind out of me.

"Jolene, what's the matter with you?"

I turned my head to find Celeste Martin glaring at me.

"Sorry, Celeste. I was just … looking over my shoulder."

She inserted the key in the entrance to Talbots. "Afraid someone's going to take a shot at you again?"

"How do you know about that?" Ray had promised it wouldn't be in the news.

"The manager of the P&C goes to my church. It was all he could talk about last night at choir practice." She held the door to her store open as if waiting for me to follow her inside. I didn't want to, but then again, maybe I did.

Celeste turned on all the lights and headed to the back of the store. I tagged along behind her, clutching my bag of donuts. She locked her purse under the counter and turned the key in the cash register. "I wanted to talk to you alone anyway."

"You did? What about?"

Celeste rested her hands on the counter. "There's something funny about your friend Leslie."

"What do you mean?"

She pursed her lips. "Mindy used the restroom at the Coachman when we had lunch there the other day. She noticed the feet in the stall next to her were facing the toilet while the person peed, not away from it like a lady who sits down. Mindy waited by the sinks. Your friend Leslie came out of the stall."

I didn't know what to say.

Celeste's lips compressed into a thin line of distaste. "I swear when she came into the dining room and hugged me, I felt a Willie. A big one."

Celeste had comparisons too numerous to name, including quite possibly my own father. I only had Ray. I clutched my bag of donuts even tighter, speechless.

She shrugged. "So you knew. You've always been open to the alternative lifestyles."

I could not, would not, discuss this any further. I needed a distraction. "Ah … my tan pants I bought the other day got ruined in the grocery store parking lot. Would you have another size four?"

"Let me check." Celeste disappeared into the clothes racks.

I sank down into the armchair by the dressing room. Leslie Flynn, a man? That would explain her size, homely appearance, and deep voice, but what about this guy she wanted to attract? Was she changing teams in every way?

Contrary to Celeste's catty statement, it wasn't that I was open to alternative lifestyles. I was more oblivious and uninterested—and I thought those things were private. I never discussed my feelings about Ray with anyone. It would make me feel disloyal to him. I certainly didn't discuss our sex life with anyone. That would make it less … special. It was supposed to be only between us, wasn't it? Ray was my first and only, but I knew other people approached sex differently, some very differently. In theory, I got the concept. Hell, I even watched HBO. But in practice, in the real world … ultimately, it was none of my business.

Celeste reappeared, holding my replacement tan pants.

I pulled my credit card from my wallet and offered it to her.

She smiled, clearly pleased to be selling me the same pair of pants twice within forty-eight hours. Dollar signs may have flashed on her eyeballs like the readout on a one-armed casino bandit. I thought I heard a ca-ching.

We finished the transaction without further conversation. Maybe she thought we had nothing left to say. It was more likely that she knew she'd shocked me, and she didn't want to break her spell. She did thank me when she handed me the bag. I thanked her, too. Then I ran.

Danny was in the garage with Cory when I returned to the shop. I handed out donuts and napkins and headed for my office to think.

As I walked into the room the phone rang. It was Ray.

"I checked on Leslie Flynn's brother. I don't find any record of him."

"What do you mean? I just talked to them both on the phone."

"The brother doesn't have a current driver's license or a New York State identification card. The only vehicles registered to their address are registered to Leslie."

Strange, especially considering Leslie's plans to leave Wachobe. If her brother didn't drive, how would he get around? Surely running a farm required leaving it on occasion for supplies. Maybe the bookkeeper she wanted to hire would provide his transportation as well.

I had one more question for Ray. "What kind of vehicles does Leslie have?"

"A yellow Mustang convertible and a Ford pick-up truck."

"That makes sense. One for farming, one for fun."

Ray heaved a sigh, sending a crackle over the line.

"One thing doesn't make sense, Darlin'. Leslie's driver's license says she's male."

SIXTEEN

THAT CONFIRMED IT. I filled Ray in on Celeste and Mindy's ob-
servations. "Leslie did say she was seeing Dr. Albert for the last few
months. Maybe she has some kind of gender issue."

Ray sighed. "I'm wondering if she even has a twin. Based on
this picture, she'd make one butt-ugly woman. Maybe she's a split
personality."

I could tell from the tone of his voice that he didn't look forward to confronting that. His training for the sheriff's department
only covered so much. I decided not to mention Leslie's new, improved femininity. My makeover efforts only made it harder for
him to recognize her now from the driver's license photo. "Can
you call Dr. Albert and ask him about her?"

"Dr. Albert won't tell me anything, Darlin'. Not unless Leslie
poses a danger to herself or someone else."

"I've had my doubts about his treatment of Erica. Maybe he
doesn't know Leslie's a danger." Frankly, after spending time with

her, I would be surprised to learn she was, but I didn't want to rule it out.

"Let me see what I can find out about her. I'll take this DMV photo over to The Cat's Meow when they open at noon and see if any of the girls can link Leslie to Josie ... I mean Jessica James. In the meantime, you sit tight."

That was easy for him to say, but oh so hard for me to do. I paced the showroom, circling the Ferrari until I got dizzy. When Cory left for lunch, I took Danny out for pizza. He talked about what he'd worked on with Cory that morning. I pretended to listen, all the while thinking about Leslie. When we got back to the garage, he ran off to see Cory. I went into the garage and peered over Cory and Danny's shoulders as Cory explained the steps involved in taking the dent out of Brennan's Mercedes. They tried to ignore me. I clicked around the Mercedes, running my hand over its lines.

Finally, Cory had enough. "What's wrong, Jo?"

"I'm waiting for Ray to call me."

He glanced at Danny and apparently decided not to ask any more questions.

I rocked back and forth on my heels.

Cory glared at me. The garage was his territory. The showroom was mine. I could tell he wanted me to leave them to work in peace.

The phone rang.

I ran out of the garage, skated through the showroom, and slid to a stop behind my desk in time to catch the call on the third ring. "What'd you find out?"

"Is this Asdale Auto Imports?"

"Yes. I'm sorry. This is Jolene As … Parker, the owner. Can I help you?"

"This is Maury Boor."

My heart skipped a beat. I sank on to my chair. "Emerson Maurice Boor?"

"Just Maury, please."

"Maury, I've been looking all over for you. Is Erica with you?"

"Yes."

"Can I speak to her?"

"She can't talk now."

I shot to my feet. "What do you mean, she can't talk now? Where are you?"

"I can't say. I promised Erica." He sounded defensive.

"I want to talk to my sister, and I want to talk to her now, Maury. Otherwise, I'm going to have you arrested for kidnapping."

"I didn't kidnap Erica. I married her. She's sleeping right now."

My legs buckled. I fell back into my chair. Did he say he married her? She'd never gone as far as to marry anyone before, although she'd spoken of it often enough. Maybe Maury was delusional. Or maybe he was just lying. "Wake her up and put her on, Maury. I need to speak to her. Now!"

"No! She's right, you don't care about her." His voice was filled with disgust.

I saw red. No, I didn't care about her. All the fights I had with Ray to convince him to allow Erica to live with us. All the times I'd dragged her out of some bar or out from underneath some sleazy guy. All the bills I'd paid. All the nights of sleep I'd lost. All those visits to the psych center to hold her hand while she got better. I wanted to reach right through the phone and take all my frustrations out on Maury with one well-placed punch.

But that wasn't possible. Instead, I took a deep breath and tried to reason with him. "I haven't seen my sister in days, Maury. Her apartment is trashed. She left her medicine. I need to know that she's okay."

"She's not."

My throat constricted. I choked out, "How so?"

"She just sits in a chair all day. She won't eat. She won't leave the room. She won't let me touch her." His voice strangled.

A tear burned my eye. I blinked it away, fighting to remain calm. "Maury, you're a nice guy. You were always nice to Erica in high school. I know you care about her. She needs to come home. She needs to see her doctor. She needs her medicine. She needs medicine every day, Maury, or she can't function well. She has to have her medicine. Do you understand?"

"She doesn't want to come home."

"Then you have to make her, Maury. Or call an ambulance. The paramedics will take her to a hospital to be evaluated."

"No! She'd never forgive me."

"She'll forgive you, Maury. She always forgives me. She just doesn't like to admit that she needs help. Please, you can't take care of her alone. She needs medical attention. Just tell me where you are. I'll come and help you. Please, Maury. She's my baby sister." I blinked as tears flooded my eyes.

"I'll talk to her."

The phone beeped incessantly in my ear. He'd hung up.

I checked the incoming number record. It read "private caller."

I rested my forehead in my hands. Tears washed my palms.

Erica was my baby sister. In fact, I thought of her as my baby, period. I'd been responsible for her since she was seven and I was twelve. I was the one she came to when she was in pain, for all the comforting hugs, band-aids, and love she needed. Why had she picked Maury, of all people, to turn to now?

The familiar wave of guilt arrived in a rush. Because I hadn't been there for her. For months, I'd thought only of myself. I'd let her down. Everyone needed someone to count on. I had Ray and Cory and my college roommate Isabelle, who I'd call now except for the fact her family was on a two-week holiday cruise. But Erica only had me, and I hadn't been there for her. So she'd found herself a substitute. Maury.

I grabbed a tissue and dried my eyes. Too bad Maury was a wacko. No doubt he wanted her to love him as much as she needed him to care about her. But would he love her enough to bring her home or at least call the doctor?

The phone rang again. I grabbed it. "Maury?"

Two seconds ticked by before I heard a response. "No, Jolene, it's Ray."

"Oh, Ray." I couldn't get the words out fast enough to explain. He made me slow down and repeat myself.

"He called this line within the last ten minutes?"

"Yes."

"Let me see what I can find out from the phone company. I'll call you right back."

I hung up and watched the clock tick. One minute, two, three, five, eight.

The phone rang again.

"It was a cell phone. There's no quick way to know where he was calling from now."

I pounded on my desk in frustration. "Erica needs her medication, Ray."

"I know, Darlin'. Maury will figure that out soon enough. You know how she is when she's depressed. He'll do the right thing. Give him time."

"What if he doesn't?"

"He will."

"What if he's a killer?"

"Jolene, we have no reason to believe he's responsible for Jessica James' death."

I thought back over the last two weeks. Something bothered me. Something Gumby said the night Danny and I visited his father at the county jail— "What about the flowers?"

"What flowers?"

"Gumby said Jessica James' kitchen table had flowers on it. What if Maury gave her roses, too? That would tie him to the murder."

When Ray spoke, I could hear the irritation in his tone. "They weren't roses. It was live houseplants, an African violet and some other white flower. I know you like to play amateur detective, Jolene, and I'm relieved to see you taking an interest in something other than …"

I filled the silence with the word "Myself."

"Exactly, but do you really think I'd miss a clue like a bouquet of roses? Do you?"

"I'm sorry, Ray." And I was sorry, for more than questioning him. I was sorry for checking out the last few months, for ignoring my sister, my business, and my few but valuable friends—Cory,

Isabelle, and of course, Ray, who did double duty as my best friend and husband. "I just can't believe Erica actually married Maury."

"Let's wait until we hear confirmation about that from her. It doesn't sound like the marriage got consummated, even if she did say 'I do.'"

I didn't appreciate the mental image his words brought to mind. I did, however, like the possibility of an out for Erica.

For the moment, I hung my hopes on that technicality and remembered what Ray had originally set off to investigate. "Did you find out anything at The Cat's Meow about Leslie?"

"Just confirmation of what we already knew. Her brother comes there often, and she was there last week, for the first time, to cover his bounced check."

"Has her brother ever ... touched any of the girls?"

"Apparently not. He sits in the back row, buys the expected number of drinks per hour, and tips well. Erica was the first person who ever paid much attention to him, from what the girls said. They think he's shy."

"Oh." A quiet one, automatically a suspect.

But this time, oddly enough, Ray didn't seem to think so. "I'm more interested in your friend, Leslie. I'm going to talk to her."

"About what?"

"About the fact that her driver's license says she's a male, not a female."

"That's not a crime, is it?"

"No, Jolene, it's not a crime."

"If you pull in her driveway, you're going to scare her to death."

"Only if she's guilty of something."

"Ray, everyone slows down when they see a sheriff's car behind them on the highway, even when they're not speeding. Everyone stops to look when a sheriff's car drives down their street. A sheriff's car in her driveway will scare her. She'll think you're coming with bad news or something."

"So what's your suggestion?"

"Come pick me up, and we'll ride out there together in the Lexus. I'll introduce you to her." Leslie was my new friend. I couldn't sic Ray on her without feeling guilty. This way, I could help frame the questions and draw some conclusions about her for myself. Because Ray was right about me as usual, I did like playing amateur detective. Cory and Danny would never miss me.

Ray's tone turned sarcastic. "And what reason will we give for stopping by?"

I thought for a moment. "Fresh brown eggs."

SEVENTEEN

THE COUNTRY ROADS LEADING to the Flynn farm curved and tilted and rolled up and down and all around. Ray swooped through every turn and rocketed over every hill, clearly enjoying the opportunity to drive my Lexus. At times we were airborne, and Ray would let out a little whoop like he was enjoying the thrill ride. I, on the other hand, felt carsick.

We passed a Mennonite farmhouse. I knew this because of the lack of electrical wiring to the house, the black buggy parked in front of the barn, and the long line of ankle-length, flowered-print dresses, blue jeans, and dress shirts on their laundry line. A quarter mile farther down the road, I spotted the farmer running his tractor in the field. He waved from the cab of his tractor when I looked at him. He wore a black hat even inside the cab. I wondered, as I often had, why tractors were acceptable to them while a car was not.

I asked Ray.

"They lead a simple life. I think cars are considered distracting, showy, and unnecessary."

I'd never make it in their world. Neither would Ray.

Leslie's family farm overlooked the lake with a magnificent view of both the water and the hills surrounding it. Their white Victorian home with black shutters and covered porches on the front and side had very little adornment other than electrical wires, but perhaps that was due to the time of year. It also had no landscaping. The grass grew to the home's edges and a couple feet up the sides, brown with the onset of winter. Their driveway was gravel and mud. The red barn to the right of the house listed to one side. The steel barn behind it held most of the cows, while farm equipment rusted in between the steel structure and another low, ramshackle building covered with tar paper. Brown pastures fenced with barbed wire reached far back into the property.

Horse droppings lined the road abutting the Flynn's front yard. Perhaps a gift from their neighbor and one of the negatives associated with the Mennonites' simple horse and buggy life.

As Ray pulled into the drive, I pointed with glee to the sign at the end of the drive offering fresh brown eggs for two dollars a dozen.

He rolled his eyes and parked behind the black Ford 4x4 in the driveway. The bed of the truck was filled with buckets, bags, tools including a hoe and an axe, and clumps of hay. A hunting rifle hung in the rear window. Clearly, this was Leslie's work vehicle, unlike the shiny yellow Mustang, which was nowhere in sight.

We climbed out of the Lexus and stood, waiting for someone to greet us.

A thin gray dog the size of a miniature horse appeared from the barn and trotted closer, sniffing our pant legs. Ray reached down to give him a pat on the head. The dog bounded away, snarling then barking an alarm.

"Quiet you!" A screen door slammed behind us. Leslie walked toward us, wearing her Carhartts and work boots, minus the new wig and makeup. She flashed her newly veneered smile.

"Hey, Jolene. Never mind Rufus. He's just a grump." She sized Ray up, her gaze lingering on his gun holster. "Who's your friend?"

"This is my husband, Ray Parker."

Ray held out his hand. Leslie wiped hers on her pant leg before shaking with him.

I flashed my best saleswoman smile at her. "I told Ray you had fresh brown eggs. We thought we might buy a dozen."

Leslie glanced from my face to Ray's and back again, seeming puzzled. "Never had one before?"

"I don't think so. We buy the white ones at the grocery store."

Something I thought might be doubt twinkled in the back of Leslie's eyes, but she took a few steps in the direction of the barn. "If you two want to wait here, I'll get you a carton."

"Okay, thanks."

Ray turned to study the house, the fields, and the barn that Leslie had disappeared into. "This is a big farm. They must have help."

"I think she said they did, but ask her."

He leaned against the Lexus. "I will."

I took a deep breath. "Something smells."

Ray grinned. "Everyone thinks cow manure smells, but they haven't smelled chicken shit. And chicken coops run a close second to hog farming."

"You should know." I chucked him in the arm.

"Nice, Darlin', really nice. I'm glad you've got your sense of humor back."

I hadn't realized I'd lost it.

I shuffled my feet in the gravel and wondered how long Leslie would take to retrieve the eggs. "I thought Leslie would have on her new wig and makeup. She was so excited about it yesterday. She looks like her old self today, except for her teeth."

Ray shrugged. "She's back on the farm. If you hadn't called her Leslie, I would have thought she was a man."

"She has breasts. I could tell when she hugged me the other day. She doesn't have any facial hair."

"Her license says different." Ray continued to lean against the Lexus, his eyes glued to an enormous brown brick of manure mixed with hay drying on the far side of the barn.

"Why are you looking at that?"

He eased off the Lexus. "I was just thinking that's one place I'd never want to dig for a body."

Ew.

He went on, "Although, with the lack of oxygen in that pile, the body would probably be perfectly preserved."

Double ew. Was he trying to tell me something? "You don't have any reason to search the premises, do you?"

"No, I don't." But he continued to survey the area as though trying to think of one. "Tell her you'd like to meet her brother."

"Okay."

Leslie reappeared in the barn door, carrying a gray egg carton. She crunched down the gravel drive and held it out to me. "Here you go. They were laid this morning. Can't get much fresher than that."

"That's great, Leslie. Thank you." I fumbled in my purse, pulled out my wallet, and offered her the two dollars.

She waved me off. "After all you've done for me, they're on the house."

Ray and I thanked her again. Then Ray raised one eyebrow at me expectantly. He would let me take the lead, but only if I produced some results.

I swallowed and plowed ahead. "Leslie, I'd love to meet your brother. Is he around?"

She rubbed her chin. "He's milking right now."

Ray's eyes never left my face. I knew he was waiting for me to think fast. I did my best. "Could we go in and meet him? I've never seen the inside of a cow barn before."

Leslie picked up her boot and showed us the bottom, which was covered in mud, manure, and hay. "It's too hot and smelly in there, and you'd ruin your boots and the shine on Ray's shoes. Besides, we're a little behind. Our help quit."

I kept my gaze glued to Leslie's face. "Why?"

Leslie grinned. "I'm in the middle of a sex change, Jolene. I think that's a first for Wachobe. I scare the hell out of my neighbors. Even my brother's struggling to be supportive."

I wasn't sure whether to laugh or cry. When I glanced at Ray, he had his "good-cop, bad-cop, whatever-you-need-me-to-be-cop" expression firmly in place.

Since Leslie had opened the door, I decided to keep asking questions. "Is that why you meet with Dr. Albert?"

She nodded. "My last visit is this week. A psychiatrist has to sign off before the final operation. Mine is scheduled for next month. I'm so excited. I've been a woman my whole life, but now I'm finally going to look like one."

I couldn't think of an appropriate response.

Ray's eyes narrowed, but he held out his hand to Leslie once more. "Nice to meet you, Leslie. Thanks again for the eggs and good luck with your operation. You'll have to keep Jolene informed." He headed for our car.

Surprised, I waved the egg carton at Leslie. "Has your love interest been by for any more eggs?"

A sad expression settled over her homely features as she shook her head. "I may have to buy the Caterham after all."

I tried to think of a delicate way to phrase the question in the back of my mind. "Does he know about your … upcoming surgery?"

Her expression changed to amused. "He can't tell me and my brother apart. He thinks we're the same person. I planned on introducing myself wearing my wig and makeup this week."

"Well, like you said, we can always get you a Caterham." Although I still doubted it would make a difference. I thanked her for the eggs again and joined Ray in the car.

Leslie watched as we backed down the drive then waved as we pulled away.

I twisted in my seat to face Ray. "What do you make of her sex change?"

Ray kept his eyes on the road. "It's definitely a first."

"We didn't get to meet her brother. I didn't want to be too obvious and insist."

"That's okay, Darlin'."

I could tell from his tone of voice that it really wasn't. "How will we find out if he even exists? She said the guy she's interested in thinks they're one and the same person. What if they are?"

Ray braked suddenly, swung the car around in a U-turn and stopped roadside, parallel to the Mennonite farmer who was still in the fields. "We'll ask her neighbor. Sit tight."

He climbed out of the Lexus and headed across the field toward the oncoming tractor. The farmer slowed the tractor as he neared Ray and cut the engine.

Ray pointed in the direction of the Flynn's farm. The farmer nodded.

I saw Ray's lips moving then the farmer's. After a minute or two of conversation, Ray waved to the farmer and walked back to the car.

The Lexus sank on the left side when he got in and slammed his door. "Theory one shot to shit."

"What?"

"Leslie and her brother are *not* the same person. This guy says they're identical twins, and he's definitely seen them both at the same time as recently as yesterday."

"Identical twins means one egg?" How odd that one half of the same egg would turn out so differently.

Ray twisted the ignition key. "One egg, same sex twins. That's what I remember from biology class." He gunned the engine and took off like we were in the Indy 500.

My right leg instinctively tried to brake. Too bad the brake was on his side of the car.

He accelerated through a curve.

I gripped my door handle. I'd had enough G-forces for today. "Ray!"

"Sorry." He slowed down to fifty.

I tried not to notice the road signs recommending thirty-five miles an hour for the curves. I could take the speed. It was the curves that killed me.

Ray drummed his fingers on the steering wheel. "I'm moving Leslie and her brother up on my suspect list."

"Why? Leslie was very open with us. She's having a sex change operation, which is definitely not a crime. Her brother exists. And none of the girls at The Cat's Meow could tie either of them to Jessica James, right?"

"True, but according to the neighbor, Leslie's brother's name is Peter."

"Peter?" My heart dropped.

"That's what the guy said."

"Another P name, like on the key chain."

Ray nodded, a grim expression on his face. "Exactly, but there's more to it than that." He gestured to the fields outside my windows. "Do you know what's just over there?"

"The Flynn farm?"

Ray gave me the look, the incredulous, you-are-so-naïve look. "Yes, Darlin', but think about this farm in relation to the rest of the countryside. Think about the other side of this hill, at the bottom of the road, maybe a mile or so from here. What do you see?"

I gazed out the window. All I saw was fields, maybe a few corn-stalks on the horizon. If he turned me around twice, I'd be clue-less. "I have no idea. Tell me."

"The Cat's Meow."

EIGHTEEN

WHILE I WAITED FOR Cory and Danny to finish up in the garage, Ray headed back to the sheriff's office to discuss our findings with the sheriff and the deputy in charge of investigating Jessica James' disappearance. I could tell Ray wished he was in charge. He'd caught the scent and clearly wanted to be the one to follow the trail.

I, on the other hand, still smelled manure. The smell had attached itself to my cardboard carton of eggs, the eggs my new friend Leslie had given me. I think I had some actual manure squished in my tire treads, too. We'd probably picked some up left behind by a horse and buggy on one of the curves Ray flew through.

But just because something smells, it doesn't mean it's bad, I thought as I locked up the shop an hour later. And just because someone's different doesn't mean they're dangerous. Leslie's gender change was unusual, but it didn't necessarily indicate she had any other issues—surely not those of a killer. She simply wasn't happy with herself and had found a way to solve the problem. I couldn't see any more in her actions than that. Leslie had no reason to kill Jessica James.

And her brother had even less reason, as far as I could tell. But it bothered me that his name was Peter. Why couldn't the first letter of his name have been anything other than a P? There were twenty-five other choices, for Pete's sake.

Ha! For Pete's sake. I smiled as I slid into the Lexus where Danny waited with his backpack full of partially completed homework.

"What's so funny?"

I met his gaze in the rearview mirror. "Nothing. How far did you and Cory get on the bodywork repair?"

"Cory said we'll sand it tomorrow."

I pulled out onto Main Street and headed toward home. "Have you ever done bodywork before?"

"No."

"What'd ya think?"

"I like it. Cory said I could work on the race car with him, too, if you said it was okay."

I slowed for a turn, flipped on my signal, and watched for an opportunity, checking the rearview mirror for any suspicious cars behind me, particularly any with guns pointed out the window in my direction.

"Is it?"

I swung onto North Street. "Is it what?"

"Okay?"

"Sure, of course." I looked in the rearview in time to catch the broad smile that crossed his face. "So you guys got along okay today, huh?"

"Yeah."

"Cory's pretty nice, right?"

"He's cool."

I let it go, pleased and relieved Cory had won him over. But then, what's not to like about Cory? He was like an adorable puppy. You just had to love him.

As I made the turn onto our street, a multitude of colored and clear Christmas lights sparkled from rooflines, fences, bushes, and trees. Several windows featured lit trees as well as doors and fences with wreaths and bows. Overnight, our street had become a winter wonderland, even though the temperature said Indian summer.

I checked the rearview mirror again. My car was the only one in sight. The gunman wouldn't have much opportunity to hide from my neighbors anyway. Not a day went by that I didn't see at least one face in a window, watching Ray and me come and go. Of course, most of our neighbors were elderly. What else did they have to do? Still, I kinda welcomed the unofficial neighborhood watch program. In all likelihood, it was in place all over town now, more in the spirit of stamping out crime than saving me.

I soaked in the neighborhood decorations and felt better for it. Christmas was still my favorite time of the year, even though my mother had killed herself on Christmas Eve. I couldn't believe the season had arrived already—the wreaths with red velvet bows, the evergreen scent, the sparkling white lights, and the atmosphere of goodwill towards man. Thanksgiving had been late this year, and tomorrow was December third already. The annual Wachobe

Dickens festival had kicked off this past weekend with carolers dressed in period costumes greeting people on the streets. Now our neighborhood was getting into the spirit as well.

This would have been our second Christmas with Noelle, but the first where we could have put presents under the tree and a stocking by the fire for her. A few days from now would be her first birthday. I'd so looked forward to celebrating both events. I even had a gold bracelet engraved with her name put away in the closet for her. I'd purchased it this past summer at an art show before she'd been taken from us. I supposed I could send it to her birth-mother with a note.

But my heart broke at the thought of Noelle opening her special gift with someone other than me.

"Jolene?"

I shook my head and focused on the road, happy not to have hit anyone or anything while lost in my thoughts. "Yes, Danny?"

"Are you and Ray Jewish?"

A deep belly laugh welled and burst from my lips, erasing all my sorrows in an instant.

"No, Danny. Why do you ask?"

"You don't have any Christmas decorations. Our house is the only one on the street that doesn't."

He was an observant little man. I kinda liked the fact he'd referred to "our" house as though he belonged there, too. "The decorations are in the attic. Maybe after dinner, we can put some of them out."

"Can we get a tree?"

Sadness fell over me again like a net. Erica and I carried on the family tradition of decorating the tree two weeks before Christmas. That only gave me a few days to find her and get her straightened out. This might be one of those years where I had to decorate the tree without her, one of the years where she sat it out in the psych center instead. But I'd wait and hold out hope a little longer for her return.

I turned into our driveway, cut the ignition, and swiveled in my seat to face Danny.

"We always put the tree up fourteen days before Christmas. That way it doesn't get too dried out and the needles don't fall off before Christmas Day. You can cut one down for us this year if you want."

"Okay." He rubbed his hands together, his eyes bright. Then the light in them faded. "What about my dad?"

Poor Danny had his own heartbreaks and sorrows. We were two of a kind. I treaded lightly. "I'm not sure. He refuses to talk to the sheriff's department. If he won't tell them what happened, he can't clear his name. He'll probably have to stay in jail until he goes to trial."

Danny's chin got a stubborn set to it. "He doesn't know what happened."

"He must know if he stole the Cadillac Escalade and the Toyota Camry."

Danny averted his eyes. "He doesn't know what happened to Aunt Jessica."

I made my voice as gentle as possible, trying to mask my excitement with my sympathy. "Your dad told you about her?"

He nodded and swallowed.

"What did he say?"

"He said my mom died of pneumonia and my aunt took care of us for a while. Then they had a fight and we moved out. We didn't see her after that."

"Why did he go see her at The Cat's Meow?"

Danny's chin sunk into his chest. "I don't know. He wouldn't tell me." He raised his face to give me a fierce look. "But he said he didn't kill her. My dad would never hurt anybody. He doesn't know who did."

"Okay." I patted him on the knee. "I believe you and him. But did he drive the Toyota Camry we found her arm in?"

Danny averted his gaze once again. "I don't know if I can tell you."

That answer was as good as a yes, a yes that might send his dad away for a good many years to come.

I sighed. "I can't help you or your dad if I don't know what's going on. Neither can Ray. And we do want to help your dad, Danny. We know you love him. We know he loves you. We want you to be together."

Danny sniffled. "I miss my dad."

"Do you want to go visit him tonight?"

For an instant, Danny's eyes lit up then they dimmed. "No!"

I thought I'd misheard. "No? Why not?"

"I don't want him to know I got suspended. He'll be mad." Danny burst into tears. "I want my dad. I want my dad." He clapped his palms over his face and bent over his knees.

"Oh, Danny." I clambered over the console onto the seat next to him, gathering his quivering body into my arms. I cried right along with him, thinking about his problems and mine.

After five minutes, his tears stopped. He settled his face in my shoulder. I thought he might be falling asleep, worn out from all his emotions. I knew I felt drained.

The windows had fogged over with the evening chill. I leaned back against the seat and stared at the ceiling, savoring his closeness. I closed my eyes. It was nice to have someone to cuddle, but maybe Danny could use a chat with Dr. Albert. Maybe we all could.

The car door opened.

Danny and I jerked our heads up to look.

Ray's head appeared in the opening. "What are you guys doing in there?"

———

After dinner, Danny parked himself in front of the television to watch SpongeBob once again. I wanted to ask him to lower the volume, because if I heard the little creature's annoying laugh one more time, I might put an umbrella through the television, too. But I didn't. Instead, Ray and I went into the bedroom and closed the door to whisper with one another again. The bungalow was too small to keep our conversation from Danny any other way.

We lay down on the bed, my head resting on Ray's shoulder, my arm on his chest, his muscular arm holding me tight against his side. "What did the sheriff say?"

"He said he'd have one of the guys assigned to the investigation look into it. They're looking at over forty different guys who were regulars at The Cat's Meow and tracking credit card receipts to identify anyone who was in the club during the time Jessica James worked there. But a lot of men pay cash in clubs like that to keep it from their wives."

"Did you ever go to clubs like that?"

"In high school, the football team went once or twice."

I raised my head to look at his face. "You were underage."

Ray snorted. "Why do you think I can pick out a fake ID so fast?"

I snuggled in again. "Any other time?"

"A couple of stag parties. That's all."

"What did you think?"

"They're naked women, Darlin'. I enjoyed the view, just like any other guy."

"Did you touch?" Worse, did he sleep with them?

"No. You know I like to be the first man in." He rolled to cover my body with his and lowered his face to kiss me.

The phone rang.

Ray dropped the F bomb. His full weight—more than twice mine—slumped onto me.

"Get off, get ... awph," I gasped.

With a sigh of resignation, he rose and crawled across the bed to pick up the phone.

I watched the annoyance on his face morph to interest. He swung his legs onto the floor and glanced at me. He raised his eyebrow.

A few more seconds passed as he listened.

I heard SpongeBob's laugh through the walls. Where was my umbrella anyway? We could upgrade to a flat screen.

Ray hung up. He ran his hand over his hair and rubbed the back of his neck.

"What?" I sat up and shoved his shoulder. "What?"

"They found Jessica James' body."

"Where?"

"A few miles from the apartment where she was killed, just outside the radius the sheriff's office searched. She was buried about four feet under, in a plastic garbage bag, naked and in pieces. A hunter stumbled over her. The animals had been after her."

I wasn't even going to ask what he meant by "in pieces." My stomach was already churning. "Just like you said."

He tipped his head. "I knew they wouldn't find her in the middle of the road."

"How did she die?"

"Preliminary findings point to strangulation, but the medical examiner won't issue his report until tomorrow."

"So that's all?"

"There's more." Ray glanced toward the bedroom door.

I leaned closer and breathed, "What?"

"They found a car remote lying in the leaves about five yards from the body. The deputy from the other county just left our evidence garage. It matches the Toyota Camry Danny stole from the psych center lot. It has a partial print on it."

"And?"

Ray grimaced as if it pained him. "Danny's father may be charged with murder."

NINETEEN

My heart filled with dread. "What are we going to tell Danny?"

"Nothing yet."

"What if it's in the paper tomorrow?"

Ray scratched his eyebrow and peered at me through his fingers. "We don't get the paper. Do you get it at the shop?"

"Sometimes Cory brings it in."

"Call him and tell him to leave it home tomorrow. Danny doesn't have to go back to school until Monday. By then, we'll know what to tell him."

"His classmates already know his father's in jail."

"I'm not surprised. How do you know?"

"I saw Bernie at The Lincoln House. His son Jacob is in Danny's class. He said another kid told Jacob on the bus."

Ray stretched out on the bed again. "It's one thing to be in jail for car theft, but it's a whole different game when your father's in jail for murder, especially of a female relative."

"That kid was already teasing Danny about you. I can't imagine what they'll say about his real dad."

"We'll just have to tell him to hold his head up high and ignore them."

I stretched out next to him, my body rigid with tension. "Oh, Ray, you said yourself he's impulsive. He cried in the car today. I don't know if he can take any more pressure."

"What's your suggestion?"

"I thought about making an appointment for him with Dr. Albert. He could tell Dr. Albert the whole truth. Dr. Albert wouldn't tell us, but maybe he could give Danny some direction or at least some support."

Ray thought about it for a minute. "That's a good idea, Darlin'. Dr. Albert works miracles on your sister. Let's hope he can help Danny, too."

I lay silent next to Ray, thinking about the doubts I'd had about Dr. Albert's treatment of Erica. She was avoiding Dr. Albert now, but prior to her disappearance, she'd gone the longest time ever content and employed. Not to mention she always seemed upbeat when she came out of his office. It wasn't him causing the problems. It was her.

In the morning, I'd give him a call about Danny.

Ray broke into my thoughts. "The sheriff doesn't want me involved in the investigation. Period. Exclamation point. That's why he called. He said if we had any further suspicions about Leslie Flynn or her brother, we need to talk to him directly. We're not to pay any more calls on them."

I stiffened. "I don't work for the sheriff, Ray."

"I know."

"I don't like being told what to do, especially by him." The sheriff didn't leave his office very often, unless an on-camera opportunity arose. I'd lost respect for him years ago. But Ray didn't share my feeling, so I kept it to myself.

"I'm just telling you what he said. I'm the only one sworn to obey."

I lifted my head and gazed into Ray's amused eyes. "Are you trying to tell me something?"

"No."

But the twinkle in his eye said otherwise.

———

The next morning I phoned Dr. Albert. His receptionist said he didn't have any openings this week and gave me the runaround. I insisted on speaking to him directly. She grudgingly took a message.

He called back within an hour. "Were you calling about your sister? I'm willing to make another appointment for her this week, but it would be better if you escort her. She didn't show up this Wednesday."

"She's missing." I rattled off the whole sordid tale, including all I knew about Maury Boor. "He's not a patient of yours, is he?"

"I couldn't tell you if he was."

I got the feeling from his tone that Maury wasn't a patient. "What do you think of his behavior, the roses and the stalking?"

"I'd say he's desperate for attention."

"Does that make him dangerous?"

"Not necessarily."

"Ray and I have showed his picture around town. We don't know where else to look."

Dr. Albert changed topics. "I guess I misunderstood. Did you want an appointment for yourself?"

I explained about Danny and his father. Dr. Albert listened without interruption. He had a question when I finished.

"Did you talk with Social Services about making an appointment for him with me?"

"No."

"You'll need to call them first for authorization."

"Really?"

"I'm afraid so."

No way would I do that. A conversation with Social Services might get him labeled as a troubled child—if he wasn't already—or, worse, removed from our home. Ray and I were still a safe haven for him. Besides, I kinda liked having him around. From all indications, Danny liked it here, too.

I hung up disappointed and frustrated. I only wanted to help Danny. Why did bureaucracy always mess things up?

Danny sat at the table, working on his assignments when I walked into the kitchen. I wondered if Ray had gotten him going this morning or if he'd taken the initiative himself. Either way, I was pleased.

"Did you eat breakfast?"

He didn't look up. "Ray made eggs. Brown eggs."

"How were they?"

"Okay."

I poured a glass of juice and peeled the lid off a container of yogurt. I ate leaning against the sink. "How's the homework coming along?"

"I'm almost done. I have to study for a geography test." Danny glanced at the clock. "What time are we leaving for the shop?"

"In fifteen minutes."

He nodded. His pencil moved more quickly over the page. Impressed, I left him alone to finish.

On the drive to work, Danny talked nonstop. Most of his sentences started with the words "You know what, Jolene?" and ended with something Cory had told him about cars. I even learned a few things. But once we reached the shop, I was delighted to hand him off to Cory. The constant conversation, after all my months of solitude, was a little more than I could take. He'd talked our ears off last night, too, while we unpacked the outdoor Christmas decorations and hung them up.

I went in my office and closed the door, breathing a sigh of relief.

The phone ruined my peaceful retreat.

"Jolene? This is Maury Boor. Is this a bad time?"

A bad time? Was he nuts? "Maury, where's Erica?"

"She's here. She's really ... not well."

Where had I heard that before? "What's she doing?"

He lowered his voice to a whisper, "She's curled up on the floor in the corner, sucking on her hair."

"Call an ambulance, Maury. I'll meet you at the hospital."

"I can't."

"What do you mean, you can't? If you love Erica, you have to do what's right for her. You can't help her. She needs medical attention."

"She said she'd never speak to me again if I had her locked up."

"Maury, she always says that. No one really *wants* to spend time in the psych center, but she needs to."

"I can't do it. Can you come?"

"Where are you?"

He gave me an address an hour outside of Wachobe, an apartment complex. He said they were in apartment 4B.

I hung up.

Should I call an ambulance to meet me there? They'd undoubtedly arrive and take her before I could make it. I might not get to see Erica for days if I did it that way, and I needed to see her, if only to verify with my own eyes that she would be all right. I decided no ambulance.

Should I call Ray? He'd want to question Maury, which might further aggravate Erica and the whole situation. The apartment complex wasn't in our county, so he'd have to get off duty. I didn't want him to get in any more trouble. I'd gotten him in enough hot water in the last year. I decided no Ray.

I did tell Cory exactly where I was going and if I didn't call him within two hours, for him to call Ray. Two hours would give me more than enough time to drive there, assess the situation, and get whatever help Erica needed. Of course, if Maury was a serial killer luring me to my death, he'd have time enough to accomplish that, too. But this was geeky Maury Boor. I'd take the chance.

I hugged Danny goodbye. He didn't seem to mind the hug, although he didn't reciprocate.

I roared out of the parking lot. With a little extra pressure on the Lexus' gas pedal, I made it to the apartment complex in forty-five minutes.

It sat fifty feet off a county road, the only building in sight. The rectangular, stucco four-story building had only one car in its parking lot—a white Honda Prelude. I parked next to it and observed the sheets and beach towels that substituted for curtains in all the apartment windows. Erica had really moved on up this time.

The apartment building had an exterior staircase that ran up the center of the building. Signs indicated the B apartments were on the right, A to the left. I went right.

By the top of the second flight of stairs, I realized I was out of shape. By the third, I huffed and puffed. By the time I reached Maury and Erica's door, I had to lean on the railing and rest. If Maury attacked me, I'd have no air left to put up a fight.

After a minute of deep breathing, I approached the apartment and knocked.

The door flew open as if Maury'd been standing just on the other side.

I got a glimpse of his baby-cheeked face before he reached for me. I tried to move back, but he was too quick. He pulled me into a hug. "Thank God you're here."

I suffered his embrace for all of a second. "Let go of me, Maury. I want to see Erica."

He stepped out onto the landing, closing the door behind him. "I didn't tell her I called you."

"It doesn't matter." I tried to push past him, but he had grown since high school. He outweighed me by at least seventy pounds.

"Can you pretend you found us on your own?"

"What?"

He licked his lips. "Please? I don't want her to hate me."

"She won't hate you. Now get out of my way."

Maury blocked me again. "She hates you."

That stopped me cold. I blinked back tears. "She didn't say that."

"She said she doesn't love you anymore because all you do is lock her up in the hospital."

For all of a second, his words bothered me. Then reality kicked in. "Maury, the opposite of love is not hate. The opposite of love is indifference. Now get the hell out of my way."

He opened the door all the way and stood aside.

I rushed in. The living room was empty, the kitchen littered with takeout boxes and paper plates. It smelled like dirty feet and, oddly enough, lemons. I headed for the door off the living room. I pushed it open.

Sheets and blankets were clumped in the center of the bed and clothes were strewn all over the floor, some of them Erica's. I whisked the covers off the bed. No Erica.

I checked the corners of the room. No Erica.

I peeked in the bath, which smelled of wet towels and lavender. She was here someplace.

I bent to check under the bed. I heard a whimper.

I stood and tipped my head to see behind the bedroom door.

Erica.

She wore tattered jeans and a pink sweater, her feet bare, her tangled blonde hair covering her eyes.

I crept closer, pushed the door aside, and knelt in front of her. "Erica? Sweetie?"

She pulled her feet closer to her body.

I reached out and smoothed the hair from her face.

Her eyes were puffy and red with mascara circles the size of mini donuts. She held a hank of hair in her fingers as she sucked on it.

"Oh, Erica."

She didn't acknowledge me.

I pulled out my cell phone and called Dr. Albert's emergency number. He said to bring her in as soon as possible.

I sat cross-legged in front of her and took her free hand in mine. It was like ice. I rubbed it gently. "Everything will be fine. Don't worry. We'll take care of you."

She let out a sigh and murmured something.

"What? I didn't hear you."

Her gaze met mine. She pulled the hair from her mouth.

"Mom said you would come."

TWENTY

I RODE IN THE backseat with Erica. Maury drove his Honda Prelude. Dr. Albert met us at the door of the psych center. He touched Erica's shoulder, then mine, joining us in a pseudo triangle. "I'll take her from here. Everything's going to be fine. She'll call you in a few days."

Where had I heard that before?

The last five times I'd checked her in.

I kissed Erica and ran my hand down her cheek before the attendants rolled her away. She sucked harder on her hair.

Maury started to chase after her. The guard blocked him. "I'm sorry, sir. You can't go with her."

He looked at me, bewildered and forlorn. "I'm her husband."

I slid my arm through his and tugged him in the direction of the cafeteria. "Let's talk about that."

While Maury purchased coffee for himself and a Snapple iced tea for me, I dialed Cory to let him know everything had gone according to plan. Then I dialed Ray and filled him in. He was more concerned about Maury than Erica.

"How's he behaving?"

"He's lost, Ray. He's the same geek he was in high school, just taller and better looking."

"Where were they?"

I described the apartment to him. From my brief glimpse, the furniture had been old, the carpets threadbare, and the house-keeping less than desirable, but I wouldn't say dirty, just used. "He still claims they're married."

"Ask to see the marriage certificate. We can verify with the officiant and witnesses."

I rushed Ray off the phone because Maury appeared with our drinks in hand. He set mine in front of me, put his down, and reached for mine again. He took off the shrink wrap and popped the cap before returning it to me.

He smiled as he sat. "I don't want you to chip a nail."

I was torn between "Aw, shucks, how considerate" and "Do I really look like I'd care?" I settled for a simple "Thanks."

He sipped his coffee and glanced around the room, which had only a few other occupants seated on plastic chairs. "Is this where Erica will eat?"

"She'll eat in her room."

"Is the food any good?"

"It's pre-chewed. You know, mashed potatoes, Jell-O, pudding. I'm not sure why. The patients have mental problems, not gastro-intestinal."

"She hates it here."

I took a long swig of my iced tea while I tried to formulate a response he might understand. He hadn't spent the last fifteen years coping with Erica's issues. I had.

"Sometimes she's been known to think of it as a resort and spa. When her life doesn't go the way she wants, she'll do … something to get herself admitted."

His eyes told me he was wounded. "She was happy with me."

I couldn't argue. I didn't know for sure. "She has to take her medicine every day, Maury, or she starts to act differently. Sometimes she's wild and takes too many risks, and sometimes she's like this. Without the medication, she's unpredictable." I decided not to mention "suicidal." I still wasn't sure of the reason behind all of her suicide attempts. Some had been pretty lame for a girl of her ingenuity. Of course, Dr. Albert didn't agree with me on this, and he was the expert. I only knew Erica needed professional help.

"Is it because of your mom?" He stared at his coffee cup, twisting it between his hands. "Because she killed herself? Is that why Erica acts this way?"

Life should be so simple. "Erica has been diagnosed as bipolar. That's why she takes the medicine. I'm sure our mother's death created issues for her, too. She didn't always get along with our father, and she had difficulties with school. I can't really categorize all her behavior for you. I'm not even sure Dr. Albert can, but maybe you can talk with him later and see what he says. She's … unpredictable, like I said. But loveable."

His eyes met mine. "I love her. I've always loved her, even in high school."

"I remember all the times you asked her out."

He blushed and cast his eyes on his coffee cup again. "Erica didn't want to go out with me then. She said I was too short, but I think it was because I was a geek." He looked up at me through his eyelashes as if waiting for me to respond.

I didn't know what to say.

He pulled himself taller in the chair and squared his shoulders. "But I grew. I wear contacts now. I look good."

I had to smile. "You do look good, Maury." His dark hair had a fashionable cut, tight on the sides, spiky on the top. His skin was clear, which it didn't used to be. But then, in high school, whose skin was? No longer hidden by thick glasses, his brown eyes didn't look as fearful as they used to. Of course, the football team wasn't here. He might still jump in a locker to avoid them if they appeared. "Do you have a job?"

He slumped again. "Not at the moment."

"Are you really married to my sister?"

"Yes! We went to Niagara Falls. It was very romantic. I have pictures."

I didn't like the sound of Niagara Falls. That's where my parents went on their honeymoon. It would be just like Erica to follow in Mom's footsteps. "Do you have a marriage certificate?"

"At the apartment. Why? Do you want to see it?"

"Yes, Maury, I do."

———

About a mile away from the psych center, the sparse homes in the surrounding area disappeared in the side view mirror, and I realized I was alone in a car with a man I'd thought had the potential to be a serial killer. Alone, and headed in the direction of an even more isolated place, his apartment. Worse, I hadn't told Cory or Ray that it would be necessary for Maury to drive me back to my car. It would take them awhile to figure out where to look if I didn't come home today.

I glanced at the side view again. No other cars in sight. At least I didn't have to worry about getting shot at, unless Maury had a gun. I had considered him a possibility for my assailant at the grocery store parking lot, and here I was letting him drive me around. I'd like to think I was brave, but I knew I was more like stupid.

I glanced at him.

His eyes were on the road, his posture rigidly upright, hands gripping the wheel firmly in the ten and two o'clock position.

Geek.

The hills and trees flew by the window. I had no idea where we were. I knew how to get to the psych center from Wachobe and how to get to Maury's apartment from there, too. But I had no idea how to get from the psych center to Maury's. He could be driving in the opposite direction. I wouldn't know. One stretch of farmland looked pretty much like the next.

Ray's words came back to haunt me. *You have to watch out for the quiet ones.*

My heartbeat accelerated. I felt my armpits dampen, then a trickle of sweat ran between my breasts. A few more minutes and I'd be short of breath with a full-blown anxiety attack. I recognized the symptoms. I'd had a few over the past few months. And here I was ready to hyperventilate without a paper bag.

Maury made a right turn and his apartment building came into sight.

I took a deep cleansing breath like Dr. Albert had suggested. My heartbeat slowed.

Maury parked next to my Lexus. Why, in an otherwise empty lot, do we always park next to the one car in it? Are we so afraid to stand out from the crowd?

Maury got out of the car and took off at a fast pace for the stairs. He didn't even check to see if I was behind him.

Hard to believe he planned to attack me when he didn't even care if I came inside. I huffed and puffed my way up the four flights of stairs again, my knees snapping and popping as I tried to catch up with Maury. For thirty-eight, my body was sure going south, in more ways than one.

As we reached the top of the stairs, I could see the door to Maury's apartment stood open. We may have left it that way. Surely no one would want to steal any of his meager possessions.

He rushed inside and across the living room and began to dig through a stack of magazines and newspapers, leaving me to close the door behind us. I thought about leaving it open in case I had to scream for help, but with the empty parking lot, what would be the point? I closed it, leaning against it in case I needed to flee.

"Here it is!" Maury waved the white document in triumph. He strode across the room with more confidence and held it out to me.

It was all there in black and white. I repeated the clergyman's name in my head over and over, not wanting to pull out a piece of paper and write it down in front of Maury like I didn't trust him or something. After all, he was my new brother-in-law. He was family now.

What was the old saying? You can pick your friends but not your family? How appropriate.

"Congratulations." I hoped he didn't hear the sarcasm in my voice.

He beamed. "Thanks."

"I'll tell Dr. Albert to have Erica call you as soon as she's allowed." I glanced around the room, looking for a phone. "What's your number here?"

"I use my cell."

"Okay." I took out a piece of paper and wrote down his number. Then I quickly added the clergyman's and witnesses names, too, and shoved the paper back in my purse. "Well, I guess that's it. I'm sure we'll be in touch."

Maury blinked.

I opened the door and stepped out onto the landing.

"Hey, Jolene?"

I turned back.

He was leaning on the door frame, one hand in his pocket. "Is Erica allowed to get flowers? Do you think she would like roses?"

How special. I managed a weak smile. "Why don't you wait a few days? Maybe take something when you go to see her. But you know, Maury, that reminds me. Did Erica tell you about her friend Josie Montalvo?"

Okay, so I told a little white lie, but I figured he'd be more inclined to answer if he thought Erica was involved.

He shook his head. It was hard to tell for sure, but he didn't seem to recognize the name.

I tried again. "Actually, that's her stage name. Her real name is Jessica James. She was a stripper at The Cat's Meow."

His expression morphed into recognition. "Erica didn't mention her, but I know The Cat's Meow."

"Do you know any of the girls who worked there?"

"Not really."

"Do you go there?"

He stiffened. "Not anymore. I'm a married man."

I resisted the impulse to roll my eyes. He'd as much as admitted to visiting the club, just "not anymore."

"Erica will be pleased you feel that way, but she doesn't have any objections to an unmarried man having a good time. Did you ever go there and ..."—how could I put this delicately—"have a good time with one of the girls?"

Revulsion washed over his face. He reached for the door. "Those girls are nothing but trash, Jolene. I wouldn't touch them with a ten-foot pole." He slammed it shut.

Revolting, untouchable trash. That's what he'd said.

How come his answer didn't make me feel any better?

TWENTY-ONE

I DROVE BACK TO the shop, wondering about Maury's statements. It probably wasn't so unusual to be both attracted and repelled by the dancers at the club. Like Ray said, men liked to look. Most men might even want to touch, but if their brain could overpower their sex drive, they probably wouldn't want to touch one of those girls, who, let's face it, had more fingerprints on them than a doorknob. If they did touch, they might feel remorse and shame afterwards. The few that teetered on the mental edge might want to stamp out the source of their shame—the girl. That was an old story, but history does repeat itself. Was it now Maury's story? Had Maury, unable to attract a nice girl even with attention and roses, succumbed to the temptations of a prostitute, then killed her in a fit of disgust?

I tried to picture him doing that.

Instead, I saw the captain of the football team stuffing Maury in a locker while the rest of the team cheered him on. Erica had told me that story one day when she came home from school.

She'd cried. She couldn't believe they had been so cruel. In fact, she'd been the one to release Maury from the locker. Erica had a kind heart.

Maury could have years of anger built up inside. Now that he was physically able, had he taken it out on someone weaker than himself?

Stranger things have happened.

Like my sister marrying Maury.

What were ya thinking, Erica?

I pulled into the parking lot behind Asdale Auto Imports and entered the shop through the garage to find Danny sitting in the race car while Cory explained all the instrumentation to him. Cory looked up with questions in his eyes when I appeared.

"Hey, Jo. How's Erica?"

"Dr. Albert admitted her to the psych center. She'll call in a few days."

Cory nodded. He knew the drill. "What about Maury?"

"He's my new brother-in-law."

"Huh." He didn't seem all that surprised, but then again, he knew Erica.

"Yeah, huh." Further elaboration wasn't required. Cory would know what I was thinking. But at his age, Danny shouldn't know, and he'd been following our discussion like a tennis match. I opened my mouth to try to explain, but I didn't have the energy or the desire to hash it all over with him. It was what it was.

Instead, I gave Danny what I hoped was an encouraging, care-free smile and started toward my office. I'd set an example of how to take life in stride. Besides, if we discussed the issue any further,

I might let a swearword, or two, go—not the example I wanted to set. "Any calls?"

"Just one. Celeste called. You're supposed to call her back."

I couldn't believe my ears. "Celeste Martin?"

"Is there any other?"

Thank God, no. This was a first. I don't believe Celeste had ever called me. In fact, since high school, the only time we spoke was when I went in her store or ran into her somewhere—except, of course, for the time I confronted her at home about dating my father. She certainly had never, ever called me. But, then, I didn't ever have any gossip to share. I wondered if that was what she was after now.

Curious, I walked through the showroom into my office and shrugged off my jacket. As I reached for the coat rack to hang it, I caught sight of Celeste crossing the street in my direction. She must have been watching Main Street for my car.

I froze.

She didn't wait for the light. She didn't wait for the oncoming automobile, either. She held out her left arm in the "stop" position and walked right in front of it. It halted inches from her kneecaps. She didn't spare the driver a glance.

The bells jingled on the front door when she breezed through. Her heels clicked across the showroom floor. "Jolene, you didn't call me back."

I shook off my shock and finished hanging my coat on the rack. "I just walked in, Celeste. Is something wrong?"

"Your sister has been admitted to the psych center."

"Oh." So much for patient confidentiality. "I know. I delivered her there myself."

For a moment, Celeste appeared deflated. Then she fluffed up again. "She married Maury Boor."

I sat behind my desk and gestured for Celeste to sit down as well. "I know. He told me."

She sniffed.

"How did you hear?" I leaned forward, curious to unlock Celeste's secrets for a change.

She seemed to consider a moment before deciding to answer. "Mindy's cousin Emma works at the florist shop. Maury came in and purchased a dish garden for your sister. He asked to have it delivered to the psych center, along with a card that read 'Like our love, this will grow forever. Your husband, Maury.'"

There you have it. Sweet as saccharine.

Celeste continued, "Emma was shocked."

I waited for more.

Celeste examined her fingernails as if she hadn't left me hanging.

I got it. She needed me to admit I didn't know something. "Why was Emma shocked, Celeste?"

"Because Maury always buys roses, lots of roses. He's bought so many roses for so many women Emma thinks he's crazy."

I cringed. Another certifiable in the Asdale clan after all my years of trying to avoid it. "Literally?"

Celeste shrugged. "Well, no, but he tries too hard. He buys roses for girls he doesn't even know yet. Emma tried to explain to him once that he might want to get to know a girl first before he gives her flowers. He didn't seem to get it. She said he's spent thousands on roses in the shop over the years."

I laughed, the kind of laugh that said I surrendered to the gods who thought this loon belonged in my family. "Wow."

"He's bought a couple dish gardens before, too. Emma said they're handmade wooden planters that looked like a wishing well with an African violet, white gerberas, prayer plants, and godseffiana. Very pretty, apparently."

I realized my lips had parted in astonishment. My thumb was black as car grease. I had absolutely no idea what she was talking about, but it sounded lovely—although no more unique than the roses, apparently. "I'm sure Erica will appreciate it."

Celeste looked at me. Stared, really.

I forced myself not to squirm. "I appreciate your keeping an eye out for Erica and Maury. It was very … nice"—I almost gagged on the word—"of you to rush right over. Thank you."

She didn't blink. She didn't leave, either, which is what people normally do after I thank them.

I tilted my head. "Was there something else, Celeste?"

"How's your new friend Leslie?"

Oh, I got it. Payback time. I would have to give information if I wanted to receive it. No wonder grapevines were so tough to cut. "She's fine. She's having a sex change operation next month." There—that would get her, and I didn't feel like I was talking out of school. Leslie had been quite upfront about it.

Celeste rose and looked down her nose at me. "I know."

———

Celeste stopped traffic on her way back across the street, too. This time I wished the oncoming car might have at least given her a nudge and soiled her perfectly creased pants.

I hadn't given her the satisfaction of asking how she already knew Leslie Flynn was having a sex change operation. Perhaps she just surmised after her brush with Leslie's big Willie. Or maybe Leslie had been in to Talbots to buy more clothes and shared the information as casually as she had shared it with Ray and me the other day. Or, better yet, maybe Celeste's sister's best friend's brother's wife's child from her first marriage was slated to be the Flynn's new bookkeeper. Whatever. It didn't matter.

I was more annoyed with my new brother-in-law Maury. He hadn't listened when I told him to wait to get Erica flowers. Flowers must be some kind of compulsion with him. Once again, I wondered if he'd ever sought therapy.

I dialed Ray's phone number to fill him in on Erica and Maury.

"Hey, Darlin'. How's Erica?"

"Married." I read him the clergyman's name and the names of the two witnesses.

"Did you look them up in the phone book?"

"Not yet. Hold on." I pulled it out and thumbed through the pages. "They're not local, but Maury said they honeymooned in Niagara Falls. He and Erica could have stopped anywhere between here and there to get married."

"Didn't your parents honeymoon there?"

"Yes. That's what makes me think they really got married. Like mother, like daughter."

"So where's Maury now?"

"I'm not sure. I left him at his apartment, but he apparently went out and bought Erica a dish garden to be delivered to the psych center. I have it from a very reliable source that the card read, 'Like our love, this will grow forever.'"

"I thought he was a rose man."

"With the occasional dish garden. It sounded very nice. An African violet, white gerberas, prayer plants, and some other God-like plant."

"An African violet?"

"Yes."

"What are white gerberas?"

"I don't know. I'm not even sure how to spell it."

"What's a prayer plant look like?"

"I don't know. Hold on." I pulled up Google and typed the words on the search line. A few clicks later, a picture of a flower-less, broad-leafed plant with pink veins appeared. I described it to Ray.

"Do you know where he bought it?"

"No, but I can call Celeste and ask if you want. She did say it was in a handmade wooden planter shaped like a wishing well."

"A wishing well?" Ray sounded excited.

"Yes. Why?"

"Give me the number at the store. I'll call her myself."

I flipped through the phone book again and gave him the number at Talbots. "Why are you interested in this dish garden, Ray?"

"Because it sounds exactly like the one I saw sitting on Josie … I mean, Jessica James' kitchen table in the apartment where she was killed."

My fingers clenched the edge of my desk. "Are you saying Maury might have killed her?"

"That's what I'm going to check out. Don't hold dinner."

I hung up the phone and rocked back in my chair. What would I tell Erica if Maury turned out to be a killer? She hadn't discussed him with me in years, but I had to wonder if this time she had truly fallen for him. She'd been engaged on and off a half dozen times at least, always to undesirable men, always spur of the moment, often during one of her manic states. All those engagements had run out of gas almost as fast as they had begun. When she sunk into depression, had she finally joined forces with the most undesirable man of all? If that were the case, I wondered how it would affect her. Could Dr. Albert put a spin on a disaster of this proportion that would make her feel better? Or would Erica's kind heart and bad judgment cause her to love Maury anyway? If Maury turned out to be a killer, would Ray and I be driving both Erica and Danny to weekly prisoner visits in the future like one big happy family?

I'm sure Ray would love being related to a convicted killer.

The good news was Danny's father couldn't be a killer if Maury was. The bad news was, either way, Danny or Erica would be hurt. It was like the age-old question, if you could only save one of your children, which one would you pick? I wanted both my "children" to be happy. I crossed my fingers that Ray wouldn't find a connection to Maury.

Then I wondered if the partial print on the Camry's remote had been matched to Danny's father. If it did match, he would remain the prime suspect in Jessica James' death, linked to the car in which her arm was found, to The Cat's Meow where Danny's father visited her, and to her Cadillac Escalade that he obviously stole. Not to mention the fact that they were related. Pretty substantial evidence compared to a dish garden.

I rocked in my chair and stared out the window of the showroom. I watched as the sun disappeared and gray clouds moved in, signaling a significant change in the weather. When the first snowflake fell a few minutes before closing time, I shook off my thoughts and fears and walked into the garage.

Cory had the hood off Brennan Rowe's race car. The car's engine sat on an engine stand. Cory stood in the center of the empty front end, fiddling with the wiring. Danny leaned over the right fender, handing Cory whatever tool he requested. Neither one noticed my arrival.

"It's five o'clock guys. Let's call it a day, okay?"

Cory nodded and dropped to the ground to slide out from under the grill. Danny's face reflected his disappointment.

I put my hand on Danny's shoulder. "Did you do any schoolwork today?"

"It's all done. I just have to study for my tests. I can do that Sunday."

"Okay. Cory, do you want to join us for dinner tonight? Ray's working late."

He whisked plastic gloves off his hands, removed shoe covers, and wiggled out of his mechanic's coveralls to reveal khakis and a dark blue dress shirt. "No thanks, Jo. Brennan and I have a date."

For a second, I thought Danny winced. But then, his expression reverted to neutral.

I continued to try to set a good example for him. "Great. Have fun. I'll lock up."

Cory slid his coat on. "Thanks for all your help today, Danny." He turned to me. "I think Danny would make a great mechanic, but he says his dad wants him to go to college and become a doctor or something more professional."

"He could be both."

"Good point." Cory clapped Danny on the shoulder. "See ya tomorrow, Danny. Thanks for your help today."

Danny followed me around the garage and showroom as I shut off the lights and checked door locks.

I pulled my coat off the brass rack behind my office door and shrugged it on. "It started to snow. Where's your coat?"

"I didn't wear one."

"It's December. You better remember to take one from now on, no matter how warm outside it is."

Danny nodded.

I walked over to the alarm box. "I'm going to punch in the code then we have two minutes to get out."

He watched with interest as I activated the alarm.

"Okay, let's go." We darted out the door. I locked it. I jogged to the car with Danny by my side, wind whipping around us and blowing stray newspapers in our path. We scrambled inside. I cranked the heater. "It'll be warm in a minute."

Danny's teeth chattered in lieu of a reply.

Halfway home, an odd thought popped into my head. "Danny, did your dad ever buy flowers for a girl?"

I saw his expression in the rearview mirror. It was the "yeah, right lady" expression. "No. Why?"

"I was just curious. Erica got married to this guy named Maury Boor. He buys girls flowers all the time."

"Erica really got married?"

"It looks that way, Danny."

"I'm never getting married."

"Why not?"

"I don't want to. I'm going to get a dog."

I laughed. "Man's best friend."

The few miles to our house passed quickly and I pulled into the driveway, pleased to see that the timer had lit the Christmas lights we'd strung the night before. Now we were as festive as the rest of the neighborhood. At least our family had one thing going right for us.

Danny followed me to the front door, slipping on the fresh snow in his high-top sneakers. I unlocked the door to let him scoot inside the warm house. Then I fished the mail out of our mailbox, which was filled to overflowing.

I took off my coat and carried the mail into the kitchen to sort. A blue envelope caught my eye. It was addressed to Danny, in care of me.

I picked it up. The handwriting looked like a child's. It had no return address. I waved it at him. "You have mail."

His expression was stunned. "I never got mail before." He darted over to stand next to me. "Who's it from?"

I held it out to him then pulled it back, hesitant. What if it was something that would hurt him? "Do you recognize the handwriting?"

Danny shook his head.

"Could it be from your dad?"

"I've never seen my dad write."

Of course not. If he didn't read, he probably didn't write, either. "Maybe someone at the jail wrote you a letter for him. Open it and see."

Danny took the letter and flipped it over. "How?"

"Just slide your thumb in this opening here and lift the flap. Or you can rip it across."

Danny tried, but his hands shook. "Here, you open it."

I did. It was a card covered in footballs that said, "A Party …" I opened the card.

Jacob, Bernie Shubert's son, was having a sleepover party for his twelfth birthday.

Danny was invited.

TWENTY-TWO

DANNY TURNED THE INVITATION over in his hands. "Should I go?"

"Sure, why not? Ray and I know Jacob's parents. They're very nice. You know Jacob, right?"

"Yeah. We play football at lunch."

"His dad told me that. He said Jacob thinks you're pretty good."

Danny's face brightened. "He does?"

I pointed to the card. "Maybe you'll play football at the party."

"Yeah." He looked inside the card again. "But it says to bring a sleeping bag."

"You can use Ray's."

"What about a present?"

I felt like I was talking him into feeling as excited as me. "You can pick out something. I'll pay for it."

"Okay." But he sounded doubtful. He set the card on the table and went into the living room to turn on the television.

I pulled ground meat out of the refrigerator to make meatballs. As I rolled the balls, I smiled. Danny was invited to his first birthday party. I couldn't feel more delighted.

After our mother committed suicide, Erica and I didn't get many party invitations. Those we did receive were from kids whose parents made them invite us just to be nice. I knew that because the kids made a point of telling us. My mother had never been involved in school activities and she didn't encourage us to invite friends over. We were all she could handle, and in the end, she couldn't handle even that. So the invitations had always been few and far between, since people generally invited the kids with the parents they knew best to their birthdays. I didn't mind being left out, but Erica did. She'd cried many tears over it, which made me both angry and sad. I'd feared Danny's jailed father would prevent him from blending in with the kids in much the same way. Apparently, it hadn't.

Then it occurred to me. Bernie might have had a hand in this. It might be another pity invitation. Maybe Jacob invited Danny because Bernie insisted. If Danny found out, he would be hurt, too.

Tears burned my eyes. Why did life have to be so uncertain?

I finished rolling the meatballs and put the frying pan on the burner. There wasn't much I could do but encourage Danny to go to the party and have a good time. I'd hope for the best.

Danny and I ate dinner. He had two helpings of spaghetti and, after asking me to identify the spinach, chewed and swallowed his serving of that without complaint. I tried to talk to him about school and the work he did with Cory. He gave short answers designed to discourage conversation. He wasn't a teenager yet, but he'd picked up all the mannerisms.

After he carried his own dish to the sink, I didn't ask him to clear the table or wash dishes. Ray would have. I preferred to do it myself, alone.

When I heard SpongeBob come on, I hid in our bedroom and tried to read. The pages blurred as I worried first about Danny, then his father, then Erica, and finally even Maury. I glanced at the clock. Seven p.m. and still no Ray.

I thought about calling him on his cell phone, but didn't want to disturb him. Maybe he'd find out something tonight that would answer some of my concerns.

I must have fallen asleep. I awoke at nine-thirty to find Ray standing next to me.

I sat up. "Is Danny in bed?"

"He is now. He was watching television when I got home. He's all excited about Jacob's birthday party."

"He is?" I filled Ray in on my concerns. "Do you think it will be okay?"

"Sure. You know Bernie. He can't stand it if everyone isn't having a good time. Danny will have a blast. It'll be good for him." Ray disappeared into the closet.

I got out of bed and followed him. "What did you find out about the flowers?"

He took off his uniform and tossed it in the clothes hamper. "I saw the dish gardens. They look like the one on Jessica James' kitchen table, but the only other one the florist remembers Maury purchasing besides Erica's was delivered to a girl in Canandaigua. I called her. She and Maury dated for a while, then she broke it off."

"So Maury didn't give one to Jessica James."

"I don't think so, unless he paid cash and no one at the florist shop remembers. But they're pretty fascinated by Maury, so it's hard to believe they'd forget." He pulled on a pair of jeans.

"Did you ask them who else bought a dish garden recently?"

"I did. They're compiling a list of customers. I asked them to fax it to the department. That's all I can do for now. Remember, I'm not supposed to be investigating Jessica James' death."

Ray headed toward the kitchen. "Anything left from dinner?"

"We had spaghetti. I'll warm some up for you." I pulled the leftover dishes out and made up a plate for the microwave.

He sat at the breakfast bar and watched me.

After I slid his plate into the microwave, I leaned against the breakfast bar, my face inches from Ray's. "Did you hear any more about the partial print on the Camry's remote?"

"It's not Mr. Phillips' print."

Relief washed through me. Danny's father couldn't be tied to the killing, at least not yet. "Whose is it?"

"They're still running matches and gathering prints from the car dealership employees. They ruled out Mr. Phillips immediately."

"Is the investigation focusing on him?"

"They're pushing him hard to talk. His lawyer wants a deal, but the prosecutor isn't offering one. They think they have a motive."

"What?"

"Jessica James' will. She left everything to her closest relative—Danny."

The microwave dinged as if on cue. I pulled Ray's steaming plate out and set it in front of him. "I don't understand how that gives his father a motive."

"Think, Darlin'. Danny is a minor, so his legal guardian, Mr. Phillips, is probably in charge of the inheritance until Danny reaches eighteen. He might have killed her for the money, house, and possessions."

"He did get caught in her Cadillac Escalade. Maybe he thought he was entitled to it."

Ray shoved a forkful of spaghetti in his mouth and chewed for a minute. "That's the part that bothers me. I can't believe he'd let himself be found in the car after he killed her. He doesn't strike me as stupid."

"All criminals make mistakes eventually, don't they? Isn't that how you catch them?"

"This guy's been caring for Danny for ten years, Jolene. He hasn't been arrested in all that time, although he has a very spotty work record. It doesn't fit."

I let Ray eat the rest of his dinner in peace. I could tell his mind was churning through the events of the last few days, looking for the missing link, just as I had been earlier. With any luck, when he found it, it would not lead to Danny's father.

Did that mean I was willing to sacrifice Maury Boor, my sister's husband? I guessed so. But I wished I could talk to Erica about him first. She might have some answers, too.

———

The next three days passed quietly, except for the sound of Sponge-Bob's laugh. If Danny was going to live with us for an extended period, I would need to find a better way for him to pass the time when he wasn't in school or at the shop. Either that, or he would have to watch television wearing earphones.

Ray passed his time working from dawn to dusk. From his silence, I knew the department wasn't making much progress in finding Jessica James' killer.

Sunday night Danny asked to visit his father. Ray took him after dinner. I tried to watch television while they were gone, wondering what more, if anything, Mr. Phillips would share with Danny about the stolen car, his dead aunt, and his inheritance and how Danny would react to the information. I didn't have to wait long to find out.

Ray called me at seven-thirty. "Can you pick up Danny?"

"Sure. What's wrong?"

"Danny's father has agreed to talk. His lawyer and the prosecution are on the way. The sheriff wants me here."

"Okay, I'll be right there."

I grabbed my coat and raced out the door. Snow had begun to fall heavily and an inch or so had accumulated on the roads. I had to drive the speed limit, and when I got behind more nervous drivers, even less. I arrived at the county safety building full of pent-up frustration. I found Danny alone in the squad room, slouching in a chair with an open soda can next to him.

"Where's Ray?"

Danny pointed toward the interview rooms. "In there with my dad."

I sat on a metal chair next to him. "Do you know what's going on?"

Concern flickered across his face. "My dad's telling the truth."

"Do you know what he's saying?"

"Yeah." Danny cast a final desperate glance back toward the room where his father was. "I know everything. He never left me at Chuck E. Cheese's. I was with him the whole time."

I desperately wanted to know what happened but refrained from asking. It didn't seem right to pump Danny when his father was in there laying it all on the line. Ray could tell me later.

I stood. "Are you ready to go home?"

He looked at me like I was crazy. "Don't you want to know?"

I dropped back into my seat, feeling relieved that I wouldn't have to wait but apprehensive about what Danny might say. "Sure."

He scratched his neck, leaving a dark red mark. "My dad picked up the Camry at the dealership outside Geneseo. We went to my dad's friend's house and loaded all our stuff in it. My dad said we were going to move to New York City. A friend of his had a job for him there."

Danny glanced at me out of the side of his eyes, and I knew it wasn't a legitimate job. Although Danny hadn't admitted it, I figured he knew his dad had stolen the Camry, too. I let it go and nodded, encouraging him to continue.

"We went to see my aunt. I didn't know she was my aunt. My dad said she was going to give him her Cadillac Escalade to sell. She was going to report it stolen to the insurance company."

Insurance fraud. A great way to make money, as long as no one got caught.

"We went to The Cat's Meow. Everything happened there like I said, except when I came back to the car, it was different. My soda and my backpack weren't in the back seat. My dad's baseball hat was gone, too. I thought somebody took them. My dad came out.

He thought he'd lost his remote. He looked all over the car. He noticed our stuff was gone. He wanted to know what I did with it. I told him nothing. I told him I got out of the car and when I came back, our stuff was gone. He opened the trunk. It was empty. That's when he figured out it wasn't our car, because the trunk had dirt and stuff in it. He went back inside and came out again. He said we couldn't wait for the person who took our car to come back. He said if it was a mistake, they might call the police and when the police checked, they would know it was stolen. He said if they took it on purpose, then one stolen car was as good as another. He said we'd get new stuff. My backpack had all my school stuff in it, but he said I'd be starting a new school anyway. So we left."

Danny took a swig of his soda before continuing. "My dad dropped me off at his friend's house so he could go get Aunt Jessica's car. He drove me to school the next morning in it. It was awesome. Then he got caught. Aunt Jessica reported it stolen too soon."

Timing was everything. I could imagine Danny's father's surprise when the sheriff's department cruiser pulled him over. I wondered if she had done it on purpose to spite him for some old wound or if it had been an honest mistake. Jessica wouldn't be able to tell us now.

"Jolene?"

I snapped out of my reverie. "Yes, Danny?"

"My dad didn't kill Aunt Jessica. He doesn't know who did."

"Where's the Camry your father took from The Cat's Meow?"

"In a parking lot." Danny jerked his head in the direction of the interrogation rooms. "He's going to tell them where to find it. Do you think they'll go get it?"

"I hope so, Danny."

"My dad said he would tell them who he sold all the stolen cars to. He thought they might let him go, but then we found out about Aunt Jessica." Danny's eyes filled with tears. "Do you think they'll believe him?"

I put my arm around Danny and hugged his shoulders. "I hope so."

The pressure on this poor little boy proved to be too much. He dissolved into heaving sobs.

I held him tighter and rubbed his back. He was asking the right questions. Would they believe his father? Would they want to talk to Danny, too? Maybe I shouldn't take him home yet. Maybe we should wait until they were through. But it could take hours. Then they might not want to talk to Danny. His father had had enough time with him now to coach him on this story. It did sound a little too good to be true, but then truth is stranger than fiction. Could the mix-up at The Cat's Meow be an innocent but ironic mistake? Or had the killer taken the opportunity to tie someone else to the victim?

The fact remained that someone with the initial P like Danny's father had most likely switched his car for the one Danny's father stole from the used car lot. It could have been managed by sitting next to Danny's father at the bar and laying the two sets of keys side by side. Did he do it on purpose or was it a mistake? Did the *P* stand for the man's first name or his last? Was it *P* for Peter Flynn, Leslie's brother? Had he been in The Cat's Meow Saturday night, the last night anyone remembered seeing Jessica James? Could he be the killer?

Hard to believe. The man didn't even have a driver's license, and Ray had said the DMV records didn't show a Toyota Camry registered to anyone at Leslie and Peter's home address.

Besides, Ray said the sheriff's department interviewed all the regulars. Surely Peter was on the list. I wondered who else might be on the list with the initial *P*. Maybe Ray worked with the lead investigators to check those names out.

The only positive spin I could put on the whole story was that this killer with the initial *P* who took Danny's father's car couldn't be my sister's new husband, Emerson Maurice Boor. He drove a Prelude and didn't have an initial *P*. Unless, of course, the *P* stood for Prelude. Wouldn't that be a pip? Maury might just be weird enough to think that way, but I hoped not.

Danny pulled away and wiped at his face with his fists. I dug in my purse and handed him a couple of tissues. He blew his nose loud and long like a foghorn.

The interrogation room door opened. Ray stepped out.

He crossed the room to us. "Take Danny home, Darlin'. I'll see you in the morning."

Danny stepped away from us. "What about my dad?"

Ray reached for Danny's shoulder. "Your dad is talking. He's got a lot to say, and we've got a lot of questions. Don't worry. We'll get it all straightened out."

Danny frowned, clearly doubtful.

I had doubts myself. "Why don't you go splash some water on your face in the men's room, Danny? Then we'll go home."

He shuffled off, his shoulders drooping. It was so unfair that a twelve-year-old should have to bear such a burden. Danny seemed so much older than his years.

I turned to Ray. "He told me the whole story. What's going to happen now?"

"We're going to send a patrol car to find the Camry. We'll see if we can figure out who it belongs to and we'll round him or her up for questioning."

"What about Danny's father?"

Ray shrugged. "He's definitely guilty of auto theft, but if he helps bust up a ring, he might be able to avoid a jail sentence. And if what he says is true about the Escalade, I'm not sure the D.A. will prosecute since his aunt left all her property, including the car, to Danny."

"So he might be released?"

"Anything's possible, but one thing's for sure. We're one step closer to finding our killer."

TWENTY-THREE

RAY HADN'T COME HOME by the time Danny and I needed to leave for school the next morning. Danny begged me to let him take the day off. I tried to call Ray at the department and on his cell phone, but he didn't answer. I left a message, wondering what was so pressing that he'd been up all night. But I insisted Danny go to school, telling him it would only make the time pass that much faster. Besides, he had a spelling test and a geography test to take, and I didn't want him kicked out of school.

When I pulled into the school turnaround, I shut off the ignition and looked over my shoulder at Danny. He made no move to get out of the car.

"Danny, I'll pick you up today same as always. By then, we should know what's going on. Just do your best in school, and don't worry. Your dad will be fine."

He met my gaze with anguish in his eyes. "I told my dad about my suspension and about taking Erica's car. He didn't get mad. He was too worried about Aunt Jessica."

"Well, now that he's told the truth, he shouldn't have to worry about that anymore. When they find the other Camry, it should lead them to the person who killed her. And that's not your dad, right?"

Danny nodded then his lips turned up in a rueful grin. "I told my dad what you said."

Surprised, I tried to recall what it might have been. "What'd I say?"

"You know."

"I'm not sure what you're referring to. I say a lot of things, Danny."

"When you said, 'What were ya thinkin'?' You know, when I took Erica's car and when I got in the fight."

"Oh." I smiled. "What did he say?"

"He said that was a good question. He wanted to know the answer."

"What did you tell him?"

"I told him I wasn't thinking."

An honest answer. How often do we all do things without thinking them through? At twelve, Danny was entitled to a few more mistakes than we adults. "Okay, well, listen, think hard when you're taking your tests today, so you can tell your dad all about your good grades later. I'm sure Ray will take you to see him tonight."

Danny's face brightened considerably. He hopped out of the car without another word. Two boys approached him and greeted him. They headed toward the building together, scuffing their feet and talking.

As I watched Danny walk into the building, my cell phone rang. I thought it might be Ray, but when I checked the display, I didn't recognize the number.

"Hello?"

I waited, straining my ears and thinking it must be a wrong number. "Hello?"

I heard a sigh. I knew that sigh. "Erica?"

More silence. "Erica, if it's you, say something. Otherwise, I'm going to hang up and I won't answer again."

"It's me. Who else do you know in the tower?"

"I didn't recognize the number."

"You should have it memorized by now."

I tried not to respond in the same combative manner she was addressing me. It was hard, because I was the one with the right to be pissed. Erica had stopped taking her medicine, failed to show up for her doctor's appointments, lost her job, and run away to marry a geek. I swallowed hard and tried to be congenial. "I take it you're feeling better."

"I hate it here."

"What does Dr. Albert say? How long do you have to stay?" I left off the words "this time."

"He might let me come home in a couple days, if someone stays with me to monitor my medication."

For the last fifteen years, that would have been me or Ray. Now Maury was in the picture. "Did you marry Maury?"

Another sigh, this time heavy enough to make the line crackle. "Yes."

"How do you feel about that?"

"You sound like Dr. Albert. You know, I don't like Dr. Albert anymore. He's really not even that good-looking."

He was, but again, I didn't want to argue. "What about Maury, Erica? Are you planning on living with him?"

"Of course. He's my husband."

"So, you love him?"

She heaved another sigh. "Of course."

Her response didn't make me feel any better. It was the same response I would have gotten if I asked her if she wanted me to bake chocolate chip cookies. "You're going to live in the apartment where I found you?"

This time she hesitated. "Can we live in the apartment on Wells Street?"

"Sure, if you can afford it." I hated to start trouble, but I wasn't going to pay Maury's bills. He would have to step up.

Erica caught my less than subtle implication. "Maury got a new job."

"Where?"

"He's going to be a delivery man for a florist shop."

I didn't know whether to laugh or cry. "That sounds like a great job for him."

I doubted it would pay the rent, but Erica could get another job, too. She never had trouble getting jobs, just keeping them. She and Maury had that in common.

Erica continued, "I have to see Dr. Albert once a week. He has an opening on Thursdays starting next week."

"Do you want me to drive you?"

"I can drive myself."

"All right. Cory's fixing the Porsche for you. I'll tell him to hurry."

Erica remained silent so long that I thought she'd hung up. Then she asked, "Do you still have Danny?"

"Yes, but I'm not sure for how much longer." I told Erica the whole story about the stolen cars, Jessica James' death, the possible suspects, and the news from last night. "Ray still hasn't called me. I'm not sure if Danny's father will be released or not. Even if he is, he doesn't have a home or a job, unless he can move into the aunt's house. It seems like he should be required to have both before he can take Danny, but that's up to Social Services, I guess."

Erica wasn't interested in Danny. "That redheaded guy, Peter, he used to visit another psychiatrist in the building on Wednesdays. I talked to him in the elevator sometimes."

"He told you his name was Peter?"

"He told me when I saw him in The Cat's Meow."

The night she asked him if he was big all over. "Are you sure it was the same guy? Leslie was a patient of Dr. Albert's. She saw him once a week. A lot of people get the two of them confused. They're identical twins."

"He recognized me. He said 'Hello' first."

I didn't know what to make of that. Could both Leslie and her brother be in treatment? If so, what was Peter being treated for? I started to ask Erica if she knew, but she said the orderly wanted her to hang up.

I tried Ray again. Still no answer at either number. I dialed again and connected with the operator, who said Ray was on patrol. Was he working a back-to-back shift? He was too tired to drive safely. Maybe he'd slept at the office or in his car. Maybe they were so close to solving Jessica James' case that he didn't want to miss it.

I drove home, stopping at the corner store to purchase a newspaper. I wanted to know what, if anything, had been reported about Jessica James' death.

I found no reference to her murder in the local paper. I did spot advertisements for two damaged cars, a Mercedes and a BMW, that I would have loved to purchase and have Cory repair for resale in my showroom. Too bad all my inventory dollars were tied up in a very pricey Ferrari with its own ghost riding eternal shotgun.

At home, I tried to watch Regis and Kelly, but even with all their charms, they couldn't hold my attention. Reading a book was out of the question. All my housework had been completed over the weekend.

After checking my cell phone for the tenth time to make sure I hadn't missed Ray's call, I had to get out of the house. I decided to take back the sweaters Celeste had forced on me the other day. After the superior way she'd behaved in my office, I figured I didn't owe her anymore.

I walked into Talbots twenty minutes later with my shopping bag full of sweaters. The assistant manager, a woman old enough to be my mother, was behind the counter. She greeted me warmly. I could tell she thought she should know my name but it wasn't coming to her.

She found it on the sales receipt. "Oh, you're Jolene Asdale. I'm sorry, Jolene Parker. Someone was just here looking for you."

"Really?" I couldn't imagine why anyone would look for me here. I came in here once a season, if that.

She began entering information in the register and scanning the tags on the sweaters. "She was looking for Celeste, too. She wanted to give you both fresh chickens to thank you for helping her pick out clothes or something like that. I can't remember her name, but she had red hair."

"Was her name Leslie Flynn?"

The assistant manager nodded. "That's it. Seemed like a nice woman. I told her today was Celeste's day off and that your shop was always closed on Mondays. She said she'd come back tomorrow."

I signed for my return. The woman sealed my old and new receipt in an envelope. She thanked me, as though returning clothes was as helpful to the store as purchasing them. I knew Celeste wouldn't feel that way, but what she didn't know wouldn't hurt her.

In my car, I debated between heading home, driving to the county safety building to look for Ray, or calling Leslie Flynn. At home, I'd have nothing to do but look at the walls. Chasing after Ray was not appropriate. He was busy. I needed to respect that. Besides, if the sheriff found out I was following Ray on the job, Ray might get in trouble again. We didn't need that.

I decided to call Leslie. I didn't know what all was implied by "fresh chicken," but it was thoughtful of her to think of us. Ray and Danny had enjoyed the eggs.

I checked my cell phone log and found her phone number. She answered on the fourth ring.

"Leslie, it's Jolene. I was just in Talbots. The assistant manager said you were looking for me."

"Hey, Jolene. I've got fresh chickens in a cooler for you. I realized the other day that I hadn't done enough to thank you and Celeste. I knew you were interested in the eggs, so I figured most of your chickens had come from the grocery store in the past, too. I know the store labels often say 'fresh' but fresh really means killed and plucked today."

"Killed" brought all sorts of undesirable pictures to mind. I liked the sound of "plucked," though. I wondered about all the chicken's innards, but was too afraid to ask.

Leslie continued, "I have two whole roasters for you and Ray and one for Celeste. I can bring them back into town tomorrow, or you and Ray can stop by today and pick yours up if you have time."

I didn't want to admit that I had nothing but time, or that Ray wasn't allowed to visit her farm anymore. "Ray's working, but I can stop by this morning, if that works for you."

"Good. I'll put a pot of coffee on."

TWENTY-FOUR

As I DROVE TOWARD the Flynn farm, it occurred to me that no one had ever given me a gift like this before. Candy and baked goods, yes. Casseroles when my parents died. But never an uncooked chicken. I supposed amongst farming families this type of gift was more common and appreciated, even welcomed if they didn't raise chickens of their own. I wondered if it would taste better than the ones from the grocery store. With any luck, Ray would cook the chicken for me. It would taste better if he did. Of course, I wouldn't be inviting Erica and Maury over to dine with us, not with the way Erica felt about chickens.

The thin gray dog the size of a miniature horse greeted me in Leslie's driveway as I stepped out of the Lexus. I took a step away from the car. The dog positioned itself between me and the house. I waited, never one to brave an unknown dog.

The thought flashed through my mind that maybe I shouldn't have come out here. But that was silly. Leslie had invited both Ray and me. She was a friend. But her grumpy dog was another story.

I avoided eye contact with it and tried to stay calm. I didn't want it to sense my fear.

Leslie appeared in the side doorway seconds later. Once again, she wasn't wearing her wig. She had on her old Carhartt overalls and a green plaid shirt. "Come on in, Jolene."

I stepped around the dog. It growled.

I glanced at Leslie for support.

"Rufus. Quiet. Go in the barn."

The dog slinked off, tail between its legs.

Leslie hugged me and offered to hang up my coat. I watched as she threw it on a wall hook next to her Carhartt jacket. I hoped my coat wouldn't smell like manure when I put it on later.

I stepped over the piles of dirty and worn boots in the hall beyond the entryway and followed her into a sunlit kitchen with a picture window overlooking the barn and fields.

"I was putting a fresh pot of coffee on. Sit down." Leslie gestured to the oval oak table in the middle of the kitchen.

I hadn't planned on staying long, but the kitchen seemed welcoming enough with its blue and white tiled floor and bright yellow walls. Spotless, too. I took a seat at the table.

She pulled a couple of coffee cups from the cupboard. "We can take our coffee in the sunroom when it's ready."

I could see a wide doorway and hints of foliage beyond it at the far end of the cheerful kitchen. Something smelled earthy and warm. I also smelled apple pie.

"I've got a pie in the oven to go with the coffee." She opened a white foam cooler that sat on the counter, a cooler very much like the one we'd found Jessica James' arm inside days ago. "Wait 'til you see what I've got in here."

I cringed, fearing she'd pull out a severed limb. Ridiculous since these coolers were common everywhere and used for food, fishing, and …

Leslie pulled out a naked, headless chicken.

"O-o-o-h." My heart started beating again. I tried to smile appreciatively.

Leslie squinted at me. "What's the matter?"

"Nothing. I'm just used to buying chicken breasts."

"Not a roaster?"

I shook my head. "Are you sure that's a chicken? It's huge."

Leslie fluffed up with pride. "We don't even give them growth hormones."

Yet another side to farming that I knew nothing about. I decided not to ask.

She slapped the chicken down on the cutting board. "I can chop it into pieces. You can use the breasts now and freeze the rest. Just make sure you eat some of it fresh today."

"Okay." I could bake a chicken breast. That was not beyond me.

Leslie pulled open a kitchen drawer. She took out a cleaver with a blade approximately four inches by eight inches. She started to sharpen it.

The blade zipped in and out of the sharpener, making a slight grated noise. For some reason, my hands started to sweat. "Is that what you use to chop chickens?"

Leslie continued to sharpen it. "It's a Chinese cleaver. It can chop anything. Chicken, beef, vegetables. It can go right through bone."

A visual of this cleaver hacking Jessica James into pieces flashed through my head.

Perspiration broke out in my armpits. I thought I might be sick. I fumbled for my purse, trying to think of an excuse to leave.

Leslie ran her finger over the blade. "There. It's ready." She held it out to show me, twisting the blade from side to side. It caught the sunlight streaming in through the kitchen window and blinded me.

I closed my eyes and tensed.

The cleaver dropped with a whack. I opened my eyes to see Leslie push the right wing of the chicken to the side of the cutting board. She raised the cleaver again.

I looked away, chiding myself. I had no reason to fear this woman. She had offered me a fresh chicken in friendship, for Pete's sake.

A check secured with a magnet to the stainless steel refrigerator caught my eye.

I glanced at Leslie, who continued to whack away at the poor defenseless chicken.

I stood up and leaned to get a better look at the check.

It was made out to The Cat's Meow and dated for the Saturday of Jessica James' disappearance. Peter Flynn was scrawled in bold letters on the signature line.

"He still owes me."

I turned to find Leslie gesturing to the check with the meat cleaver. She missed my chest by inches.

Alarmed, I dropped in my chair.

"Ooops. Sorry." Leslie resumed chopping the chicken. "Peter hasn't paid me back yet for covering that check. He and I keep the farm funds separate from our personal accounts. His personal account is drained, according to him."

"Is he home? I still haven't met him." Not that I was sure I wanted to.

"No, he's at the grocery store, buying chew. I swear he goes there once a day. If he's not spending his money on drinks, it's chew."

She chopped off the final piece, a drumstick, and took plastic freezer bags out of the drawer. "I'll put the breasts in one bag and the thighs, drumsticks, and wings in another. How's that sound?"

"Fine." My voice was a croak. Peter went to the grocery store once a day? Had he in fact been there the day I got shot at?

Leslie turned and studied me. "You have a weak stomach, don't you?"

I half-nodded, thinking of Erica's words earlier today regarding the redheaded man: "He used to visit another psychiatrist in the building on Wednesdays."

Erica couldn't have been referring to Leslie. Leslie saw Dr. Albert, not another psychiatrist. Erica had to have met Leslie's brother, Peter, in the elevator. The brother I'd never met. The brother who lived here on this farm with access to meat cleavers. The brother who frequented The Cat's Meow and had no money. Could he have spent it all on alcohol and chew? Maybe he'd spent it on some of the girls, maybe even the ones willing to meet him outside the club. Maybe one like Jessica James, who was driving a new Cadillac Escalade.

Leslie was speaking to me. "I'll keep the innards. You probably don't know what to do with them. We'll boil them up for the dog."

I watched as she loaded the dark purplish heart and assorted organs into a pot and filled it with water. She turned it on to boil. My nose twitched. My stomach rolled.

Leslie walked over to the refrigerator with the plastic bags in hand. "I'll put these in here for now and put them back in the cooler for you when it's time to go home."

She closed the door. "Come on out in the sunroom and see the flowers. They'll perk ya right up."

I knew I should make excuses and leave, but I didn't want to offend her.

I followed her obediently across the kitchen and out the door. Instantly, the temperature rose twenty degrees. I found it more difficult to breathe.

The sunroom was actually a greenhouse filled with potted plants on shelving. Flowering plants and ferns, tall and short, all sucking the oxygen out of the air in the room. It was a heady experience, especially to someone prone to allergies like me.

A wicker furniture set occupied the middle of the floor: a couch, two chairs, and a coffee table. The cushions were blue with sunflowers. They looked home sewn. I wondered if Leslie or her brother had the decorating and floral talents.

Leslie pointed to one of the chairs. "Sit down, Jolene. Make yourself comfortable. I'll serve the coffee and pie out here as soon as it's ready."

"Great, thank you." I dropped into the chair facing the doorway. Then I spotted them. I tried not to let my distress show.

I took a deep breath. I needed to know if Leslie really was a friend—or the enemy. "So, Leslie, are you the gardener in the family?"

She laughed. "Not me. My brother grows all these. He also makes those cute planters over there by the door."

The cute planters shaped like wishing wells. The ones that held African violets, prayer plants and other florals I couldn't identify. I swallowed the bile that rose in the back of my throat.

"Does he sell them?"

"Sure does. One of the florists in town stocks them. We also sell them here, along with the fresh eggs, if you know someone who might like one."

My mouth felt dry. I shivered, even though the greenhouse had to be eighty degrees. I didn't know if I was sitting in the house of a killer—or just the florist to a killer. Either way, it spelled a funeral for me.

Could Leslie's brother be the killer? If so, I wasn't safe here. I slid to the edge of the chair cushion, ready to make my excuses. I needed to call Ray.

Leslie chattered on, clearly not sensing anything amiss. "The last one we sold was to that man who liked the Caterhams, the man I told you about."

I blinked. "You never told me his name, Leslie."

"It's Maury. Maury Boor."

I slumped in the chair. Maury Boor. My sister had married an axe murderer, and I would get to be the one to tell her. "It's a little warm in here, Leslie. Could I trouble you for a glass of water?"

"Sure." She lumbered to her feet and disappeared into the kitchen.

I wanted to weep, but after all my perspiring, I didn't have any fluids left. Besides, how would I explain my breakdown to poor, sweet Leslie? I certainly didn't want to be the one to tell her that the love of her life had married my sister—and killed a woman just days before that.

Leslie reappeared, holding a glass of water in her hands. The gray dog trotted in at her heels. She held the glass out to me without a word.

"Thank you." I drank it down.

She continued to stand over me. The dog had settled at her feet, watching me.

I set the empty glass on the coffee table and studied her. Something was different. Had her shirt been blue earlier or was it just a trick of the lighting? "Is everything okay, Leslie?"

"Here's the pie. Peter, now that you've introduced yourself, go get the coffee, will you? I couldn't fit it all on the tray."

The person standing over me who I thought was Leslie took a few steps back and smiled. His teeth were crooked, not the pretty veneers Leslie had gotten. "Sure, Les."

He turned and went through the door, passing his sister, who balanced a tray as she crossed the room to me. My purse dangled from her arm.

She smiled and set the tray down. "I hope Peter introduced himself. I told him you were in here, admiring his planters."

My lips parted, but no sound came out. The resemblance was uncanny. Without the veneers, I'd never have known the difference between the two. Although something about Peter's smile had made me uncomfortable, creeped out actually.

Leslie held out my purse. "Your cell phone was ringing. You might have a message."

"Thank you." I set the purse next to me on the chair, still reeling. Was Peter the killer? Or was Maury? Maury's initials didn't match the key chain in the Camry. Peter's did.

Leslie busied herself with slicing the pie. She used a ten-inch knife.

I couldn't take my eyes off it. This house was well-armed with cutlery.

Leslie set a piece of pie in front of me. "Here you go, Jolene."

"Thanks, Leslie." I pulled out my cell phone and noticed the message announcement. "Do you mind if I get my message? It might be the school calling about Da... our foster child."

Or it might be Ray with an update on Jessica James' killer. Please don't let him say I was sitting down to coffee with a killer.

Leslie's eyebrows flew up in surprise. "I didn't know you and Ray had a child. By all means, go ahead."

As I dialed the number and waited for my message, Peter carried in a tray with two cups of coffee on it. The dog was still at his heels.

Peter set one cup in front of me and one by Leslie then set the sugar and creamer in between us. "Here you go, Les. I'll be outside."

"Don't you want pie?"

"I'll have some with dinner." He walked out with the dog behind him.

I glanced at Leslie as I entered my password. "Please, go ahead, enjoy. Don't wait for me." I wasn't going to drink the coffee anyway. I never drank the stuff. I'd have to pretend to take a sip or two, just to be polite. Then I'd run like hell.

Leslie smiled and picked up her coffee cup. She sank back in her chair and took a gulp.

Ray's voice came over the phone. "Darlin', I got your messages. We found the Camry last night. It had blood stains in it and some animal hairs and human hairs. It also had the old New York State license plates on it, the ones with the red Statue of Liberty in the center. We couldn't identify the owner right away.

"The DMV looked through their archives. The Camry was registered to Peter Flynn. Peter Flynn, Sr. I guess Leslie's brother is named after the father. We located a death record. He died fifteen years ago."

My gaze darted to Leslie, who had finished half her coffee and was now leaning forward to pick up her pie. Then my gaze skipped over to the ten-inch knife lying near her plate.

"We found a record for her brother Peter. He had a driver's license. He lost it after a drunk driving accident, the third in a string when he was a teenager. I'm on my way to question the girls at The Cat's Meow again to see if they remember him driving a Camry. We're also requesting a search warrant for the farm. He may be our man. I'll try you again later."

When Ray stopped talking, I almost sobbed out loud. Never had I wanted him with me more.

The gray dog trotted into the room again and sniffed the table. Leslie looked up from her pie in surprise. "Bad dog, Rufus. Lie down.

She glanced over at me. "Peter lets Rufus eat table food. He should have taken him back outside."

I clicked my cell phone shut and nodded, smiling weakly. Ray had said they found animal hairs in the Camry. Could they have been gray dog hairs? I wondered if they had found any hairs on Jessica James' body as well. It would probably take them weeks to run them through the city's crime lab. I doubted Wachobe's cases took priority.

"Is everything all right? Aren't you going to eat your pie?"

I realized Leslie was staring at me. She looked the same as all the other times I'd seen her. She seemed just as friendly and nice. I still felt an overwhelming desire to snatch up my purse and run.

Too bad the dog now lay in my exit path, watching me with his big yellow eyes. Too bad he looked big enough to swallow me whole.

I picked up my pie and took a bite, the cell phone still in my hand.

Leslie smiled happily and took her coffee cup in hand.

I ate the piece of pie, except for the crust, while she finished her coffee. It was a good pie. I told her so, hoping it wouldn't be my last.

"I have to be going, Leslie. I have to pick Danny up at school." I waggled the cell phone at her as if in explanation.

"Well, I'm glad you stopped by. I never get to have coffee with a friend. Let me get the chicken for you."

Leslie stood. She grabbed the arms of her chair.

She sat again. "I feel woozy."

When I stood up to help her, the dog leapt to its feet and growled. I didn't dare touch Leslie. "Are you all right, Leslie?"

"I don't know. Let me lean back for a second."

I watched as she shifted her weight back in the chair. Her eyes closed.

I waited for a few seconds. "Leslie? Leslie?"

I reached for her. The dog inched toward me and growled again.

I dropped my hand to my side.

Leslie's lips parted.

She snored.

Peter appeared in the doorway.

"I guess you're not a coffee drinker, Mrs. Parker."

TWENTY-FIVE

"No, I'm not." My response was automatic as my gaze darted around the room, searching for another exit. I spotted a door in the far corner, but it was barricaded by plants. The only way out of this room was past Peter ... and his dog.

"That's too bad. Leslie said you were interested in my planters. They told me at the florist shop that your husband had requested a list of all the customers who bought one." Peter stuck his hands in his pockets and rocked back and forth on his heels. "I guess I should have thought to take back the one I gave Josie."

It was as good as a confession. Peter had killed Jessica James a.k.a. Josie Montalvo.

My hands started to shake. I thought I might throw up my pie. I swallowed multiple times and fought for control.

Peter's gaze never left me. He didn't make any moves toward me, either.

I wondered if I could flip open my cell phone and surreptitiously dial 911. My gaze dropped to my hand.

Peter noticed.

He lumbered into the room and grabbed the cell phone from me. He picked up my purse, too. Then he returned to his position in the doorway.

He flipped the lid on my cell open and shut, open and shut, over and over again until I was ready to scream.

Abruptly he stopped. "You should have drunk the coffee. All I wanted was a head start."

Funny, that's all I wanted, too.

I heard a car door slam. I sucked in my breath and prayed. Could it be Ray?

I twisted my head toward the driveway. A woman and a toddler stood on the gravel, looking toward the house. Another egg customer.

Peter spotted them, too. "Rufus. Guard."

The dog leapt to its feet, teeth bared.

Peter disappeared and reappeared seconds later in the driveway. He spoke to the woman and headed in the direction of the barn. I lost sight of him.

I thought about screaming. My lips parted.

The dog growled. Saliva dripped from its lips and hit the vinyl floor, forming a puddle.

If I screamed, I would be endangering a woman and a child, not to mention myself. Rufus might be trained to go for the neck.

I sat instead.

Leslie snored on next to me, oblivious.

The dog watched me, still growling, but didn't come any closer. The coffee table was between us. It seemed like a very flimsy safety net to me.

I thought about placing my drugged cup of coffee on the floor in the hopes Rufus would lap it up. But the coffee cup was so small and Rufus was so big. He'd probably spill it, if he'd even break the guard command.

Then I noticed all the plants had water saucers under them. I reached to my right.

Rufus barked and snarled, lunging forward.

I closed my eyes, said another quick prayer, lifted a plant and pulled out the saucer.

Rufus snarled and lunged again, saliva dripping on the table now.

Hands shaking, I reached for my coffee cup.

Rufus growled but didn't lunge.

I flipped the coffee into the saucer. Then I grabbed the crust I'd left on my plate and added it to the mixture.

Rufus' saliva had pooled on the table. He wasn't growling anymore.

No way was I going to hold the dish out to him. He could take my hand off with one lunge.

I placed the saucer on the floor and used my foot to slide it over to him.

He growled, snapping at my toes.

I pulled back.

He sniffed the dish once. A second time. Then he stuck his face in and lapped it all up.

I watched as Peter brought the woman an egg carton and accepted her money. She said something to him. He responded.

Rufus was still on his feet, smacking his chops. The coffee and piecrust were gone.

The woman opened the back door to the car, still talking to Peter as she strapped her child into the car seat. Peter nodded, looking toward the house.

She said something else. Peter faced her.

Rufus swayed. He blinked. He swayed again.

Then he lowered himself onto his front paws. He dropped to his haunches.

A second later he was on his side, snoring in chorus with Leslie.

I grabbed the knife off the table. I looked out the window. The woman's car was gone. Peter was nowhere in sight.

I listened. The house seemed silent. Maybe Peter was still outside.

I tiptoed across the room and flattened myself against the edge of the doorway. The house remained silent but I was afraid to move.

Now would be the perfect time for Ray to show up with his search warrant. But somehow I didn't think I could be that lucky.

I decided to risk taking a look into the kitchen.

I eased myself around the edge of the door and let one eye take a peek.

The kitchen was empty. The only sound was the tick of a round clock with a rooster on its face. My purse and cell phone lay on the table.

I darted across the room and grabbed them up. I ran for the door, the purse, phone, and knife pressed tight to my chest.

Only a few more feet and I'd be out of the house. My gaze flicked to the window, keeping a nervous eye out for Peter. Too nervous.

I tripped over a shoe and started to fall. I let go of everything I held so that I could use my hands to break my fall.

As my hands and knees hit the floor, the cell phone bounced once and landed inside a rubber boot caked with mud. The knife skittered across the tiles and under a bench. The contents of my purse spilled onto the hallway carpet runner. I lost a few seconds catching my breath.

When I was able, I grabbed my car keys and left the rest of my things on the floor. I leapt to my feet, stopped at the door, and looked out the window.

No one in sight.

I listened. Besides the occasional rustle of leaves from a gust of wind and the distant moo of a cow in the pasture, the day was silent. Nothing to indicate Peter was nearby.

Now was the time to make my break. I took a deep breath, burst through the door, and ran for the Lexus, pumping my arms like an Olympic track star.

I got halfway there.

Hands dug into my stomach as they swung me off my feet. In a second, I was airborne. The keys flew from my fingers and smacked into the Lexus' windshield. I screamed in fear and despair.

Peter hustled me across the gravel drive toward the barn, holding me two feet off the ground. I kicked and screamed. My heels made contact, drumming his kneecaps. He didn't seem to notice. I tried to twist my body so I could hit him in the head. He just twisted me back. I was like a bundle of hay to him.

Of course, he was like a tractor to me.

The barn was dark. At first, I couldn't see anything. My eyes adjusted. I caught sight of stacks of foam coolers, two refrigerators, bales of hay, buckets of all shapes and sizes, and drums filled with farming tools like pitchforks and shovels. Horse stalls lined both sides of the barn. Empty horse stalls.

I kept on struggling, but I was running out of air as his hands squeezed my torso.

He tossed me into a horse stall. I landed hard on my knees. As I scrambled to my feet, he locked the door.

I could see his shoulders and face above the wall of the stall. I was too short to see anything else outside it. The walls were about my height with iron bars that reached three feet higher. It made the perfect jail cell. No way would I be climbing out of here.

Now what? Where are you, Ray? I need you.

Peter said, "You never should have made friends with my brother. No one else wanted anything to do with him. I tried to warn you off. Most people who get shot at tend to stick close to home, not go around butting their noses into other people's business." With that, he walked away.

Believe me, I was sorry I had befriended Leslie. But hindsight is twenty-twenty.

When I could no longer hear Peter's footsteps, I rushed up to the door and pushed on it. I kicked it. It didn't even wiggle. I reached for the top of the wall and tried to pull myself up to see out. I managed to get an inch off the ground before I dropped. Even at my current light weight, I couldn't do it. Pull-ups never were my thing, and my muscles were weak from months of inactivity.

I heard the Lexus turn over. Good. Maybe he'll steal my car and Ray would find me here later.

No such luck. The Lexus pulled inside the barn. He shut off the engine.

I heard the car door slam and more footsteps. The sound of a creak wafted to my ears from the loft overhead.

A metal trough banged into the bars on my stall. It appeared to descend from the loft. I heard a noise like a garage door lifting. Then another noise like raindrops on a metal rooftop.

Something dropped to the floor at my feet. Corn kernels.

I looked up and watched as a rush of kernels flew off the end of the trough and showered the floor of the stall. They kept coming, covering the floor.

I realized Peter's plan. He was going to bury me alive!

Heart beating out of control, I scrambled to the wall and tried to claw my way up it again as the kernels poured into the stall. They were a foot deep now. Each time I dropped to the floor, I slipped and slid. I lost my grip on the wall. I realized I was screaming when I sucked in a cloud of corn dust and choked.

The kernels kept coming. The dust made my eyes water and my throat burn. I couldn't breathe.

I was knee deep now, struggling to move. My legs were mired in corn. My eyes burned.

I gagged. The air was too full of dust and particles. The oxygen was gone. My lungs strained for a breath of air.

Tears welled in my eyes.

The realization hit me.

I was going to die.

TWENTY-SIX

My chest felt tight. The pressure on my legs was growing. I couldn't feel my feet. I kept my eyes closed but my mouth opened involuntarily, trying to suck in air. All I got was a mouth full of corn dust, which made me panic just that much more. I was lost. *I love you, Ray.*

My fingers clawed uselessly, desperately, at the stall walls.

Then I felt it. The smallest knothole in the wood, maybe big enough for a toehold.

I struggled to lift my right leg out of the kernels. Holding my breath, I bent and unzipped my boot, letting it drop onto the rapidly rising corn.

It took me three tries but I fit my bare toe in the knothole. Summoning all my strength, I heaved myself upward. My big toe cramped but held my weight.

I grabbed the bars, coughing and sputtering. Then I puked corn dust all over my shirt.

My eyes burned when I tried to open them. I gripped the bars tightly with one hand while I rubbed at my eyelids with the other. My tears washed away some of the dust but more came to replace it as the corn kernels kept falling. Soon they would reach my knee-caps at this height, too.

I opened my eyes a slit and tried to see through my tears. Was Peter still in the barn?

Unable to see or hear him, I attempted to swing my still-booted foot onto the top of the stall wall. It took me five tries but finally I managed to pull myself into a kneeling position between the bars. After a moment of rest, I got my feet flat on the stall wood and swung over the top of the bars. From there, I looked at the eight-foot drop to the floor.

In elementary school, I had thought nothing of jumping off the top of the slide. Of course, my bones were a lot less old and brittle then. On the other hand, the stall below had hay on it. Perhaps it would cushion my fall.

I slid off my other boot. Heels planted on the top of the wooden stall, I crouched as low as possible to shorten my drop and let go of the bars.

I landed on my feet and immediately fell forward, smacking my knees for a second time that day on the floor beneath the hay. Winded, I lay still and listened for Peter.

The corn kernels trickled to a halt. The barn was silent.

Pain shot through my ankles as I pulled myself slowly to my feet. If Peter came after me now, he'd have no trouble catching me. My ankles would give out in a chase.

I limped toward the barn door and yelped as an enormous form filled the doorway.

It was Peter.

I backed into the barn, whimpering.

He came after me.

"Jolene, it's me. It's Leslie."

I squinted, trying to make out the color of the shirt. Even in the dim barn light and with my sore eyes, I could tell it was green. I let out a sob. "Peter tried to kill me."

"I know. I'm so, so sorry. He's not … quite well." Leslie held out her hand to help me up. "Come on, let's get you some air."

Not quite well? Was that like a little bit pregnant? Her excuses sounded familiar, though I couldn't say why.

I let her lead me out of the barn. My eyes closed involuntarily. The sun was too bright and they were too damaged.

"Stand right here. I'll get some water to rinse your eyes."

I waited for her, afraid when I no longer heard the noise of her footsteps and afraid when I did. My heart beat so loud I feared it would burst.

She touched my arm, making me jump. "Lean your head back and I'll pour the water over your eyes. It will make it better."

I did as she asked then felt like I was drowning when the water ran up my nose.

I pulled away, snorting.

She pressed a towel into my hands. "Here, Jolene. Just blot your eyes gently."

When I finished, my eyes were still sore but I could see. Peter was lying crumpled by the barn entrance, a huge goose egg on his brow. A shovel lay abandoned on the ground next to him.

I backed away, pointing, my lips moving without sound.

Leslie glanced at him. "Don't worry. He's out cold."

When I had last seen her, she was, too. Apparently, their large bodies could take quite an onslaught and still bounce back quickly.

She took a step in my direction and held out her hands, palms up. "I'm sorry he attacked you. He hates so much the idea of me becoming a woman." She closed her eyes. "So much."

When her eyes opened, I thought they looked desperate. She took another step toward me. "He goes to a psychiatrist about it. He can't stand the thought of me … changing my body and leaving him. He despises anyone who provides me with any sort of support, including you, my psychiatrist, and my surgeon. I thought he was coming around, but …" Leslie heaved a sigh, the kind of sigh that says "I was so wrong. Don't worry. I'll see that he gets the proper care."

I wasn't worried. Within minutes, I planned to have Ray ensure Peter got the proper care, courtesy of the state of New York, for many years to come.

Peter's eyelid twitched.

I backed toward the farmhouse door. "We need to call 911 right now. Right now, Leslie!"

"Okay, okay." She glanced over her shoulder at him. "I just don't want the police to hurt him."

Was it my imagination or had Peter opened his eye and looked at us? I jumped back a foot, shaking my head.

Frankly I didn't care if the police killed him, as long as they kept him away from me. "I'll call Ray."

I turned and ran for the house, yanking the door open then turning to lock it behind me, praying neither of them were carrying a key. Darting into the kitchen, I scanned the counters and the walls for the phone.

A white cordless hung on the far wall. I raced to it and dialed 911.

The operator answered. I stammered my name and the address of the Flynn farm. "Peter Flynn tried to kill me. I think he killed Jessica James. Can someone come right away?"

"Yes, ma'am. I'm sending a sheriff's deputy now."

"Send more than one. He's a big man."

"Yes, ma'am."

"Can you call my husband, Ray Parker? He's a deputy sheriff."

"Yes, ma'am. I know your husband. I'll call him now."

The doorknob jiggled. Someone banged on the door. The glass broke.

My hands started to shake. "Hurry, hurry. He's coming in the house."

I dropped the phone and started pulling out drawers, looking for the Chinese meat cleaver. It was in the sink, with bits of chicken flesh still on it.

I wrapped my fingers around the handle and held on tight.

No one came inside the house.

Instead, I heard sounds of a struggle outside: metal clanging, grunting, feet scrambling for footholds in the gravel.

Creeping toward the door with cleaver in hand, I was ever so careful not to trip on the shoes and boots in the hallway. I looked through the hole in the glass.

Peter had a pitchfork. Leslie had the shovel. They were circling one another.

Peter spoke first. "Les, you don't understand. Just let me go. I'll leave town."

"You can't go. You need help."

Peter's face twisted in anguish. "It's too late for that."

Leslie shook her head. "It's not too late. The doctor will help you."

"You don't understand."

Leslie waved the shovel at him. "What don't I understand?"

He jumped back seconds before she connected with his protruding stomach. "I killed a woman."

Leslie took a few steps back. "Jolene is not dead. She's in the house, calling the police."

Peter started to cry, great heaving, blubbering sobs. "Not ... Jolene."

Leslie's shovel dropped a few inches. "Then who?"

"Jo ... sie Mon ... tal ... vo."

I could almost see the wheels turning in Leslie's head. "That dancer from The Cat's Meow? The one I read about in the paper? You said you didn't know her. YOU TOLD ME you didn't know her."

Peter nodded, tears still streaming down his cheeks.

"WHY?"

Peter shook his head. "I don't know. I don't know." His chest heaved as another sob burst from his lips.

Leslie lowered her shovel. "Put the pitchfork down, Peter. We'll talk about it. Whatever happened, we can work it out. Together."

"We can't. We can't. She's dead. I killed her. I didn't mean to ... I mean, I didn't want to." He fell to his knees, the pitchfork lying useless beside him.

Leslie moved toward him. "Why did you kill her, Peter?"

"I thought she liked me. She slept with me. I gave her money, but she said I was special. I thought she might want to marry me.

I didn't want to be alone. You were leaving me." Peter covered his face with his massive hands. "I told her about you. She listened. I thought she cared."

Leslie moved a little closer. "Why did you kill her, Peter?"

Peter dropped his hands. He raised his tear-streaked face to Leslie's. "I told her about you and how much I loved you and how much it hurt me that you didn't want to be twins anymore."

He gasped for breath. A moan followed.

I felt a chill run down my spine. He sounded like a wounded animal. I almost felt sorry for him. Almost.

"She laughed at me, Les. She laughed. She said, 'What's the big deal? Who cares? So what if your sister wants to … to get … to get … her … peter … whacked off?'"

With a heartbroken wail, he crumpled to the ground at Leslie's feet.

Leslie knelt and gathered him in her arms.

As he sobbed into her chest, she smoothed his hair and murmured, "It's okay. It's okay. I'll stay with you. Don't worry, I'll be right here. You're my brother. I'll take care of you."

Then she lifted her gaze to mine and I knew what I had seen in her.

A little bit of me.

———

Gumby, Ray, and Tony , another officer, showed up minutes later, lights flashing. They got out of their respective cars, guns drawn, and looked at Peter and Leslie huddled in the driveway. By this time, the two of them didn't look much like a threat. More like a meltdown.

Gumby took the precaution of kicking the pitchfork and shovel aside.

I dropped the Chinese cleaver, unlocked the door and stepped out.

Ray holstered his weapon as he strode over to me. "Are you all right?"

I nodded, more of a reflex than an actual response. I was alive. Numb, but alive.

He glanced at Leslie and her brother. "We're arresting Peter, right?"

"Yes. He killed Josie Montalvo. They had a relationship of some kind." Clearly, not the good kind. Not the healing kind.

Ray looked at the two brothers again. "Which one is Peter, for sure?"

I sighed. "The one in the blue shirt. The one without the veneers." Without the boobs. Soon, without the brother.

Ray slid his cuffs off his belt. He walked over to Leslie and Peter. "We're going to have to take Peter in, Leslie. Can you step back, please?"

Leslie let go of Peter and stood. Ray slapped the cuffs on Peter, who didn't resist as Ray led him to Tony's patrol car and put him in the back. Tony holstered his gun. He listened to Ray for a moment then climbed into the car. He turned his lights off and backed down the driveway.

Gumby approached Leslie. "We're going to need a statement from you. Can you accompany me, please?"

Leslie glanced my way. She mouthed, "I'm so sorry." Then she followed Gumby to his car. He turned off his lights and backed out.

Ray met me at the base of the steps. "What happened?"

I shook my head. Tears started to flow.

I pressed my forehead against his chest.

Without another word, his arms encircled me and held on tight.

———

Erica called at eight o'clock that night. I answered the phone, because Ray and Danny were in the middle of playing poker, a game I never understood. A flush, a straight. They sounded like plumbing issues. Ray and Danny were playing for M&Ms. Danny was winning. I'd have to cut off the game soon or the sugar and caffeine from the chocolate he was winning would keep him up all night.

"Can you pick me up tomorrow at eleven? Dr. Albert said he would be in to sign the release papers then."

Just like Erica. No greeting. No apology. Just demands. It was okay with me, though. I'd missed her. "Sure. Doesn't Maury want the honor?"

"He has to work. He has a new job, remember?"

"Oh, sure." In floral delivery. I stifled a giggle. It wasn't really funny that my sister had married a man who tried to woo every woman he met with roses. It certainly wouldn't be too funny when she found out about it.

I sure wasn't going to be the one to tell her.

"Can you help me clean out the apartment and move all our stuff to Wells Street?"

"Sure."

"Tomorrow?"

"Sure."

"Can I hang out with you the next couple days, until Maury has time off?"

"Sure."

"Can I have five hundred bucks?"

"No!"

"Just checking." She hung up.

After we tucked Danny into bed, Ray led me into the bedroom. He closed the door and sat on the bed, patting the spot next to him.

I snuggled beside him. "What's up?"

"Danny's father is going to be released tomorrow. They're not going to charge him with anything."

"Does that mean Danny will be leaving us?" Leaving our home, leaving us, leaving me. I was so tired of everyone leaving me. My mom, my dad, Noelle, Erica, and now Danny. At least Erica would never leave me. She couldn't afford to.

Ray entwined his fingers with mine. "I spoke to Social Services. With the house in Newark and the aunt's cars, all Danny's father needs is a job and he can have custody of Danny. He can get in touch with Social Services, and they will ask us to give Danny to him as soon as Mr. Phillips gets his first paycheck."

I whispered, "I wasn't too happy about taking Danny at first, but I'm going to miss him."

"Me, too." Ray kissed the back of my hand.

I tried not to think about having to say goodbye to Danny. Instead, I remembered Leslie's face as she watched her brother taken away in handcuffs. It made me feel worse.

"What's going to happen to Peter Flynn?"

"Leslie got him a lawyer. I think the lawyer will plead not guilty by reason of temporary insanity."

"Do you think he'll get off?"

"It depends on the psychiatric evaluations, his attorney's skill, the trial jury, and the alignment of the moon. I'm sure it doesn't hurt that Peter was already seeing a shrink. But he did try to kill you in addition to Josie Montalvo. He won't walk, but he might spend the rest of his days in a psychiatric facility."

Let's hope they didn't put him in the same one Erica frequented. I would not care to run into him again.

"Did he say why he was driving around with Jessica's arm in a cooler?"

"He found it in the back of the truck when he got home. It must have slid out of the bag, and he missed it in the dark. He planned to put it with the rest of her body after his psychiatrist appointment on Wednesday."

Imagine his surprise when he came out of his appointment and found it missing. "Did he take Danny's father's car from The Cat's Meow on purpose?"

"He said not. He was drunk and agitated to see Josie talking with another man when he thought he was her one and only. He sat right next to Danny's father at the bar, and they had both laid their keys on it. He picked the wrong set up when he left the bar and was too far gone to notice."

"When did he kill her?"

"Sunday night, same day Danny's father took her Cadillac Escalade."

Her death was too horrific to think about. It was one reason I couldn't buy a temporary insanity plea. Peter Flynn had walked out of Jessica James apartment after choking her to death, grabbed the axe, and gone back inside to chop her up piece by piece and toss her remains into a garbage bag.

I pushed those images away and closed that mental drawer forever. "I wonder if Leslie will go ahead with her surgery."

"I don't know, Darlin'. If she truly thinks she'd be happier as a woman then she'll have to, won't she?"

I guessed so. But as much as I liked her, I wouldn't be visiting her at the farm again to find out. In fact, her farm might very well be the first and last I ever set foot on. I certainly didn't plan on ever eating corn again and I'd think twice about chicken, too.

Something else had been bothering me. "Did you notice the similarities between Leslie and her brother and Erica and me?"

Ray raised his eyebrow. "No. I don't see any."

I looked at him in shock. "You don't? Leslie's brother is mentally ill and causing trouble, my sister is mentally ill and causing trouble. Leslie's caring for her brother. I'm caring for my sister."

Ray squeezed my hand. "Leslie is an enabler. You're an enforcer."

"A what?"

"An enforcer. Erica would have been a lot worse off without you. I don't think we can say the same for Leslie and Peter. Leslie knew her brother had an alcohol problem. She knew her brother was driving without a license for years. She didn't report him. She didn't stop him."

"Yes, let's talk about that. How did all you big, bad deputy sheriffs miss him driving over the hills all these years?"

Ray grimaced. "Oh, sure, now it's my fault. Let's just say we missed it and leave it at that."

"I suppose you're right about Leslie. She even let him drive her truck around." When the sheriff's department returned to the farm with a search warrant, it hadn't taken them long to ascertain that the axe in the bed of Leslie's truck had been used to dismember Jessica James.

"But I don't think Leslie would have ignored the facts that he shot at me or killed Jessica James if she had known."

"She has been very cooperative . . . and supportive to her brother. It's a fine line to walk."

I knew all about that line. Erica had pilfered from convenience stores, taken money from her co-workers' purses, and even driven the getaway car in a movie theater robbery. But that was before her medication got straightened out, before she grew up. Of course, she did "borrow" a car from my garage last year . . .

I hugged Ray's arm and willed my worries away. "Yes, it is."

TWENTY-SEVEN

Two weeks later Ray and I stood on our front porch with Danny as his father carried Danny's new suitcase to the old gray Cavalier left to him by his aunt. The way the car bucked and snorted as it idled, I feared it might not make it back to Newark.

A foot of snow had blanketed the town last night. The air had chilled our cheeks red seconds after we stepped outside to say our final goodbyes.

I grabbed Danny's jacket lapels and pulled them tighter around his neck. "Call us once in awhile and let us know how you're doing. We want to hear from you."

Danny nodded but didn't meet my eyes.

I let go, thinking I was embarrassing him.

Ray pulled Danny into a hug. "Be a good kid. Make good choices. Follow the rules." He let go of Danny and bent down to look him in the eye. "And know we're here for you, whenever you need us."

I gazed skyward, trying to contain the tears that threatened. As soon as Danny left, I planned to tell Ray in no uncertain terms, no more foster children. I couldn't take the heartache again. Problem was Ray might start in on me about having a child of our own again. Given the way everything had been going lately, that idea appealed to me less and less, not that it ever really had.

A few good things had occurred. Danny's father had gotten a job as a dishwasher. He'd also gotten a tutor from Literacy Volunteers. Two steps in the right direction.

He and Danny had already sold the Cadillac Escalade for thousands below sticker price. But the money would help.

Unfortunately, the house in Newark had come with a hefty mortgage and a home equity loan to be repaid. Danny's father had said they would have to sell it. He hinted that the house wouldn't sell for as much as the bank was owed. I couldn't quite figure out how such a thing had happened. It made no sense to me that Danny's aunt had borrowed more money than she could repay. It also made no sense to me that the bank had lent it to her. That sounded criminal. But then, lots of things don't always make sense to me.

It did make it all the more painful to let Danny go. His future didn't look as bright as we'd originally thought.

His father seemed cheerful enough. He came back to the porch and shook Ray's hand one more time.

I reached for Danny and hugged him tight. "You're welcome here anytime."

He hugged me back. Tight. It took him a few seconds to let go.

When he followed his father down the sidewalk, he looked back. I thought I saw tears in his eyes.

Of course, I might have been fooled by all the tears in mine.

―――

We had to make some adjustments to our Christmas plans, what with the addition of Maury to our family.

In the years when Ray and I had been separated, Erica and I had spent Christmas with my best friend Isabelle, her husband, and my godchild Cassidy. Last Christmas I'd spent with Noelle, the only Christmas I'd ever spend with her.

I would miss Danny, but I'd expected him to leave us all along. It was the unexpected departures of loved ones that I couldn't handle.

This year, Erica had invited us to dinner, and with some hesitation and an apology to Isabelle, I had accepted. Now the day had arrived and I dressed with some trepidation. Erica had never been known to cook anything more difficult than macaroni and cheese. She'd promised us prime rib and lasagna.

I wore green and made extra heavy hors d'oeuvres just in case. Ray and I drove to my old apartment with Christmas carols playing on the radio, including my favorite "I'll Be Home For Christmas."

Maury greeted us at the door and took our coats into the bedroom.

Ray took in the living room and whistled.

I stifled a laugh.

Red roses were everywhere. Roses in vases on the mantel, in pitchers on the coffee table and end tables, tucked in the Christmas tree as decorations, dried and crumbled in shallow dishes as potpourri. In addition, Erica had apparently used some of her precious wine cork and bottle cap collection to make an unusual mosaic frame for her wedding photo, which looked to have been taken outside a Vegas-like chapel. I got close enough to the photo to count the two dozen red roses she had clasped in her arms.

No sign of any dish gardens potted in homemade wishing wells—not that I ever expected to see any of those again.

When Erica appeared in the kitchen doorway, she even had a rose in her hair.

Needless to say, the aroma was heady.

Erica gestured toward all four walls. "How do you like the flowers?"

"They're amazing."

Ray cleared his throat. "Awesome."

Erica danced into the room, sweeping her long emerald skirt through the air. "Maury spoils me. He says I'm a domestic goddess."

I saw Ray's eyes bulge on that one. He was probably thinking about the fact that I taught Erica what little she knows. But I have to give the man credit, he kept it together. He got his unreadable "good cop, bad cop, anything-you-need-me-to-be cop" expression locked in place within seconds.

Maury offered us wine. Ray asked for a beer. Erica went to the kitchen to retrieve one. I followed her.

"So Maury bought all these roses for you?" A little adding machine in my head was running the numbers. No wonder they couldn't afford to pay their whole rent.

"No, oh no, these are the ones the florist discarded. They all had black spots or wilted leaves. I just pick off the dead stuff, and they look fine to me."

A shrine of discarded roses for my sister. I tried not to read anything into that.

In the living room, Erica delivered Ray's beer and perched on the arm of Maury's chair. Then the four of us sat in awkward silence, alternately eating a bite and trying not to make eye contact.

"These are good hors d'oeuvres, Jolene. Did you make them?" Maury smiled at me.

I didn't have the heart to tell him that they came in a box. "They bake up fast."

Ray cleared his throat and took a long swig of beer. The four of us continued to smile politely at one another. I wished I were anywhere else. Knowing Ray, he probably wished he was at work.

The flowers started to get to me. My nose twitched. Then it itched. I rubbed it. My eyes watered. I sneezed. And sneezed. And sneezed.

Erica curled her lip and offered me a tissue box. "Do you have a cold?"

"I think it's the flowers."

"Oh." She glanced at Maury. "Why don't we sit down for dinner?"

We followed her into the dining room. She swept a huge bouquet of roses off the table and stuffed them in the closet.

Maury, Ray, and I pretended not to notice.

With the first cut, the prime rib bled like it was still alive. I half expected to hear it moo in protest. The lasagna noodles were still brittle. Erica had tried the "no boil" method and forgotten to add extra water.

The salad looked good until it ended up swimming in the blood on my plate from the prime rib. I tried not to let my disgust show, but my expression betrayed me as usual.

Ray looked at me and buttered a roll with great care, as though it might be the only thing he planned on eating tonight.

Looking from one of us to the other, Erica burst into tears then ran into the bedroom.

Maury chased after her. I thought about joining him, but it didn't seem to be my place anymore. He'd have to be the one to reassure Erica from now on that he loved her, whether she could cook or not. For a second, I felt like I'd lost something important. Then I started to feel tremendously relieved, as though a huge burden had just transferred from me to someone else. But I felt guilty for thinking of Erica as a burden, even though she was—on occasion—a weight heavy enough for an entire mule train.

Ray offered me half his roll. "Let's invite them to dinner at our house next year."

I smiled at the man who loved me. "It's a plan."

Maury reappeared five minutes later, shoulders slumped and red-faced. Our coats were in his hand. "I think the pressure of entertaining has been too much for my wife. Would you excuse us?"

We were being sent home.

I took a minute to pack up my remaining hors d'oeuvres.

In the car, I fed them to Ray as he drove. "I'm sorry."

"Why are you sorry? You didn't ruin dinner."

"I accepted her invitation. I should have known better."

Ray shrugged. "You had to give her a chance. From now on, we're busy if she invites us for dinner."

But right now we didn't have anything to do for the rest of Christmas Day. Or anything more to eat. And all the restaurants in Wachobe were closed, as was every business. We were the only car on Main Street.

I thought for a second. "Do you want to drive by the park and look at the town Christmas tree?"

"Good idea."

A few minutes later, Ray pulled up next to the park on Main. In the center of it, a white band gazebo overlooked the lake, where the water had begun to freeze along the shoreline. A twelve-foot evergreen lit with clear lights and covered with enormous red and gold ornaments shone brightly in the dusk.

My eyes filled with tears. I had found Noelle under that tree last year, wrapped in blankets and tucked safely into her car seat, waiting for me. She had been a precious gift. Just not one meant for us.

Ray ran his finger down my cheek. "What are you thinking about?"

"Noelle."

"Oh." He reached over and lifted me across the center console and onto his lap. "I miss her, too. But she's safe and healthy and happy. I'm not as sure about Danny. I'll miss him. I won't have anyone to play poker with anymore."

I snuggled into his chest. Maybe I would try to learn the game to make Ray happy. "Danny's father seems to love him."

"I hope he loves him enough."

I did, too, but Danny wasn't on my watch anymore. I'd let him go.

I wondered how Ray felt to find himself childless once again, but I hesitated to ask. I wasn't sure I wanted to hear the answer.

I ran my finger over his lower lip. He smiled at me. "What?"

"We are without child again. You wanted at least one." It had been his one and only condition for us getting back together. I held my breath, hoping he wouldn't take my statement as an offer to conceive.

His gaze shifted to some distant point beyond the windshield. "I did say that. But I'm beginning to understand why you didn't want one. There's a lot of heartbreak and responsibility involved."

I thought of Noelle. And a lot of joy. My lips parted, "As well as—"

"Why don't we turn on some Christmas music?" Ray leaned forward and adjusted the dial. "I'll Be Home For Christmas" came on again.

This was new. For once, Ray was the one who didn't want to discuss children. I decided to respect his wishes—and count my blessings.

He cuddled me close and kissed my forehead. "This is good."

I kissed his neck and cuddled closer to him. "Yeah."

It was good for all of fifteen minutes until Ray's legs started to cramp. Then I slid back into my seat and he headed the car toward home.

We drove by Asdale Auto Imports. Cory and I had strung clear lights around the showroom window and tied a bow on the . . .

"Stop!"

Ray hit the brakes. We lurched forward and back. Ray's forehead just missed the windshield.

Ray peered out at the street in front of us. "What? Was it an animal?"

"No. Look!" I pointed to the shop window.

"I don't see anything."

"Exactly."

The Ferrari was gone.

———

Ray called Wachobe's chief of police, since the theft occurred technically in his jurisdiction. The chief wasn't too happy to leave home and hearth in order to take my report, but he did. He found it most peculiar that my alarm was still activated. So did Ray and I.

From the tire tracks in the snow, we could tell someone had opened up the front doors and pulled the car out, impossible to do without either turning the alarm off or activating it, which would have brought this situation to the chief's attention much earlier than now.

The chief asked, "Who knows your alarm code?"

Ray cocked an eyebrow at me. "You did change it, didn't you?"

He meant since last year when the dead man ended up in the Ferrari. "Yes! Only Cory and I know. That's it."

Ray pointed to my purse. "Call Cory."

Cory spent the holidays at home each year with his parents and his brother's family. He answered on the third ring. I heard voices in the background.

I didn't bother with any greetings. "The Ferrari's gone from the showroom, but the alarm is still on. Do you know where it went?"

"No shit?"

"No shit, Cory."

"I don't know, but this is cause for celebration, don't you think?"

I did, but I couldn't let the police chief and Ray know.

I wished Cory a Merry Christmas and snapped the phone shut.

Ray and I drove home in silence. On the way, it occurred to me that one more person might know my alarm code, one twelve-year-old boy who I most certainly didn't want to get in any new trouble.

Ray parked the car in our driveway. I heard singing as we got out of the car. "Do you hear that?"

Ray tipped his head, listening. "Must be carolers."

Yes ... but why did they sound like ... SpongeBob?

Ray unlocked the front door of the bungalow. I stepped inside. SpongeBob was on the television, dressed in full Christmas regalia, singing with Patrick and the whole underwater gang.

Danny was on our couch.

He was eating a peanut butter and jelly sandwich. He waved it at us sheepishly. "I let myself in."

Ray looked at the key in his hand and the lock he had just removed it from. He frowned.

But now was not the time to discuss Danny's unique talents.

I ran over and threw my arms around Danny, kissing his forehead. "What are you doing here?"

He couldn't meet my eyes. "My dad brought me."

"Where is he?" I had a feeling I knew the answer.

Danny's Adam's apple moved up and down slowly, and I felt him tremble. "He had to go away. I don't know where. Is it okay if I stay with you for a while? He didn't think you'd mind."

I wondered if the man ever planned to come back. I was positive he had my Ferrari. I knew Ray must have thought the same, so I was surprised when he made no move to call the police chief and fill him in.

Surprised and relieved. Mr. Phillips was welcome to the Ferrari. I would much rather have Danny. Apparently so would Ray.

I pulled Danny close. "We don't mind. We don't mind at all." I looked up at Ray and waited.

He smiled with genuine happiness. "Danny, you know you're my favorite poker buddy. You're welcome here anytime."

Danny stopped trembling and a big grin took over his face. "You really meant it? I wasn't sure."

Ray leaned in to ruffle Danny's hair. "One thing you can be sure of, Danny. Jolene and I mean everything we say."

———

We spent the rest of the afternoon playing poker, listening to Christmas carols, and eating peanut butter and jelly sandwiches and brownies that I baked and covered with green-tinted frosting. After I tucked Danny in for the night, he called out to me as I was about to close the door.

"Yes, Danny?"

"I almost forgot. Dad told me to give you a message."

I hoped it wasn't a clue as to where to find the Ferrari. I'd already done my happy dance alone in our bedroom while Ray and Danny set up the poker game.

In fact, I wasn't even going to ask Danny if he gave his father my alarm code. Because then I would have to thank him.

I stepped inside Danny's room and flicked on the light switch. "What is it?"

Danny sat up in bed and rubbed his eyes. "I didn't really understand it."

"What did he say?"

"He said 'Tell Jolene I was thinking college fund.'"

THE END

ABOUT THE AUTHOR

Lisa Bork lives in western New York and loves to spend time in the Finger Lakes region. Married and the mother of two children, she worked in human resources and marketing before becoming a writer. For more information, please visit her website at www.LisaBork.com.

Bork belongs to The Authors Guild; Mystery Writers of America; Sisters in Crime; and her neighborhood bookclub, the Thursday Evening Literary Society. Her debut novel, *For Better, For Murder*, was a 2009 Agatha Award finalist for Best First Novel, and the second book in her Broken Vows mystery series, *For Richer, For Danger*, was released in September 2010.

In the opening chapter, Jolene is floundering in her grief and questioning her purpose in life while Ray expects her to return to "normal." How long can one take to grieve? Does a reasonable time vary by circumstance? Is Jolene fit to help others, as she says she'd like to do, if she herself is floundering?

During the course of the story, we learn more about Jolene's marriage to Ray and her friendship with Cory. What makes these relationships strong and/or weak? What sustains these relationships?

Jolene becomes vulnerable when she responds to Danny's, Leslie's, and Maury's needs. What are some examples of that vulnerability? How can we tell if it is "safe" to help or to befriend someone else? Should vulnerability and safety even be considered when it comes to helping others or making friends?

Erica has many problems and just as many people trying to help her resolve them. Who is helping her? Who is not? Ultimately, can anyone else resolve Erica's problems, or is she going to have to help herself?

Parenting is an issue in this story. What are some examples of good versus bad parenting? Can someone be a good parent and a bad role model? What makes a good parent? How much does the child's opinion count in deciding what's best for the child?

Jolene thinks she and Leslie are alike in their relationships with their siblings. How much do they really have in common?

Does the novel end with all issues resolved? Why or why not? As a reader, are you satisfied with how the story ended? Was justice served? Is it a happy ending for all involved?